A Text Book of

WEB
TECHNOLOGIES

FOR
M.C.A. : MANAGEMENT : SEMESTER - II
SUBJECT CODE : IT22

AS PER NEW REVISED SYLLABUS

SNEHAL JOGLEKAR

M.Sc. (Computer Science)
Lecturer, M.E.S.'s Abasaheb Garware College
Pune

NIRALI PRAKASHAN
ADVANCEMENT OF KNOWLEDGE

N3187

Web Technologies (MCA - Sem. II)   **ISBN 978-93-5164-983-0**

First Edition   :   January 2016

©   :   Author

Published By :

NIRALI PRAKASHAN

Abhyudaya Pragati, 1312, Shivaji Nagar

Off J.M. Road, Pune – 411005

Tel - (020) 25512336/37/39, Fax - (020) 25511379

Email : niralipune@pragationline.com

✦ DISTRIBUTION CENTRES

PUNE

Nirali Prakashan   :   119, Budhwar Peth, Jogeshwari Mandir Lane, Pune 411002, Maharashtra
Tel : (020) 2445 2044, 66022708, Fax : (020) 2445 1538
Email : bookorder@pragationline.com, niralilocal@pragationline.com

Nirali Prakashan   :   S. No. 28/27, Dhyari, Near Pari Company, Pune 411041
Tel : (020) 24690204 Fax : (020) 24690316
Email : dhyari@pragationline.com, bookorder@pragationline.com

MUMBAI

Nirali Prakashan   :   385, S.V.P. Road, Rasdhara Co-op. Hsg. Society Ltd.,
Girgaum, Mumbai 400004, Maharashtra
Tel : (022) 2385 6339 / 2386 9976, Fax : (022) 2386 9976
Email : niralimumbai@pragationline.com

✦ DISTRIBUTION BRANCHES

JALGAON

Nirali Prakashan   :   34, V. V. Golani Market, Navi Peth, Jalgaon 425001,
Maharashtra, Tel : (0257) 222 0395, Mob : 94234 91860

KOLHAPUR

Nirali Prakashan   :   New Mahadvar Road, Kedar Plaza, 1st Floor Opp. IDBI Bank
Kolhapur 416 012, Maharashtra. Mob : 9850046155

NAGPUR

Pratibha Book Distributors   :   Above Maratha Mandir, Shop No. 3, First Floor,
Rani Jhanshi Square, Sitabuldi, Nagpur 440012, Maharashtra
Tel : (0712) 254 7129

DELHI

Nirali Prakashan   :   4593/21, Basement, Aggarwal Lane 15, Ansari Road, Daryaganj
Near Times of India Building, New Delhi 110002
Mob : 08505972553

BENGALURU

Pragati Book House   :   House No. 1, Sanjeevappa Lane, Avenue Road Cross,
Opp. Rice Church, Bengaluru – 560002.
Tel : (080) 64513344, 64513355,Mob : 9880582331, 9845021552
Email:bharatsavla@yahoo.com

CHENNAI

Pragati Books   :   9/1, Montieth Road, Behind Taas Mahal, Egmore,
Chennai 600008 Tamil Nadu, Tel : (044) 6518 3535,
Mob : 94440 01782 / 98450 21552 / 98805 82331,
Email : bharatsavla@yahoo.com

niralipune@pragationline.com | www.pragationline.com

Also find us on 🅕 www.facebook.com/niralibooks

PREFACE

It gives me great pleasure in presenting this book **"Web Technologies"** designed to serve as a textbook for students of the Second Semester of Master of Computer Application (M.C.A.).

There has been significant development in recent years in the field of Computer Science. The book is a perfect blend of technology which has been a field of dramatic revolution; this subject focuses on different technologies of it.

The book is organized in such a way that it mirrors the revised syllabus. The book will be found useful by a wide section of readers, teachers and students of Business, Technology and Computer Management courses in Indian Universities. The entire book is freshly written as per the revised syllabus.

The book has its own unique features. It brings out the subject in a very simple and lucid manner for easy and comprehensive understanding of the basic concepts, its intricacies, procedures and practices. This book will help the readers to have a broader view on Web Technologies like HTML, CSS, CSS3, JavaScript, ASP etc. The language used in this book is easy and will help students to improve their vocabulary of Technical terms and understand the matter in a better and happier way.

Particular attention has been paid to making this book stimulating and highly readable. The result is a text which is clear, focused and designed to capture student interest. This text is equally suitable for courses directed at undergraduates and postgraduates.

I thank Prof. Gautam Bapat for the friendly manner in which he reviewed our script and suggested improvements from time to time, we must say he has done the editing, exceptionally well for our book.

I thank Mrs. Aabha Athavale, Mrs. Anita Panajkar for their important inputs time to time. Mr. Akbar Shaikh painstakingly attended to all the details to make this book appear good. I also thank Ms. Chaitali Takale and Mr. Ravindra Walodare,

I have given my best inputs for this book. Any suggestions towards the improvement of this book and sincere comments are most welcome on niralipune@pragationline.com.

Author

SYLLABUS

1. HTML　　　　　　　　　　　　　　　　　　　**[Weightage 25] [Sessions 10]**
　1.1　Introduction to HTML, WWW, W3C, Common HTML
　1.2　Tags and attributes, Ordered and Unordered Lists
　1.3　Inserting Image
　1.4　Client Server Image Mapping
　1.5　Text and Image Links
　1.6　Tables
　1.7　Frames
　1.8　Forms
　1.9　Introduction with text box, text area, buttons, List box, radio, checkbox etc.

2. CSS　　　　　　　　　　　　　　　　　　　　**[Weightage 20] [Sessions 5]**
　2.1　Introduction to Style Sheet
　2.2　Types of Style Sheets
　2.3　Inline, External, Embedded CSS
　2.4　CSS Border, Margin, Positioning, Color, Text, Link, Background, List, Table, Padding, Image, Display Properties
　2.5　Use of Id and classes in CSS
　2.6　use of <div> and <span>
　2.7　Introduction of CSS3 : Gradients, Transitions, Animations, Multiple Columns

3. Javascript　　　　　　　　　　　　　　　　**[Weightage 30] [Sessions 15]**
　3.1　Concept of script, Types of Scripts, Introduction to javascript
　3.2　Variables, identifiers constants in javascript and examples of each
　3.3　Operators in javascripts, Various types of javascript Operator
　3.4　Examples on javascript Operators
　3.5　Control and looping structure, Examples on Control and Looping Structures (if, if...else, for, while, do while, switch, etc.)
　3.6　Concept of Array, How to use it in javascript, Types of an array, Examples
　3.7　Methods of an Array, Examples on it
　3.8　Event Handling in javascript with Examples
　3.9　Math and Date Object and Examples on it
　3.10　String Object and Examples on it, and some Predefined Functions
　3.11　DOM Concept in javascript, DOM Objects
　3.12　Window Navigator, History Object and its Methods
　3.13　Location Object with Methods and Examples
　3.14　Validations in javascript, Examples on it

4. ASP　　　　　　　　　　　　　　　　　　　　**[Weightage 25] [Sessions 10]**
　4.1　Introduction to ASP
　4.2　How to Install IIS
　4.3　ASP syntax, Variables, Procedures
　4.4　ASP Forms
　4.5　ASP Session and Cookies
　4.6　ASP Global.asa
　4.7　ASP Objects - Request, Response, Application, Server
　4.8　ASP Database Related Operations – Insert, Retrive, Update, Delete.
　　　Programs on Database related operations

CONTENTS

Chapter 1...

HTML

Contents ...

1.1 Introduction

- Web technologies are related to the interface between web servers and their clients. This information includes markup languages, programming interfaces, languages and standards for document identification and display.

- The World Wide Web abbreviated as WWW or W3 and commonly known as the Web.

- WWW is a system of interlinked hypertext documents accessed via the Internet. With a web browser, one can view web pages that may contain text, images, videos, and other multimedia, and navigate between them via hyperlinks.

- HyperText Markup Language (HTML) is the main markup language for displaying web pages and other information that can be displayed in a web browser.

Web Site:

- Web site is a set of related web pages containing content such as text, images, video, audio, etc.

- A website is hosted on at least one web server, accessible via a network such as the Internet or a private local area network through an Internet address known as a Uniform Resource Locator (URL). All publicly accessible websites collectively constitute the World Wide Web (WWW).

Web Pages:

- A web page is a document, typically written in plain text interspersed with formatting instructions of Hypertext Markup Languages like HTML, XHTML.

- A webpage may incorporate elements from other websites with suitable markup anchors.

- The pages of a website can usually be accessed from a simple Uniform Resource Locator (URL) called the web address.

- HTML documents describe web pages. HTML documents contain HTML tags and plain text. HTML documents are also called web pages.

- There are two types of web pages:

(i) Static Web Pages:

- o A static web page sometimes called a flat page/stationary page is a web page that is delivered to the user exactly as stored, in contrast to dynamic web pages which are generated by a web application.

- o Consequently a static web page displays the same information for all users, from all contexts, subject to modern capabilities of a web server to negotiate content-type or language of the document where such versions are available and the server is configured to do so.

- o Static web pages are often HTML documents stored as files in the file system and made available by the web server over HTTP.

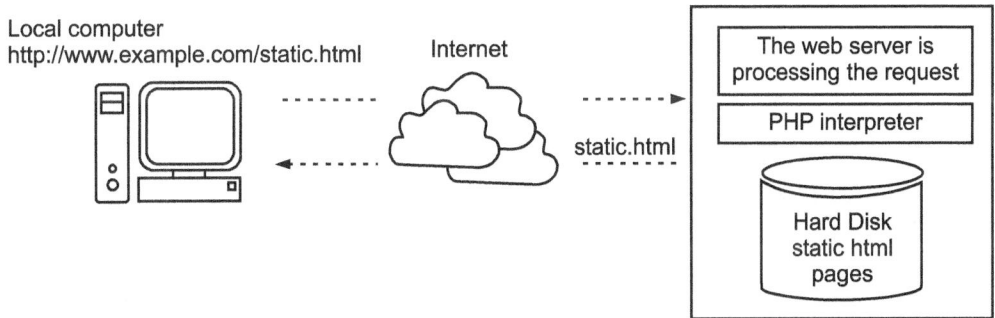

Fig. 1.1: Static web page is delivered to the user exactly as stored

Advantages:

1. Quick and easy to put together, even by someone who does not have much experience.
2. Ideal for demonstrating how a site will look.
3. Cache friendly, one copy can be shown to many people.

Disadvantages:

1. Difficult to maintain when a site gets large.
2. Difficult to keep consistent and up to date.
3. Offers little visitor personalization (all would have to be client side).

(ii) Dynamic Web Pages:

- A dynamic web page is a web page with web content that varies based on parameters provided by a user or a computer program.

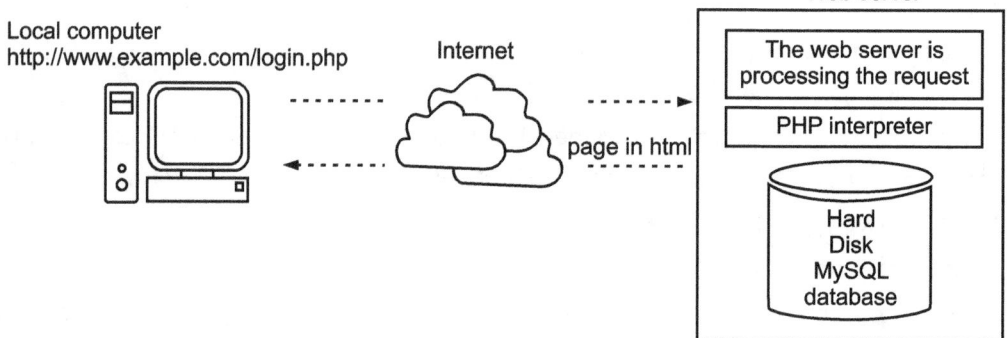

Fig. 1.2

- Dynamic web page: example of server-side scripting (PHP and MySQL).
- Typically written in various scripting languages or technologies such as ASP, PHP, Perl or JSP.

Advantages:

1. Offers highly personalized and customized visitor options.
2. Database access improves the personalized experience.
3. Scripts can read in data sources and display it differently depending on how it is run.

Disadvantages:

1. Personalized pages are not very cache friendly.
2. Requires a basic minimum knowledge of the language being used.
3. Scripts need more consideration when uploading and installing, particularly to Unix-related servers.

Web Publishing:

- Web publishing, or "online publishing," is the process of publishing content on the Internet.
- It includes creating and uploading websites, updating webpages, and posting blogs online and the published content may include text, images, videos, and other types of media.

- In order to publish content on the web, you need three things:
  1. web development software,
  2. an Internet connection, and
  3. a web server.
- The software may be a professional web design program like Dreamweaver or a simple web-based interface like WordPress.
- The Internet connection serves as the medium for uploading the content to the web server.
- Large sites may use a dedicated web host, but many smaller sites often reside on shared servers, which host multiple websites.

1.2 WWW

- The term WWW refers to the World Wide Web or simply the Web.
- The World Wide Web consists of all the public Web sites connected to the Internet worldwide, including the client devices (such as computers and cell phones) that access Web content.
- The WWW is just one of many applications of the Internet and computer networks.
- WWW is defined as **"the type of system designed for the hyper text documents that are used with the help of internet technology for the sake of searching and for different purposes of the benefit of the mankind is called as the World Wide Web or WWW."**

OR

- **"The World Wide Web is the universe of network-accessible information, an embodiment of human knowledge."**
- Different types of data or the pages are used or accessed with the help of www such as images, documents and also different types of media files.
- The World Web is based on technologies like: HTML (Hypertext Markup Language), HTTP (Hypertext Transfer Protocol) and WEB servers and Web browsers.

How Does the WWW Work?
  1. Information or data is stored in WWW as documents called web pages.
  2. Web pages are files stored on computers called web servers.
  3. Computers reading the Web pages are called web clients.
  4. Web clients view the pages with a program called a web browser like Internet Explorer, Chrome, and Firefox and so on.

1.3 W3C

- W3C Stands for the World Wide Web Consortium.
- W3C is an international consortium of companies involved with the Internet and the Web.
- The W3C was founded in 1994 by Tim Berners-Lee, the original architect of the www.

- The organization's purpose is to develop open standards so that the Web evolves in a single direction rather than being splintered among competing factions.
- The world wide web consortium exists to realize the full potential of the Web.
- The W3C is an industry consortium which seeks to promote standards for the evolution of the Web and interoperability between WWW products by producing specifications and reference software.
- W3C was created by the inventor of the web and is organized as a member organization and W3C is working to standardize the web and it creates and maintains www standards.

1.4 HTML

- HTML stands for HyperText Markup Language.
- HTML is the "mother tongue" of your browser.
- HTML was invented in 1990 by a scientist called Tim Berners-Lee.
- HTML is the most widely used language to write Web Pages. As its name suggests, HTML is a markup language.
  - Hypertext refers to the way in which web pages (HTML documents) are linked together. When you click a link in a web page, you are using hypertext.
  - Markup Language describes how HTML works. With a markup language, you simply "mark up" a text document with tags that tell a Web browser how to structure it to display. A markup language is a set of markup tags and the tags describes document content.
- Since, the early days of the web, there have been many versions of HTML, they are given below:

Version	Year
HTML	1991
HTML+	1993
HTML 2.0	1995
HTML 3.2	1997
HTML 4.01	1999
XHTML 1.0	2000
HTML5	2012
XHTML5	2013

- HTML can be edited by using a professional HTML editor like: Adobe Dreamweaver, Microsoft Expression Web and CoffeeCup HTML Editor.

HTML Page Structure:
- Fig. 1.3 shows page structure of HTML.
- A web page is also known as HTML page or HTML document.
- HTML files are text files featuring semantically tagged elements.
- HTML filenames are suffixed with .htm or .html extensions.

- A web page is marked by an opening <html>tag and a closing </html> tag and is divided into the following three major sections:
  1. **Comment Section (optional):** This section contains comments about the web page. It is important to include comments that tell us that is going on in the web page.
  2. **Head Section (optional):** The head section is defined with a starting <head> tag and closing </head> tag. This section usually contains a title for the Web page as shown in the Fig. 1.3.
  3. **Body Section:** The body section comes after the head section. The body section contains the entire information about the web page and its behaviour.

  A web page outline containing these three sections and the opening and closing HTML tags is illustrated in Fig. 1.3.

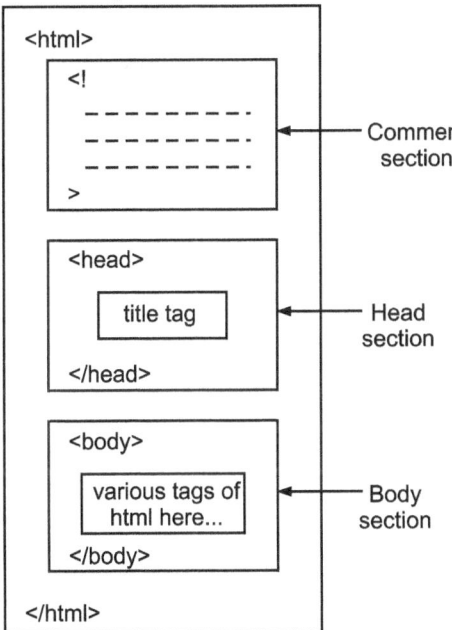

Fig. 1.3: Web page template

HTML Elements:
- HTML elements are the fundamentals of HTML.
- HTML documents are simply a text file made up of HTML elements and these elements are defined using HTML tags. A complete tag, having an opening <tag> and a closing </tag>.
- Every tag in HTML contains some attributes, which provide additional information about HTML elements. Attributes provide additional information about an element.
- Attributes are always specified in the start tag and come in name/value pairs like: name="value".
- HTML element has three basic parts i.e., opening tag, element content and closing tag.

Creating HTML Document:

- Creating an HTML document is easy. To begin coding HTML we need only two things: a simple-text editor and a web browser.

- Notepad is the most basic of simple-text editors and we will probably code a fair amount of HTML with it.

- Here, are the simple steps to create a basic HTML document:

    1. Open Notepad or another text editor.
    2. At the top of the page type <html>.
    3. On the next line, indent five spaces and now add the opening header tag: <head>.
    4. On the next line, indent ten spaces and type <title> </title>.
    5. Go to the next line, indent five spaces from the margin and insert the closing header tag: </head>.
    6. Five spaces in from the margin on the next line, type<body>.
    7. Now drop down another line and type the closing tag right below its mate: </body>.
    8. Finally, go to the next line and type </html>.
    9. In the File menu, choose Save As.
    10. In the Save as Type option box, choose All Files.
    11. Name the file template.htm.
    12. Click Save with .htm or .html extension.

Program for creating a html document.

```
<!DOCTYPE html>
<html>
<head>
<title>
</title>
<body>
<h1>Nirali Prakashan</h1>
<p>Textbook Publication Firm.</p>
</body>
</head>
</html>
```

Output:

Nirali Prakashan

Textbook Publication Firm.

- In above example or program:
  - o The DOCTYPE declaration defines the document type. The <!DOCTYPE> declaration helps the browser to display a web page correctly.
  - o The text between <html> and </html> describes the web page.
  - o The text between <body> and </body> is the visible page content.
  - o The text between <h1> and </h1> is displayed as a heading.
  - o The text between <p> and </p> is displayed as a paragraph contents.

1.5 HTML Tags

- Tags are the instructions that are embedded directly into the text of the document.
- An HTML tag is a single to the browser that it should do something other than just throw text upon the screen.
- By convention all HTML tags begin with an open angle bracket (<) and end with a close angle bracket (>).
- **Syntax of tag:** `<tag_name>content… </tag_name>`
- HTML tags tells, our browser which elements to present and how to present them. Where the element appears is determined by the order in which the tags appear.

1.5.1 Types of Tags

- HTML tags can be of two types:
  1. **Paired tags:** A tag is said to be paired tag if it, along with a companion tag, flanks the text.

     In paired tags, the first tag () is often called the opening tag and the second tag () is called the closing tag. The opening tag activities the effect and the closing tag turns the effect off.
  2. **Singular tags:** The second type of tag the singular tag or stand-alone tag. A stand-alone tag does not have a companion tag . For example <br> tag will insert a line break. This tag does not require any companion tag.

Common HTML tags:

1. HTML <!DOCTYPE> tag:

- The HTML <!DOCTYPE> tag is used for specifying which language and version the document is using. This is referred to as the Document Type Declaration (DTD).
- In HTML5, the <!DOCTYPE> declaration is much simpler than in previous versions of HTML, like this:

  ```
  <!DOCTYPE html>
  ```
- The <!DOCTYPE> declaration must go right at the top of the page, before any other HTML code.

2. **<html> Tag:**
- The <html> tag represents the root of an HTML document.
- The <html> tag is the container that contains all other HTML elements (except for the <!doctype> tag which is located before the opening HTML tag).
- All other HTML elements are nested between the <html> and </html> tags.
- The <html> tag tells the browser that this is an HTML document.

Syntax: `<html>............</html>`

Attribute	Description
1. `Manifest`	This attribute specifies the address of the document's application cache manifest and the value must be a valid URL.

3. **<title> Tag:**
- The <title> tag is used for declaring the title, or name, of the HTML document.
- The title is usually displayed in the browser's title bar (at the top) or the <title> tag defines a title in the browser toolbar. It is also displayed in browser bookmarks and search results.
- The title tag is placed between the opening and closing <head> tags.

Syntax: `<title>........................</title>`

4. **<head> Tag:**
- The <head> tag is used for indicating the head section of the HTML document.
- The <head> tag is a container for all the head elements and must include a title for the document, and can include scripts, styles, meta information, and so on.

Program for common HTML tags.

```
<!DOCTYPE html>
<html>
<head>What is meant by Web Technologies?
<title>Web Technologies</title>
<body>
<p>Web technologies related to the interface between web servers and
their clients. This information includes markup languages,
programming interfaces and languages, and standards for document
identification and display.</p>
<p>Parts of Web Technologies:<br>
1. HyperText Markup Language (HTML) is the main markup language for
   displaying web pages and other information that can be displayed
   in a web browser.<br>
2. Cascading Style Sheets (CSS) is a style sheet language used for
   describing the presentation semantics (the look and formatting) of
   a document written in a markup language.<br>
3. JavaScript (JS) is an open source client-side scripting language
   commonly implemented as part of a web browser in order to create
   enhanced user interfaces and dynamic websites.</p>
</body>
</head>
</html>
```

Output:

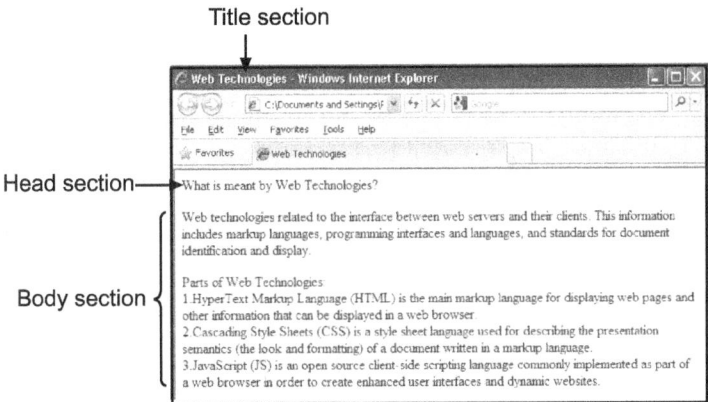

Title section

Head section

Body section

5. <body> Tag:

- The <body> tag defines the document's body.
- The <body> tag is used for indicating the main content section of the HTML document. The body tag is placed between the </head> and the </html> tags.
- The <body> tags contains all the contents of an HTML document, such as text, hyperlinks, images, tables, lists, etc.

  Syntax: <body>................</body>

- Attributes of <body> tag:

	Attribute	Value	Description
1.	alink	color	This attribute specifies the color of an active link in a document
2.	background	URL	This attribute specifies a background image for a document
3.	bgcolor	color	This attribute specifies the background color of a document
4.	link	color	This attribute specifies the color of unvisited links in a document
5.	text	color	This attribute specifies the color of the text in a document
6.	vlink	color	This attribute specifies the color of visited links in a document

Following example shows use of <body> tag.

```
<!DOCTYPE html>
<html>
<head>
<title>HTML <body> tag</title>
<body style="background-color:orange">
<p>Document content goes... here.</p>
</body>
</head>
</html>
```

Output:

Document content goes... here.

1.5.2 Text Formatting Tags

- The HTML tags are used for formatting text are called as text formatting tags.
- Following are the text formatting tags used in HTML.

1.	`<b>`	`<b>` tag defines bold text. Anything that appears in a `<b>`...`</b>` element is displayed in bold. **Syntax:** `<b>......</b>`
2.	`<em>`	The `<em>` tag is used for indicating emphasis. The `<em>` tag surrounds the word/term being emphasised. **Syntax:** `<em>......</em>`
3.	`<i>`	The content of the `<i>` tag is usually displayed in italic. The `<i>` tag can be used to indicate a technical term, a phrase from another language, a thought, or a ship name, etc. **Syntax:** `<i>......</i>`
4.	`<small>`	The `<small>` tag defines smaller text (and other side comments). The content of the `<small>` element is displayed one font size smaller than the rest of the text surrounding it. **Syntax:** `<small>......</small>`
5.	`<strong>`	The `<strong>` tag is used for indicating strong importance for its contents. The strong tag surrounds the emphasized word/phrase. **Syntax:** `<strong>......</strong>`
6.	`<sub>`	The `<sub>` tag defines subscript text. Subscript text appears half a character below the baseline. Subscript text can be used for chemical formulas, like H_2O. **Syntax:** `<sub>......</sub>`
7.	`<sup>`	The `<sup>` tag defines superscript text. Superscript text appears half a character above the baseline like 10^5. **Syntax:** `<sup>......</sup>`
8.	`<ins>`	The `<ins>` tag defines a text that has been inserted into a document. **Syntax:** `<ins>......</ins>`
9.	`<del>`	The `<del>` tag defines text that has been deleted from a document. **Syntax:** `<del>......</del>`
10.	`<u>`	The `<u>` tag usually results in the text being underlined. Anything that appears in a `<u>`...`</u>` element is displayed with underline, **Syntax:** `<u>......</u>`
11.	`<strike>`	Anything that appears in a `<strike>` tag is displayed with strikethrough, which is a thin line through the text like, ~~strikethrough.~~ **Syntax:** `<strike>......</strike>`
12.	`<big>`	The content of the `<big>` element is displayed one font size larger than the rest of the text surrounding it. **Syntax:** `<big>......</big>`

Example for text formatting tags:

```
<!DOCTYPE html>
<head>
<title> HTML <i> <b> <u> example</title>
</head>
<body>
<p>Nirali Prakashan</p>
<font size="4">Wecome to <b>Nirali Prakashan.</b> <br/></font>
<font size="2"><i>Nirali Prakashan</i> is a textbook publication
firm.<br/></font>
<font face="verdana" color="black">Nirali Prakashan <u>publised more
than 3500 book titles.</u></font>
</body>
</html>
```

Output:

Nirali Prakashan

Wecome to **Nirali Prakashan.**
Nirali Prakashan is a textbook publication firm.
Nirali Prakashan <u>publised more than 3500 book titles.</u>

Example for subscript and superscript tags:

```
<!DOCTYPE html>
<head>
<title> HTML <sub> <sup> example</title>
</head>
<body>
<h3> Mathematical Formula</h3>
<p>2<sup>10</sup>+ LOG<sub>10</sup><sup>5</sup></p>
</body>
</html>
```

Output:

Mathematical Formula

$2^{10}+ LOG_{10}{}^5$

HTML "Computer Output" Tags: Following table shows various types of computer output tags.

	Tag	Description
1.	`<code>`	The `<code>` tag is used for indicating a piece of code. The code tag surrounds the code being marked up. **Syntax:** `<code>.........</code>`
2.	`<kbd>`	`<kbd>`tag defines keyboard input text or keystroke. **Syntax:** `<kbd>.........</kbd>`
3.	`<samp>`	`<samp>`tag defines sample computer code. Syntax is: **Syntax:** `<samp>.........</samp>`
4.	`<var>`	It defines a variable. **Syntax:** `<var>.........</var>`

5.	`<pre>`	The HTML `<pre>` tag is used for indicating preformatted text. The code tag surrounds the code being marked up.
		Browsers normally render `<pre>` text in a fixed-pitched font, with whitespace in tact, and without word wrap.
		Syntax: `<pre>.........</pre>`

Attributes	Value	Description
`width`	`number`	This attribute specifies the maximum number of characters per line.

Example for <pre>tag:

```
<!DOCTYPE html>
<head>
<title>HTML <pre> tag Example</title>
<body>
<pre>This text has
been formatted using
    the HTML pre tag. The brower should
        display all white space
as it was entered.
</pre>
<pre width="30">
Text in a pre tag is displayed in a fixed-width
font, and it preserves both        spaces        and
line breaks
</pre>
</body>
</head>
</html>
```

Output:

```
This text has
been formatted using
    the HTML pre tag. The brower should
        display all white space
as it was entered.


Text in a pre tag is d i s p l a y e d in a f i x e d - w i d t h
font, and it preserves both        spaces        and
line breaks
```

- **HTML Citations, Quotations, and Definition Tags:**

Tag	Description
1. `<abbr>`	The HTML <abbr> tag is used for indicating an abbreviation, like "WWW" or "NATO". **Syntax:** `<abbr>...........</abbr>`
2. `<address>`	The HTML <address> tag defines the contact information for the author/owner of a document or an article. **Syntax:** `<address>...........</address>`
3. `<bdo>`	This tag defines the text direction. The <bdo> tag is used to override the current text direction. **Syntax:** `<bdo dir=" ">...........</bdo>` <table><tr><th>Attribute</th><th>Value</th><th>Description</th></tr><tr><td>1. dir</td><td>ltr rtl</td><td>It specifies the text direction of the text inside the <bdo> element</td></tr></table>
4. `<blockquote>`	This tag defines a section that is quoted from another source. The HTML <blockquote> tag is used for indicating long quotations (i.e. quotations that span multiple lines).
5. `<q>`	The HTML <q> tag defines a short quotation. Browsers normally insert quotation marks around the quotation using <q>tag. **Syntax:** `<q>...........</q>` <table><tr><th>Attribute</th><th>Value</th><th>Description</th></tr><tr><td>1. cite</td><td>URL</td><td>Specifies the source URL of the quote</td></tr></table>
6. `<cite>`	The HTML <cite> tag is used for indicating a citation. **Syntax:** `<cite>...........</cite>`
7. `<dfn>`	The HTML <dfn> tag is used for indicating a definition. The <dfn> tag surrounds the word/term being defined. **Syntax:** `<def>...........</def>`

Example for HTML citations, quotations and definition tags:

```
<!DOCTYPE html>
<title> HTML <dfn> <strong> <cite> <code>  example</title>
<head></head>
<body>
<p>Nirali Prakashan</p>
This is <strong>important</strong>. It <strong>really is important.
<strong>And this is even more important!</strong></strong>
<p><dfn>Definition</dfn>: To define the meaning of a word, phrase or
term.</p>
<p>Have   you   heard   that   <dfn><abbr   title="HyperText   Markup
Language">HTML</abbr></dfn> is the predominant markup language for
Web pages?</p>
According to <cite title="HTML & XHTML: The Definitive Guide.
Published    by    Nirali    Prakashan">Chuck    Musciano    and    Bill
Kennedy</cite>, the HTML cite tag actually exists!<br>
To create a new array, type the following: <code>var faq = new
Array(3)</code>
</body>
</html>
```

Output:

```
Nirali Prakashan

This is important. It really is important. And this is even more important!

Definition: To define the meaning of a word, phrase or term.

Have you heard that HTML is the predominant markup language for Web pages?

According to Chuck Musciano and Bill Kennedy, the HTML cite tag actually exists!
To create a new array, type the following: var faq = new Array(3)
```

Block level tags:
- Most HTML elements are defined as block level elements or as inline elements.
- Block level elements normally start (and end) with a new line when displayed in a browser.

(i) <!--...--> comment Tag:
- The comment tag is used to insert comments in the source code.
- Comments are not displayed in the browsers.
- Comments can be inserted into the HTML code to make it more readable and understandable. Comments are ignored by the browser and are not displayed.

Example for comment tag:

```
<html>
<title> HTML comment </title>
<!-- The level 4 heading goes here -->
<h4>How to comment out your code.</h4>
<h3>!--....-- tag used for comment and they are simply there for the
programmer's benefit.</h3>
<!-- The text goes here -->
<p>This code demonstrates the HTML code to hide your comments.</p>
</html>
```

Output:

```
How to comment out your code.

!--....-- tag used for comment and they are simply there for
the programmer's benefit.

This code demonstrates the HTML code to hide your comments.
```

(ii) HTML heading tags:

- The HTML <h1> to <h6> tags are used to define HTML headings. <h1> defines the most important heading. While <h6> defines the least important heading.

Syntax:
```
<h1>...........</h1>
<h2>...........</h2>
<h3>...........</h3>
<h4>...........</h4>
<h5>...........</h5>
<h6>...........</h6>
```

Attribute	Value	Description
1. align	left center right justify	Align attribute specifies the alignment of a heading.

Example for HTML heading tags:
```
<!DOCTYPE html>
<head>
<title> HTML headings example</title>
<body>
<h1 align="center">This is heading 1 Nirali Prakashan</h1>
<h2 align="left">This is heading 2 Nirali Prakashan </h2>
<h3>This is heading 3 Nirali Prakashan </h3>
<h4 align="right">This is heading 4 Nirali Prakashan </h4>
<h5 align="left">This is heading 5 Nirali Prakashan </h5>
<h6 align="center">This is heading 6 Nirali Prakashan </h6>
</body>
</head>
</html>
```

Output:

> # This is heading 1 Nirali Prakashan
> ## This is heading 2 Nirali Prakashan
> ### This is heading 3 Nirali Prakashan
> #### This is heading 4 Nirali Prakashan
> ##### This is heading 5 Nirali Prakashan
> ###### This is heading 6 Nirali Prakashan

(iii) <p> Tag:

- HTML documents are divided into paragraphs.
- The HTML <p> tag is used for defining a paragraph.

Syntax: <p>...........</p>

Attribute	Value	Description
1. align	left right center justify	Align attribute specifies the alignment of the text within a paragraph.

(iv) \
 Tag:

- The HTML \
 tag is used for specifying a line break.
- The \
 tag is an empty tag. In other words, it has no end tag.

    Syntax: `<br/>`

Example for \<p> and \
 tags:

```
<!DOCTYPE html>
<head>
<title> HTML paragraph example</title>
<body>
<p>A technical definition of the World Wide Web is all the resources
and users on the Internet that are using the Hypertext Transfer
Protocol (HTTP).
<br>W3C (World Wide Web Consortium), an international consortium of
companies involved with the Internet and the Web.<br> HTML is a
markup language. A markup language is a set of markup tags and the
tags describes document content </p>
<p align="center">HTML stands for Hyper Text Markup Language.
</p>
<p>Hypertext <br> Text displayed on screen which can be accessed
usually by a mouse click or key press. Apart from text, it can
display other cool stuff like images, tables, frames etc.
</p>
<p align="left">Markup Language <br>  Language which is used to
structure data and present it to the user.
</p>
<p align="left">HTML is a language for describing web pages.</p>
</body>
</head>
</html>
```

Output:

A technical definition of the World Wide Web is all the resources and users on the
Internet that are using the Hypertext Transfer Protocol (HTTP).
W3C (World Wide Web Consortium), an international consortium of companies involved
with the Internet and the Web.
HTML is a markup language. A markup language is a set of markup tags and the tags
describes document content

HTML stands for Hyper Text Markup Language

Hypertext
Text displayed on screen which can be accessed usually by a mouse click or key press.
Apart from text, it can display other cool stuff like images, tables, frames etc.

Markup Language
Language which is used to structure data and present it to the user.

HTML is a language for describing web pages.

(v) \<center> Tag:

- The \<center> tag is used to center-align text.

(vi) Non breaking Spaces:

- Suppose we were to use the phrase "14 Angry Men." Here we would not want a browser to split the "14" and "Angry" across two lines:
- A good example of this technique appears in the movie "14 Angry Men."
- In cases where we do not want the client browser to break text, we should use a nonbreaking space entity ( ) instead of a normal space.
- For example, when coding the "14 Angry Men" paragraph, we would use something similar to the following code:

```
<p>A good example of this technique appears in the movie
"14 Angry Men."</p>
```

(vii) <div> Tag:

- The <div> tag defines a division or a section in an HTML document.
- The <div> tag is used to group block-elements to format them with CSS.

Syntax: `<div>............</div>`

Attribute	Value	Description

1. `align`	`left`
	`right`
	`center`
	`justify`
		Align attribute specifies the alignment of the content inside a <div> element

Example for <div> tag:

```
<!DOCTYPE html>
<title> HTML div example</title>
<head></head>
<body>
<div style="background-color:orange;text-align:center">
<p>Nirali Prakashan</p>
</div>
<div style="background-color:pink;text-align:center">
<p>Pragati Group</p>
</div>
</body>
</html>
```

Output:

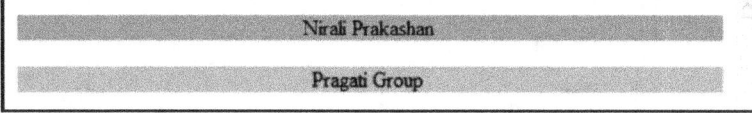

(viii) <span> Tag:

- The HTML <span> tag is used for grouping and applying styles to inline elements.
- The <span> tag provides a way to add a hook to a part of a text or a part of a document. The <span> tag provides no visual change by itself.
- The difference between the <span> tag and the <div> tag is that the <span> tag is used with inline elements whilst the <div> tag is used with block-level content.

Syntax: `<span>............</span>`

Example for <span> tag:
```
<!DOCTYPE html>
<head> span tag </head>
<title> HTML span tag example</title>
<body>
<p>The   <span   style="color:red">span   tag   is   used   with   inline
elements</span> and the <span style="color:purple">div tag</span> is
used with block-level content.</p>
 </body>
</html>
```
Output:

> span tag
>
> **The** span tag is used with inline elements **and the div tag is used with block-level content.**

(ix) <hr> Tag:

- Horizontal rules are used to visually break up sections of a document. The HTML <hr> tag is used for specifying a horizontal rule in an HTML document.
- The <hr> tag creates a line from the current position in the document to the right margin and breaks the line accordingly.
- The <hr> tag is used to separate content (or define a change) in an HTML page.
- The intention behind the <hr> tag is that it indicates a paragraph-level thematic break.

Syntax: `<hr/>`

Attribute	Value	Description
1. align	left center right	This attribute specifies the alignment of a <hr> element.
2. noshade	noshade	This attribute specifies that a <hr> element should render in one solid color (noshaded), instead of a shaded color.
3. size	pixels	This attribute specifies the height of a <hr> element.
4. width	pixels %	This attribute specifies the width of a <hr> element.

Example for <hr> tag.
```
<!DOCTYPE html>
<head>
<title> HTML <hr> example</title>
</head>
<body>
<p>This is paragraph one and should be on top</p>
<hr align="right" width="50%">
<p>This is paragraph two and should be at middle</p>
<hr size="7">
<p>This is paragraph two and should be at bottom</p>
<hr width="80%" size="12" noshade>
</body>
</html>
```

Output:

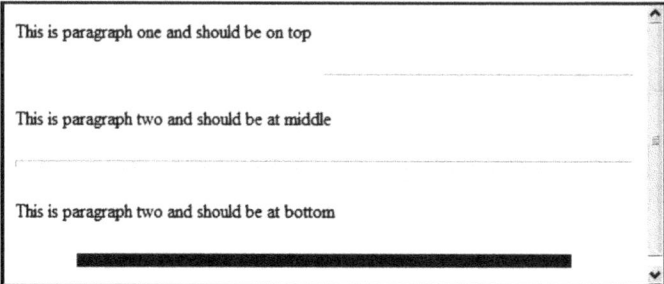

(x) HTML Marquees:

- A HTML marquee is a scrolling piece of text displayed either horizontally across or vertically down your web site page depending on the settings. This is created by using HTML tag <marquees>.

Syntax:
```
<marquee attribute_name="attribute_value"....more attributes>
One or more lines or text message or image
</marquee>
```

- A HTML marquee can have following attributes:
  1. `width`: how wide the marquee is. This will have a value like 10 or 20%etc.
  2. `height`: how tall the marquee is. This will have a value like 10 or 20% etc.
  3. `direction`: which direction the marquee should scroll. This will have value either up, down, left or right.
  4. `behavior`: what type of scrolling. This will have value scroll, slid and alternate.
  5. `scrolldelay`: how long to delay between each jump. This will have a value like 10 etc.
  6. `scrollamount`: how far to jump. This will have a value like 10 etc.
  7. `loop`: how many times to loop. The default value is INFINITE, which means that the marquee loops endlessly.
  8. `bgcolor`: background color. This will have any color name or color hex value.
  9. `hspace`: horizontal space around the marquee. This will have a value like 10 or 20%etc.
  10. `vspace`: vertical space around the marquee. This will have a value like 10 or 20%etc.

Example for HTML marques
```
<!DOCTYPE html>
<head>
<title> HTML marquee tag</title>
</head>
<body>
<marquee>This is basic example of marquee tag in HTML</marquee>
<br />
<br />
<marquee width="50%">This example will take only 50% width</marquee>
<br />
<br />
<marquee  direction="right">This  text  will  scroll  from  left  to
right</marquee>
</body>
</html>
```

Output:

```
This is basic example of marquee

This example will take onl

This text will scroll from left to right
```

(xi) <font> Tag:

- <font> tag is used to add style, size, and color to the text on your site.
- The <font> tag specifies the font face, font size, and font color of text.

Syntax: `<font>............</font>`

Attribute	Value	Description
1. `color`	`rgb(x,x,x)` `#xxxxxx` `colorname`	This attribute specifies the color of text.
2. `face`	`font_family`	This attribute specifies the font of text.
3. `size`	`number`	This attribute specifies the size of text.

Example for <font> tag:

```
<!DOCTYPE html>
<head>
<title> HTML <font> example</title>
</head>
<body>
<p><h2>Nirali Prakashan</h2></p>
<font size="4" color="red">Wecome to Nirali Prakashan. <br/></font>
<font size="2" color="blue">Nirali Prakashan is a textbook
publication firm.<br/></font>
<font face="verdana" color="black">Nirali Prakashan publised more
than 3500 book titles.</font>
</body>
</html>
```

Output:

```
Nirali Prakashan

Wecome to Nirali Prakashan.
Nirali Prakashan is a textbook publication firm.
Nirali Prakashan publised more than 3500 book titles.
```

1.5.3 List Tags

- We can list out our items, subjects or menu in the form of a list. HTML gives us three different types of lists, i.e. an unordered list (This will list items using bullets), a ordered list (This will use different schemes of numbers to list your items) and a definition list (This is arrange your items in the same way as they are arranged in a dictionary).

1. Unordered Lists:

- An unordered list is a collection of related items that have no special order or sequence.
- The most common unordered list, we will find on the Web is a collection of hyperlinks to other documents.

- Unordered list is created by using <ul> tag. Each item in the list is marked with a butllet. The bullet itself comes in three flavors: squares, discs, and circles. The default bullet displayed by most web browsers is the traditional full disc.

2. Ordered Lists:

- The typical browser formats the contents of an ordered list just like an unordered list, except that the items are numbered instead of bulleted.
- The numbering starts at one and is incremented by one for each successive ordered list element tagged with <li> tag.
- Ordered list is created by using <ol> tag. Each item in the list is marked with a number.

3. Definition Lists:

- HTML and XHTML also support a list style entirely different from the ordered and unordered lists we have discussed so far - definition lists.
- Like the entries we find in a dictionary or encyclopedia, complete with text, pictures, and other multimedia elements, the Definition List is the ideal way to present a glossary, list of terms, or other name/value list.
- Definition List makes use of following three tags.
  - <dl> - Defines the start of the list.
  - <dt> - A term.
  - <dd> - Term definition.
  - </dl> - Defines the end of the list.

1. <meta> Tag: [Oct. 11]

- Meta elements are typically used to specify page description, keywords, author of the document, last modified, and other metadata. The <meta> tag always goes inside the head element. Metadata is data (information) about data.
- The HTML <meta> tag is used for declaring metadata for the HTML document. Metadata will not be displayed on the page, but will be machine parsable.

Syntax: `<meta name = string content = string>`

Attributes	Value	Description
1. `charset`	`character_set`	This attribute specifies the character encoding for the HTML document.
2. `content`	`text`	This attribute specifies gives the value associated with the http-equiv or name attribute.

3. `http-equiv`	`content-type`
	`default-style`
	`refresh`
		This attribute specifies provides an HTTP header for the information/value of the content attribute.

4. `name`	`application-name`
	`author`
	`description`
	`generator`
	`keywords`
		This attribute specifies a name for the metadata.

5. `scheme`	`format/URI`	This attribute specifies a scheme to be used to interpret the value of the content attribute.

- Metadata can include document description, keywords, author etc. It can also be used to refresh the page or set cookies.
- The <meta> tag is placed between the opening/closing <head> tags.

Example for <meta> tag:

```
<!DOCTYPE html>
<head>
<title>Meta Refresh Example</title>
<meta http-equiv="refresh"
          content="5;url=/html_5/tags/html_meta_tag_example.cfm" />
</head>
<body style="background-color:#ff9900;">
<p>Watch me redirect to another page in 5 seconds...</p>
</body>
</html>
```

Output:

Watch me redirect to another page in 5 seconds...

2. <li>List Tag:

- The <li> tag defines a list item.
- The <li> tag is used in ordered lists (<ol>), unordered lists (<ul>), and in menu lists (<menu>).

Syntax: <li>.........</li>

Attributes	Value	Description
1. type	1 A a I i disc square circle	This attribute specifies which kind of bullet point will be used.
2. value	number	This attribute specifies the value of a list item.

3. <ul> Unordered List Tag:

- An unordered list is a collection of related items that have no special order or sequence.
- The most common unordered list we will find on the Web is a collection of hyperlinks to other documents.
- An unordered list starts with the <ul> tag. Each list item starts with the <li> tag. The <ul> tag defines an unordered (bulleted) list.

Syntax: <ul>.........</ul>

Attributes	Value	Description
1. compact	compact	This attribute specifies that the list should render smaller than normal.
2. type	disc square circle	This attribute specifies the kind of marker to use in the list.

Example for <ul> tag.

```
<!DOCTYPE html>
<body>
<head><h3>An Unordered List Example</h3>
<h4>Disc bullets list:</h4>
<ul type="disc">
 <li>Apples</li>
 <li>Bananas</li>
 <li>Lemons</li>
 <li>Oranges</li>
</ul>
<h4>Circle bullets list:</h4>
<ul type="circle">
 <li>Apples</li>
 <li>Bananas</li>
 <li>Lemons</li>
 <li>Oranges</li>
</ul>
<h4>Square bullets list:</h4>
<ul type="square">
 <li>Apples</li>
 <li>Bananas</li>
 <li>Lemons</li>
 <li>Oranges</li>
</ul>
</body>
</head>
</html>
```

Output:

An Unordered List Example

Disc bullets list:

- Apples
- Bananas
- Lemons
- Oranges

Circle bullets list:

- o Apples
- o Bananas
- o Lemons
- o Oranges

Square bullets list:

- Apples
- Bananas
- Lemons
- Oranges

- We can also nested unordered list as follows:

```
<!DOCTYPE html>
<body>
<h4>A nested List:</h4>
<ul>
  <li>Coffee</li>
  <li>Tea
    <ul>
    <li>Black tea</li>
    <li>Green tea
      <ul>
      <li>China</li>
      <li>Africa</li>
      </ul>
    </li>
    </ul>
  </li>
  <li>Milk</li>
</ul>
</body>
</html>
```

Output:

4. <ol> Ordered List Tag:

- The typical browser formats the contents of an ordered list just like an unordered list, except that the items are numbered instead of bulleted.
- An ordered list starts with the <ol> tag. Each list item starts with the <li> tag. Each item in the list is marked with a number.

Syntax: <ol>............</ol>

Attributes	Value	Description
1. compact	compact	This attribute specifies that the list should render smaller than normal.
2. reversed	reversed	This attribute specifies that the list order should be descending like 9,8,7...
3. start	number	This attribute specifies the start value of an ordered list.
4. type	1 A a I i	This attribute specifies the kind of marker to use in the list.

Example for <ol> tag:

```
<!DOCTYPE html>
<head>
<body>
<head><h3>An Ordered List Example</h3>
<h4>Numbered list:</h4>
<ol>
 <li>Apples</li>
 <li>Bananas</li>
 <li>Lemons</li>
</ol>
<h4>Letters list:</h4>
<ol type="A">
 <li>Apples</li>
 <li>Bananas</li>
 <li>Lemons</li>
</ol>
<h4>Lowercase letters list:</h4>
<ol type="a">
 <li>Apples</li>
 <li>Bananas</li>
 <li>Lemons</li>
</ol>
<h4>Roman numbers list:</h4>
<ol type="I">
 <li>Apples</li>
 <li>Bananas</li>
 <li>Lemons</li>
 </ol>
<h4>Lowercase Roman numbers list:</h4>
<ol type="i">
 <li>Apples</li>
 <li>Bananas</li>
 <li>Lemons</li>
 </ol>
</body>
</head>
</html>
```

Output:

An Ordered List Example

Numbered list:

1. Apples
2. Bananas
3. Lemons

Letters list:

A. Apples
B. Bananas
C. Lemons

Lowercase letters list:

a. Apples
b. Bananas
c. Lemons

Roman numbers list:

I. Apples
II. Bananas
III. Lemons

Lowercase Roman numbers list:

i. Apples
ii. Bananas
iii. Lemons

5. Definition Lists:

- A definition list is a list of items, with a description of each item.
- The <dl> tag defines a definition list. <dl> tag is used to provide a list of items with associated definitions.
- Every item should be put in a dt and its definition goes in the dd directly following it. This list is typically rendered without bullets of any kind.
- The definition list is the ideal way to present a glossary, list of terms, or other name/value list.

    Syntax: <dl>............</dl>

- Definition List makes use of following two tags.

    (i) <dt>: The dt tag is used inside dl. It marks up a term whose definition is provided by the next dd. The dt tag may only contain text-level markup.

    (ii) <dd>: The <dd> tag is used inside a dl definition list to provide the definition of the text in the dt tag. It may contain block elements but also plain text and markup.

Example for definition list

```
<!DOCTYPE html>
<body>
<h4>A Definition List:</h4>
<dl>
   <dt>Coffee</dt>
   <dd>Black hot drink</dd>
   <dt>Milk</dt>
   <dd>White cold drink</dd>
</dl>
</body>
</html>
```

Output:

```
┌─────────────────────────────────────────┐
│ A Definition List:                       │
│                                          │
│ Coffee                                   │
│         Black hot drink                  │
│ Milk                                     │
│         White cold drink                 │
└─────────────────────────────────────────┘
```

HTML Linking

- The real power of HTML is its ability to link to the other documents and pieces of text, images, video or audio.
- Links are usually highlighted or underlined in a document so that we know of their existence. Clicking on the link opens up the document for viewing.
- Web pages can contain links that directly goes to other pages and even specific parts of a given page. These links are known as hyperlinks.
- Hyperlinks allow visitors to navigate between web sites by clicking on words, phrases, and images. Thus, we can create hyperlinks using text or images available on our any web page.

- A hyperlink (or link) is a word, group of words, or image that we can click on to jump to a new document or a new section within the current document.
- When we move the cursor over a link in a web page, the arrow will turn into a little hand.

(a) <a> Anchor Tag:
- The HTML <a> tag is used for creating a hyperlink to another web page.
- The <a> tag can be used in two ways:
    1. To create a link to another document, by using the href attribute
    2. To create a bookmark inside a document, by using the name attribute
- The <a> tag defines a hyperlink, which is used to link from one page to another.
- By default, links will appear as follows in all browsers:
    o An unvisited link is underlined and blue,
    o A visited link is underlined and purple, and
    o An active link is underlined and red.

Syntax: `<a href="Document URL">............</a>`

Attributes	Value	Description
1. charset	char_encoding	This attribute specifies the character-set of a linked document.
2. coords	coordinates	This attribute specifies the coordinates of a link.
3. href	URL	This attribute specifies the URL of the page the link goes to.
4. hreflang	language_code	This attribute specifies the language of the linked document.
5. media	media_query	This attribute specifies what media/device the linked document is optimized for.
6. name	section_name	This attribute specifies the name of an anchor.
7. rel	alternate author bookmark help license next nofollow noreferrer prefetch prev search tag	This attribute specifies the relationship between the current document and the linked document.
8. rev	text	This attribute specifies the relationship between the linked document and the current document.
9. shape	default rect circle poly	This attribute specifies the shape of a link.
10. target	_blank _parent _self _top framename	This attribute specifies where to open the linked document.
11. type	MIME_type	This attribute specifies the MIME type of the linked document.

Example for <a> tag:
```
<!DOCTYPE html>
<body>
<p>
<a href="default.asp">HTML</a> This is a link to a page on this
                                                    website.
</p>
<p>
<a href="http://www.google.com/">Google</a> This is a link to a
website on the World Wide Web.
</p>
</body>
</html>
```
Output:

How to create hyperlinks

HTML This is a link to a page on this website.

Google This is a link to a website on the World Wide Web.

Concept of URL:

- URLs vary depending on the location to which you are linking.
- If the file is on web, URL is longer and if file is on our local computer, URL is shorter.
- There are two types of URL:
    1. **Absolute URL:** It contains all the information which is required to identify the files on the web. It contains the protocol, hostname, folder name, file name which are all essential for linking to web sites.

        For example: http:// www.powerweb.com/facilities/index.html

        http://www.yahoo.com/download/
    2. **Relative URL:** A relative URL points to files in the same folder or on the same server. In these cases, a browser does not need the server name or protocol indicator because it assumes the files are in the folder or on the server.
- There are two types of relative URLs:
    (i)   In **Document Relative URLs**, the document address is given in relation with the originating document.
    (ii)   In **Server Relative URLs**, the document address is given in relation with the server on which the document is present.

1. Linking to a Page Section:

- We can create a link to a particular section of a page by using name attribute. Here we will create three links with-in this page itself.
- First create a link to reach to the top of this page. Here is the code we have used for the title heading HTML Text Links

```
<h1>HTML Text Links <a name="top"></a></h1>
```

- Now we have a place where we can reach. To reach to this place use the following code with-in this document anywhere:

```
<a href="/html/html_text_links.htm#top">Go to the Top</a>
```

- This will produce following link and we try using this link to reach to the top of this page:

  Go to the Top

2. Setting Link Colors:

- We can set colors of our links, active links and visited links using link, alink and vlink attributes of <body> tag. But it is recommended to use CSS to set colors of links, visited links and active links.

- Following is the example we have used for our example.

```
a:link     {color:#900B09; background-color:transparent}
a:visited {color:#900B09; background-color:transparent}
a:active   {color:#FF0000; background-color:transparent}
a:hover    {color:#FF0000; background-color:transparent}
```

3. Use an image as a link: We can also use image as link, following example shows this.

Example:

```
<!DOCTYPE html>
<body>
<p>Create a link of an image:
<a href="default.asp">
<img src="smiley.gif" alt="HTML tutorial" width="32" height="32" />
</a></p>
<p>No border around the image, but still a link:
<a href="default.asp">
<img border="0" src="smiley.gif" alt="HTML tutorial" width="32"
height="32" />
</a></p>
</body>
</html>
```

Output:

Create a link of an image:

No border around the image, but still a link:

4. Example shows jump or link to another part of a document (on the same page).

```
<!DOCTYPE html>
<body>
<p>
<a href="#C4">See also Chapter 1.</a><br/>
<a href="#C4">See also Chapter 2.</a><br/>
<a href="#C4">See also Chapter 3.</a><br/>
```

```
<a href="#C4">See also Chapter 4.</a><br/>
<a href="#C4">See also Chapter 5.</a><br/>
<a href="#C4">See also Chapter 6.</a><br/>
<a href="#C4">See also Chapter 7.</a><br/>
</p>
<h2>Chapter 1</h2>
<p>This chapter explains web</p>
<h2>Chapter 2</h2>
<p>This chapter explains web site</p>
<h2>Chapter 3</h2>
<p>This chapter explains HTML</p>
<h2><a name="C4">Chapter 4</a></h2>
<p>This chapter explains ASP</p>
<h2>Chapter 5</h2>
<p>This chapter explains Javascript</p>
<h2>Chapter 6</h2>
<p>This chapter explains CSS</p>
<h2>Chapter 7</h2>
<p>This chapter explains JQuery</p>
</body>
</html>
```

Output:

5. **Following example shows link to a mail message (will only work if we have mail installed).**

```
<!DOCTYPE html>
<body>
<p>
This is an email link:
<a href="mailto:someone@example.com?Subject=Hello%20again">
Send Mail</a>
</p>
<p>
<b>Note:</b> Spaces between words should be replaced by %20 to ensure
that the browser will display the text properly.
</p>
</body>
</html>
```

Output:

> This is an email link: Send Mail
>
> **Note:** Spaces between words should be replaced by %20 to ensure that the browser will display the text properly.

- When you click, Send Mail then following screen displays:

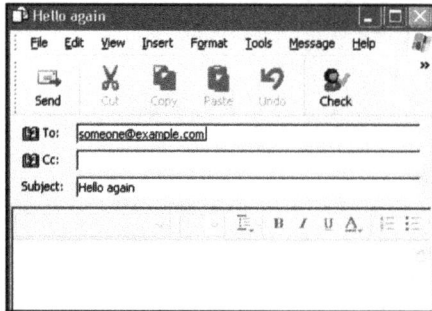

1.5.4 HTML Images

- Images are very important to beautify as well as to depicts many concepts on our web page.

- Its is true that one single image is worth than thousands of words. So as a web developer we should have clear understanding on how to use images in our web pages.

- There are basically two types of graphic programs:

  1. Bitmap based, and

  2. Vector based.

- The former comprises the image editing and painting programs while the latter refers to the drawing programs. Programs such as Adobe Photoshop, Corel Photo Paint and Painter, Macromedia Fireworks, etc. fall into the image editing and painting category.

- CorelDraw, Adobe Illustrator, and Macromedia Freehand are examples of vector-based drawing programs. Many programs, now, include tools for manipulating both types of images.

  1. **JPEG Images:** A JPEG file stands for Joint Photographic Experts Group. We would use a JPEG image for photographs, realistic scenes or other images with subtle changes in tone.

  2. **GIF Images:** Images are limited to 256 colors; they are cross-platform, which means any computer can view them. GIF files are compressed which makes them small in file size but not in dimension. GIF files unlike JPEG files do not lose quality in compression. GIF files have the .gif extension.

  3. **BMP:** Bitmap (BMP) is the standard Windows image format on DOS and Windows compatible computers. The BMP format supports RGB (red, qreen, blue) indexed-colors, grayscale, and Bitmap color modes. BMP files have the .bmp extension.

A bitmap image is made up of pixels or bits (binary digits) of information arranged on a grid. Each bit can be visualized as a dot. The number of pixels per unit of measurement, example, ppi (pixels per inch) or dpi (dots per inch) determines the resolution of the image.

4. **PDF:** Portable Document Format (PDF) is used by Adobe Acrobat. PDF files can represent both vector and bitmap graphics and can contain electronic document search and navigation features such as electronic links. The PhotoShop PDF format supports RGB, indexed-colors, CMYK (cyan, magenta, yellow and black), grayscale and Bitmap. PhotoShop has the .pdf extension.

5. **Targa**: Format is designed for systems using the true vision video board and is commonly supported by MS-DOS color applications. The Targa format supports 32 bit RGB, grayscale, and 16 bit and 24 bit RGB files without alpha channels. While saving an RGB image in this format, you can choose a pixel depth. Targa files have the .tga extension.

6. **TIFF**: Tagged-Image File Format (TIFF) is used to exchange files between applications and computer platforms. Virtually all paint programs, image editing, and page layout applications support TIFF format. Most of the older desktop scanners produce TIFF images and you should save images scanned as TIFF files unless you scan directly to PhotoShop. The TIFF format supports CMYK, RGB, and grayscale files. TIFF files have the .tif extension.

7. **PNG:** Portable Network Graphics (PNG) Pronounced "ping" was developed as an alternative to GIF. PNG files support 24-bit images and produces background transparency without jagged edges. Some older versions of Web browsers may not support PNG images. Like GIF and JPEG files, PNG files are cross-platform and compressed. PNG files can have more colors than GIF files and also compress smaller. PNG files have the .png extension.

1. **<img> Image Tag:**
- In HTML, images are defined with the <img> tag.
- The <img> tag is empty, which means that it contains attributes only, and has no closing tag.
- We will insert any image in our web page by using <img> tag.

Syntax:
```
<img src="image URL" attr_name="attr_value"... more attributes />
```

Attributes	Value	Description
1. alt	text	This attribute specifies an alternate text for an image.
2. src	URL	This attribute specifies the URL of an image.
3. align	top bottom middle left right	This attribute specifies the alignment of an image according to surrounding elements.

contd. ...

4.	`alt`	`text`	This attribute specifies an alternate text for an image.
5.	`border`	`pixels`	This attribute specifies the width of the border around an image.
6.	`crossoriginNew`	`anonymous use-credentials`	This attribute allow images from third-party sites that allow cross-origin access to be used with canvas.
7.	`height`	`pixels`	This attribute specifies the height of an image.
8.	`hspace`	`pixels`	This attribute specifies the whitespace on left and right side of an image.
9.	`ismap`	`ismap`	This attribute specifies an image as a server-side image-map.
10.	`longdesc`	`URL`	This attribute specifies the URL to a document that contains a long description of an image.
11.	`src`	`URL`	This attribute specifies the URL of an image.
12.	`usemap`	`#mapname`	This attribute specifies an image as a client-side image-map.
13.	`vspace`	`pixels`	This attribute specifies the whitespace on top and bottom of an image.
14.	`width`	`pixels`	This attribute specifies the width of an image.

Example for <img> tag.

```
<!DOCTYPE html>
<head>
<meta name="GENERATOR" content="MICROSOFT FRONTPAGE 4.0">
<meta name="PROGID" content="FRONTPAGE.EDITOR.DOCUMENT">
<title>IMAGE ALIGNMENT</title>
</head>
<body>
<center>THIS EXAMPLE IS FOR IMAGE ALIGNMENT:</center>
<p><img src = "http://images3.wikia.nocookie.net/__cb20120720034705/
christmasspecials/images/8/80/Mickey_Mouse.jpg"          width="90"
height="80" align ="TOP" border = 1> HI, I AM MICKEY, A TOP TEXT</p>
<p><img src = "http://images3.wikia.nocookie.net/__cb20120720034705/
christmasspecials/images/8/80/Mickey_Mouse.jpg"          width="90"
height="80" align ="MIDDLE" border = 1> HI, I AM MICKEY, A MIDDLE
TEXT</p>
<p><img src = "http://images3.wikia.nocookie.net/__cb20120720034705/
christmasspecials/images/8/80/Mickey_Mouse.jpg"          width="90"
height="80" align ="BOTTOM" border = 1> HI, I AM MICKEY, A BOTTOM
TEXT</p>
</body>
</html>
```

Output:

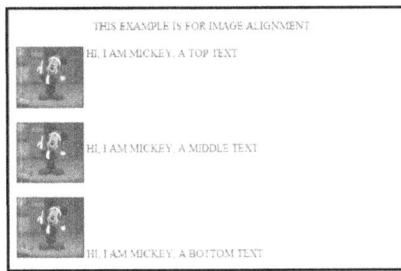

Example for image alignment:

```
<!DOCTYPE html>
<head>
<meta name="GENERATOR" content="MICROSOFT FRONTPAGE 4.0">
<meta name="PROGID" content="FRONTPAGE.EDITOR.DOCUMENT">
<title>HI</title>
</head>
<body>
<p><img src = "http://images.free-extras.com/pics/m/mickey_mouse-
1104.jpg" width="90" height="80" align ="LEFT" border = 1> HI, I AM
MICKEY, A TEXT AFTER IMAGE<br>YOU CAN WRITE A WHOLE PARAGRAPH<br>
ALSO AND CAN SEE IT AS <b>LEFT ALIGNMENT </b> </p> <br>
<p><img src = "http://images.free-extras.com/pics/m/mickey_mouse-
1104.jpg" width="90" height="80" align ="RIGHT" border = 1> HI, I AM
MICKEY, A TEXT BEFORE IMAGE YOU CAN WRITE IN <b>RIGHT ALIGNMENT</b>
SAME THAT OF LEFT ALIGNMENT</p>
</body>
</html>
```

Output:

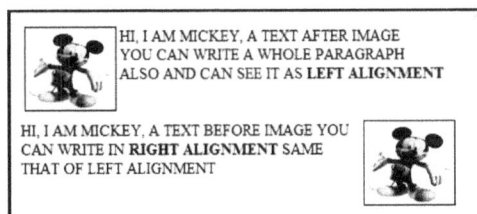

Example for image spacing:

```
<!DOCTYPE html>
<head>
<meta name="GENERATOR" content="MICROSOFT FRONTPAGE 4.0">
<meta name="PROGID" content="FRONTPAGE.EDITOR.DOCUMENT">
<title>IMAGE SPACING</title>
</head>
<body>
<p><img src = "http://www.umnet.com/pic/diy/screensaver/8/mickey-
mouse-87422.jpg" border=1 width="90" height="80">
```

```
<img src = "http://www.umnet.com/pic/diy/screensaver/8/mickey-mouse-
87422.jpg"  border=1  width="90"  height="80">  NO  VERTICLE  OR
HORIZONTAL SPACING
</p>
<p>
<img src = "http://www.umnet.com/pic/diy/screensaver/8/mickey-mouse-
87422.jpg" width = "90" height = "80" border=1 HSPACE = "20" VSPACE
= "20" >
<img src = "http://www.umnet.com/pic/diy/screensaver/8/mickey-mouse-
87422.jpg" width = "90" height = "80" border=1 HSPACE ="20" VSPACE =
"20" > 20 PIXELS VERTICLE AND HORIZONTAL SPACING FROM EACH SIDE
</p>
</body>
</html>
```

Output:

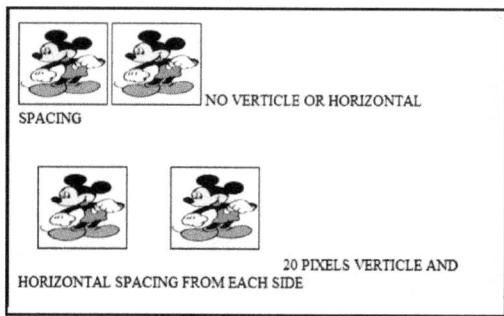

Image as a Link:

- Anything can be a link i.e. text or images. To make an image into a link we simply put the image tag inside the tag for a link.
- The tag would look like this:

```
<a href="http://www.anycartoonsite.com"><img
                                    src="z:\book\mikey.jpg"></a>
```

Example for image as link.

```
<!DOCTYPE html>
<head>
<meta  http-equiv="CONTENT-TYPE"  CONTENT="TEXT/HTML;  CHAR  SET  =
WINDOWS-1252">
<meta name="GENERATOR" CONTENT="MICROSOFT FRONTPAGE 4.0">
<meta name="PROGID" CONTENT="FRONTPAGE.EDITOR.DOCUMENT">
<title>IMAGELINK</title>
</head>
<body>
IMAGE LINK EXAMPLE
<p>
<a href = "HTTP://WWW.YAHOO.COM" ><img src = "http://images4.wikia.
nocookie.net/__cb20120710211159/cartoons/images/8/80/Mickey_Mouse.jp
g" border = "0"  width ="90" height = "80"> </a>
</p>
</body>
</html>
```

Output:

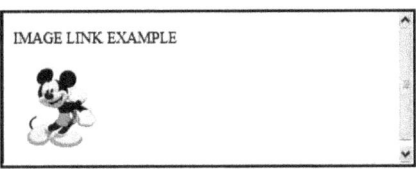

2. <map> Tag:
- The <map> tag is used to define a client-side image-map. An image-map is an image with clickable areas.
- The name attribute of the <map> element is required and it is associated with the <img>'s usemap attribute and creates a relationship between the image and the map.
- The <map> element contains a number of <area> elements, that defines the clickable areas in the image map.

3. <area> Tag:
- The <area> tag defines an area inside an image-map (an image-map is an image with clickable areas).
- The <area> element is always nested inside a <map> tag.

Attribute	Value	Description
1. alt	text	This attribute specifies an alternate text for an area.

Optional Attributes:

Attribute	Value	Description
1. coords	coordinates	This attribute specifies the coordinates of an area.
2. href	URL	This attribute specifies the hyperlink target for the area.
3. nohref	nohref	This attribute specifies that an area has no associated link.
4. shape	default rect circle poly	This attribute specifies the shape of an area.
5. target	_blank _parent _self _top	This attribute specifies where to open the linked page specified in the href attribute.

1.5.5 Image Mapping   [April 12]

- The ismap attribute specifies that the image is part of a server-side image-map (an image-map is an image with clickable areas).
- The attributes ISMAP and USEMAP are basically used to give the server side and client side image maps.
- To use the Client side image map, add the USEMAP attribute to the IMG element.

1. **Client-side image map:**
   Syntax: `<map>.........</map>`
   Attribute: `name=string`
- When we use a client-side image map, the information on the "hot spots" (clickable areas) in the image is defined here. Every selectable area should be mentioned in an `area` tag inside the `<map>` tag. The NAME attribute on the `map` tag assigns a name to the imagemap. The URL for the client-side imagemap should point to this.
- The ismap attribute specifies that the image is part of a server-side image-map (an image-map is an image with clickable areas).
- When clicking on a server-side image-map, the click coordinates are sent to the server as a URL query string.
   Syntax: `<img ismap="ismap" />`
- For example, if we have a map named "foo", we could reference to it with
   `<img src="map.gif" usemap="#tst">` if the image was on the same page.
- Client-side image maps are not widely supported yet, so try to offer a textual alternative or also use a server-side imagemap. This can be done by putting the `img` tag with the `usemap` attribute inside an A and by adding the ISMAP attribute.
- Having the imagemap data in a separate file is not as widely supported as inline data. There are two steps for creating client side image maps:
   1. Define pixel location.
   2. Create a map file within the HTML document that contains your image map.
- For creating a client side image map, we will need to specify our pixel locations as follows:
   RECTANGLE (RECT): Requires the upper left and lower right of the defined box.
   CIRCLE (CIRCLE): Requires the center point and radius (in pixels).
   POLYGON (POLYGON): Requires the co-ordinate of each vertex (point) of the area you want to define.
- Let us consider the following example to create the client side image map.

```
<!DOCTYPE html>
<head>
<meta name="GENERATOR" content="MICROSOFT FRONTPAGE 4.0">
<meta name="PROGID" content="FRONTPAGE.EDITOR.DOCUMENT">
<title> client side Image Map 1</title>
</head>
<body>
<img src="SAMPLE.GIF" usemap="#TEST">
<map name="TEST">
 <area shape="RECT" coords="26,72,145,146" href="RECT.HTML">
 <area shape="CIRCLE" coords="262,110,42" href="CIRCLE.HTML">
<area shape="POLYGON" coords="389,64,440,64,465,105,440,
                             147,389,147,365,105" href ="POLY.HTML">
 <area shape="RECT" coords="0,0,499,212" href="BASERECT.HTML">
 </map>
</body>
</html>
```

Output:

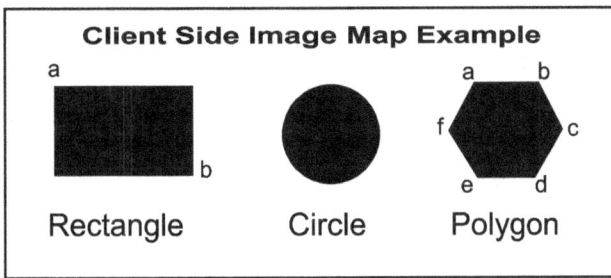

- Now in the above document we can see that the image map is created and the program is enclosing all the co-ordinates of each and every point.
- When we will click the Blue rectangle then it will take you to the rect.html file.
- When we will click the Red circle then it will take you to the circle.html file. And so on.
- If we are unable to create the proper map file nothing will happen if you click a shape.

2. Server side image map:
- The usemap attribute specifies an image as a client-side image-map.
- An image-map is an image with clickable areas.
- The usemap attribute is associated with a <map> element's name or id attribute, and creates a relationship between the image and the map.
  Syntax: `<img usemap="#mapname" />`
  Attribute values:
  1. `#mapname`: A hash character ("#") plus the name or id of the map element to use
- There are three steps for creating a server side image map:
  1. Define our pixel locations.
  2. Create an external map file.
  3. Insert a special address into the HTML document that contains our server side image map.

Step 1:
- For creating a client side image map, we will need to specify our pixel locations as follows:
  o **RECTANGLE (RECT):** Requires the upper left and lower right of the defined box.
  o **CIRCLE (CIRCLE):** Requires the center point and radius (in pixels).
  o **POLYGON (POLYGON):** Requires the co-ordinate of EACH vertex (point) of the area we want to define.

Step 2:
- Create a text (ASCII) file and save it with the extension .map. Put this file in the same directory as your HTML document that references your GIF image. In the file, we should include:
  1. A default URL. This is a location that a person will go to if she/he clicks on a part of your image map that is not a hot spot. **You must specify a default URL for your server side image map to work.** In the map file that follows, the default URL is **line 1**. **Note:** Your tags (i.e., default, rect, circle, and poly) must be in lowercase.

Step 3:

Insert a special address into the HTML document that contains our server side image map. This address should include:

1. The anchored hyperlink reference (A HREF) that specifies the location of the external map file and server side image map program on the NCSA Web server. In the address that follows, this reference is **line 1**. We will need to replace the bold text with your server and the path to our map file, respectively.

2. The GIF used for our image map. In the address that follows:

```
<a href="server.map">
<img src="server.gif" ismap>
```

1.5.6 Tables

- Tables are very useful to arrange in HTML and they are used very frequently by almost all web developers.

- Tables are just like spreadsheets and they are made up of rows and columns.

- The HTML table model allows to arrange data - text, preformatted text, images, links, forms, form fields, other tables etc. into rows and columns of cells.

- Tables are used on websites for two major purposes:
  1. The obvious purpose of arranging information in a table.
  2. The less obvious - but more widely used - purpose of creating a page layout with the use of hidden tables.

- **Using tables to divide the page into different sections is an extremely powerful tool.**

- Almost all major sites on the web are using invisible tables to layout the pages.

- **The most important layout aspects that can be done with tables are:**
  1. **Dividing the page into separate sections:** An invisible table is excellent for this purpose.
  2. **Creating menus:** Typically with one color for the header and another for the links following in the next lines.
  3. Adding interactive form fields.
  4. Typically a gray area containing a search option.
  5. Creating fast loading headers for the page.

1. <table> Tag:

- The <table> tag defines an HTML table.

- An HTML table consists of the <table> element and one or more <tr>, <th>, and <td> elements. The <tr> element defines a table row, the <th> element defines a table header, and the <td> element defines a table cell.

Syntax: <table>............</table>

Attributes	Value	Description
1. `align`	left center right	This attribute specifies the alignment of a table according to surrounding text.
2. `bgcolor`	`rgb(x,x,x)` `#xxxxxx` `colorname`	This attribute specifies the background color for a table.
3. `border`	`pixels`	This attribute specifies the width of the borders around a table.
4. `cellpadding`	`pixels`	This attribute specifies the space between the cell wall and the cell content.
5. `cellspacing`	`pixels`	This attribute specifies the space between cells.
6. `frame`	`void` `above` `below` `hsides` `lhs` `rhs` `vsides` `box` `border`	This attribute specifies which parts of the outside borders that should be visible.
7. `rules`	`none` `groups` `rows` `cols` `all`	This attribute specifies which parts of the inside borders that should be visible.
8. `summary`	`text`	This attribute specifies a summary of the content of a table.
9. `width`	`pixels` `%`	This attribute specifies the width of a table.

Example for <table> tag:

```
<!DOCTYPE html>
<body>
<p>
Each table starts with a table tag.
Each table row starts with a tr tag.
Each table data starts with a td tag.
</p>
<h4>One column:</h4>
<table border="1">
<tr>
```

```
    <td>100</td>
  </tr>
</table>
<h4>One row and three columns:</h4>
<table border="1">
<tr>
  <td>100</td>
  <td>200</td>
  <td>300</td>
</tr>
</table>
<h4>Two rows and three columns:</h4>
<table border="1">
<tr>
  <td>100</td>
  <td>200</td>
  <td>300</td>
</tr>
<tr>
  <td>400</td>
  <td>500</td>
  <td>600</td>
</tr>
</table>
</body>
</html>
```

Output:

Each table starts with a table tag. Each table row starts with a tr tag. Each table data starts with a td tag.

One column:

| 100 |

One row and three columns:

| 100 | 200 | 300 |

Two rows and three columns:

| 100 | 200 | 300 |
| 400 | 500 | 600 |

2. <th> Tag:

- Table heading can be defined using <th> tag or the <th> tag defines a header cell in an HTML table. This tag will be put to replace <td> tag which is used to represent actual data.
- An HTML table has two kinds of cells:
  - **Header cells:** contains header information (created with the <th> element), and
  - **Standard cells:** contains data (created with the <td> element).
- The text in <th> elements are bold and centered by default.
- The text in <td> elements are regular and left-aligned by default.
  Syntax: <th>..........</th>

Attributes	Value	Description
1. abbr	text	This attribute specifies an abbreviated version of the content in a cell.
2. align	left right center justify char	This attribute aligns the content in a cell.
3. axis	category_name	This attribute specifies categorizes cells.
4. bgcolor	rgb(x,x,x) #xxxxxx colorname	This attribute specifies the background color of a cell.
5. char	character	This attribute specifies aligns the content in a cell to a character.
6. charoff	number	This attribute sets the number of characters the content will be aligned from the character specified by the char attribute.
7. colspan	number	This attribute sets the number of columns a cell should span.
8. height	pixels %	This attribute sets the height of a cell.
9. nowrap	nowrap	This attribute specifies that the content inside a cell should not wrap.
10. rowspan	number	This attribute sets the number of rows a cell should span.
11. scope	col colgroup row rowgroup	This attribute defines a way to associate header cells and data cells in a table.
12. valign	top middle bottom baseline	This attribute specifies vertical aligns the content in a cell.
13. width	pixels %	This attribute specifies the width of a cell.

Example of <th> tag:

```html
<!DOCTYPE html>
<body>
<h4>Table headers:</h4>
<table border="1">
<tr>
  <th>Name</th>
  <th>Telephone</th>
  <th>Telephone</th>
</tr>
<tr>
  <td>Bill Gates</td>
  <td>555 77 854</td>
  <td>555 77 855</td>
</tr>
</table>
<h4>Vertical headers:</h4>
<table border="1">
<tr>
  <th>First Name:</th>
  <td>Bill Gates</td>
</tr>
<tr>
  <th>Telephone:</th>
  <td>555 77 854</td>
</tr>
<tr>
  <th>Telephone:</th>
  <td>555 77 855</td>
</tr>
</table>
</body>
</html>
```

Output:

Table headers:

Name	Telephone	Telephone
Bill Gates	555 77 854	555 77 855

Vertical headers:

First Name:	Bill Gates
Telephone:	555 77 854
Telephone:	555 77 855

3. <tr> Tag:

- The <tr> tag defines a row in an HTML table.
- A <tr> element contains one or more <th> or <td> elements.

   Syntax: `<tr>............<tr>`

Attributes	Value	Description

1. `align`	`right`
	`left`
	`center`
	`justify`
	`char`
		This attribute aligns the content in a table row.

2. `bgcolor`	`rgb(x,x,x)`
	`#xxxxxx`
	`colorname`
		This attribute specifies a background color for a table row

3. `char`	`character`	This attribute aligns the content in a table row to a character
4. `charoff`	`number`	This attribute sets the number of characters the content will be aligned from the character specified by the char attribute

5. `valign`	`top`
	`middle`
	`bottom`
	`baseline`
		Vertical aligns the content in a table row

4. <td> Tag:

- The <td> tag defines a standard cell in an HTML table.
- The <td> tag is used to mark up individual cells inside a table row.

   Syntax: `<td>............</td>`

Attribute	Value	Description
1. `abbr`	`text`	This attribute specifies an abbreviated version of the content in a cell.

2. `align`	`left`
	`right`
	`center`
	`justify`
	`char`
		This attribute aligns the content in a cell.

3. `axis`	`category_name`	This attribute categorizes cells.

4. `bgcolor`	`rgb(x,x,x)`
	`#xxxxxx`
	`colorname`
		This attribute specifies the background color of a cell.

5. `char`	`character`	This attribute aligns the content in a cell to a character.

contd. ...

6.	`charoff`	`number`	This attribute specifies sets the number of characters the content will be aligned from the character specified by the char attribute.
7.	`colspan`	`number`	This attribute specifies the number of columns a cell should span.
8.	`headers`	`header_id`	This attribute specifies one or more header cells a cell is related to.
9.	`height`	`pixels` `%`	This attribute specifies sets the height of a cell.
10.	`nowrap`	`nowrap`	This attribute specifies that the content inside a cell should not wrap.
11.	`rowspan`	`number`	This attribute specifies sets the number of rows a cell should span.

12.	`scope`	`col`
		`colgroup`
		`row`
		`rowgroup`
			This attribute specifies defines a way to associate header cells and data cells in a table.

13.	`valign`	`top`
		`middle`
		`bottom`
		`baseline`
			This attribute specifies vertical aligns the content in a cell.

14.	`width`	`pixels` `%`	This attribute specifies the width of a cell.

Example of <td>tag:

```
<!DOCTYPE html>
<head>
<body>
<table border="1">
<tr>
<th>Name</th>
<th>Salary</th>
</tr>
<tr>
<td>Ramesh Salunkhe</td>
<td>50,000</td>
</tr>
<tr>
<td>Amar Salvi</td>
<td>70,000</td>
</tr>
</table>
</body>
</head>
</html>
```

Output:

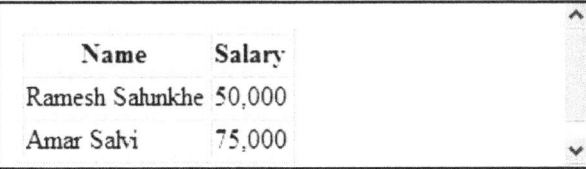

5. <caption> Tag:

- The <caption> tag defines a table caption.
- The <caption> tag is used to provide a caption for a table. This caption can either appear above or below the table. This can be indicated with the align attribute.

  Syntax: <caption>............<caption>

- The <caption> tag must be inserted immediately after the <table> tag.
- We can specify only one caption per table.

Attribute	Value	Description
1. align	left right top bottom	This attribute defines the alignment of a caption.

Example for <caption> tag:

```
<!DOCTYPE html>
<body>
<table border="1">
  <caption>Monthly Savings</caption>
  <tr>
    <th>Month</th>
    <th>Savings</th>
  </tr>
  <tr>
    <td>January</td>
    <td>Rs. 1000</td>
  </tr>
  <tr>
    <td>February</td>
    <td> Rs. 1500</td>
  </tr>
</table>
</body>
</html>
```

Output:

Monthly Savings

Month	Savings
January	Rs. 1000
February	Rs. 1500

6. Using a Header, Body, and Footer:

- Tables can be divided into three portions: a header, a body, and a foot.

- The head and foot are rather similar to headers and footers in a word-processed document that remain the same for every page, while the body is the main content of the table.

- The three elements for separating the head, body, and foot of a table are:

  o <thead>: to create a separate table header.

  o <tbody>: to indicate the main body of the table.

  o <tfoot>: to create a separate table footer.

- A table may contain several <tbody> elements to indicate different pages or groups of data. But it is notable that <thead> and <tfoot> tags should appear before <tbody>.

Example:

```
<!DOCTYPE html>
<head>
<title>Practice HTML table footer, header and body</title>
</head>
<body>
<p>Try with different footer, heard and body parts</p>
<table border="1" width="100%">
<thead>
<tr>
<td colspan="4">This is the head of the table</td>
</tr>
</thead>
<tfoot>
<tr>
<td colspan="4">This is the foot of the table</td>
</tr>
</tfoot>
<tbody>
```

```
<tr>
<td>Cell 1</td>
<td>Cell 2</td>
<td>Cell 3</td>
<td>Cell 4</td>
</tr>
<tr>
...more rows here containing four cells...
</tr>
</tbody>
<tbody>
<tr>
<td>Cell 1</td>
<td>Cell 2</td>
<td>Cell 3</td>
<td>Cell 4</td>
</tr>
<tr>
...more rows here containing four cells...
</tr>
</tbody>
</table>
</body>
</html>
```

Output:

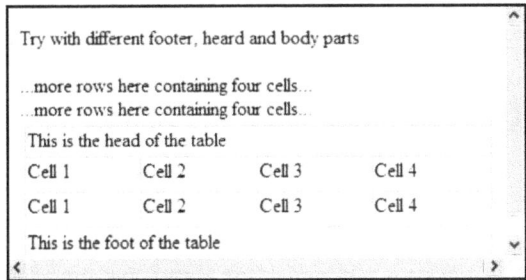

Cellpadding and Cellspacing in a Table:

- There are two attribiutes called cellpadding and cellspacing which we will use to adjust the white space in our table cell.

- Cellspacing defines the width of the border, while cellpadding represents the distance between cell borders and the content within.

Example for cellspacing:

```
<!DOCTYPE html>
<body>
<h4>Without  cellspacing:</h4>
<table border="1">
<tr>
  <td>First</td>
  <td>Row</td>
</tr>
<tr>
  <td>Second</td>
  <td>Row</td>
</tr>
</table>
<h4>With cellspacing="0":</h4>
<table border="1" cellspacing="0">
<tr>
  <td>First</td>
  <td>Row</td>
</tr>
<tr>
  <td>Second</td>
  <td>Row</td>
</tr>
</table>
<h4>With cellspacing="10":</h4>
<table border="1" cellspacing="10">
<tr>
  <td>First</td>
  <td>Row</td>
</tr>
<tr>
  <td>Second</td>
  <td>Row</td>
</tr>
</table>
</body>
</html>
```

Output:

Example of cellpadding:

```html
<!DOCTYPE html>
<body>
<h4>Without cellpadding:</h4>
<table border="1">
<tr>
  <td>First</td>
  <td>Row</td>
</tr>
<tr>
  <td>Second</td>
  <td>Row</td>
</tr>
</table>
<h4>With cellpadding:</h4>
<table border="1"
cellpadding="10">
<tr>
  <td>First</td>
  <td>Row</td>
</tr>
<tr>
  <td>Second</td>
  <td>Row</td>
</tr>
</table>
</body>
</html>
```

Output:

Colspan and Rowspan attributes in table:

- We will use colspan attribute if you want to merge two or more columns into a single column. Similar way you will use rowspan if you want to merge two or more rows.

For example:

```html
<!DOCTYPE html>
<head>
<title>Practice HTML table spans</title>
</head>
<body>
<p>Merge two or more rows or columns and then see the result:</p>
<table border="1">
<tr>
<th>Column 1</th>
<th>Column 2</th>
<th>Column 3</th>
</tr>
<tr><td rowspan="2">Row 1 Cell 1</td>
<td>Row 1 Cell 2</td><td>Row 1 Cell 3</td></tr>
<tr><td>Row 2 Cell 2</td><td>Row 2 Cell 3</td></tr>
<tr><td colspan="3">Row 3 Cell 1</td></tr>
</table>
</body>
</html>
```

Output:

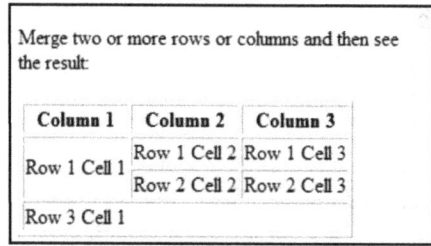

Table Backgrounds:

- We can set table background using of the following two ways:

  1. **Using bgcolor attribute:** We can set background color for whole table or just for one cell.

  2. **Using background attribute:** We can set background image for whole table or just for one cell.

Example for setting tables background.

```
<!DOCTYPE html>
<head>
<title>Practice HTML table background images</title>
</head>
<body>
<table border="1">
  <tr title="You are looking at Row 1" bgcolor="silver">
    <td>Row 1 Cell 1</td>
    <td>Row 1 Cell 2</td>
  </tr>
  <tr title="You are looking at Row 2" bgcolor="aqua">
    <td>Row 2 Cell 1</td>
    <td>Row 2 Cell 2</td>
  </tr>
</table>
</body>
</html>
```

Output:

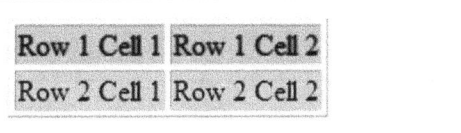

Nested Tables:

* We can use one table inside another table. Not only tables you can use almost all the tags inside table data tag <td>.
* Following is the example of using another table and other tags inside a table cell.

Example for Nested Tables:

```
<!DOCTYPE html>
<head>
<title>HTML Nested table</title>
</head>
<body>
<table border="1">
<tr>
<td>
    <table border="1">
    <tr>
    <th>Name</th>
    <th>Salary</th>
    </tr>
    <tr>
    <td>Ramesh Raman</td>
    <td>5,700</td>
    </tr>
```

```
<tr>
<td>Shabbir Hussein</td>
<td>7,500</td>
</tr>
</table>
</td>
<td>
    <ul>
    <li>This is another cell</li>
    <li>Using list inside this cell</li>
    </ul>
</td>
</tr>
<tr>
<td>Row 2, Column 1</td>
<td>Row 2, Column 2</td>
</tr>
</table>
</body>
</html>
```

Output:

Name	Salary	• This is another cell • Using list inside this cell
Ramesh Raman	5,700	
Shabbir Hussein	7,500	
Row 2, Column 1		Row 2, Column 2

1.5.7 Frames

- The term frames is used as shorthand for "a technique to display multiple documents at once". This technique is only used when the browser is running on a graphical display.

- Frames allow us to split the browser window into multiple windows that can display different pages. This will make the navigation much easier for the visitor.

- With frames, we can display more than one HTML document in the same browser window. Each HTML document is called a frame, and each frame is independent of the others.

- Frames divide a browser window into several pieces or panes, each pane containing a separate XHTML/HTML document.

- One of the key advantages that frames offer is that we can then load and reload single panes without having to reload the entire contents of the browser window.

- A collection of frames in the browser window is known as a frameset.
- The window is divided up into frames in a similar pattern to the way tables are organized: into rows and columns. The simplest of framesets might just divide the screen into two rows, while a complex frameset could use several rows and columns.
- Frames are used to display more than one document in the same window.
- Frames are defined in <frameset>, and inside it we have <frame> which defines the location of the web page to load into the frame. See the example given below to understand it clearly.

Vertical frames example:

```
<!DOCTYPE html>
<frameset cols="50%,30%,20%">
<frame src="frame1.html" />
<frame src="frame2.html" />
<frame src="frame3.html" />
</frameset>
</html>
```

Output:

This is frame1	This is frame2	This is frame3

Horizontal frames Example:

```
<!DOCTYPE html>
<frameset rows="50%,30%,20%">
<frame src="frame1.html" />
<frame src="frame2.html" />
<frame src="frame3.html" />
</frameset>
</html>
```

Output:

This is frame1
This is frame2
This is frame3

1. <frame> Tag:

- The <frame> tag indicates what goes in each frame of the frameset.
- The <frame> element is always an empty element, and therefore should not have any content, although each <frame> element should always carry one attribute, src, to indicate the page that should represent that frame.
- The <frame> tag defines one particular window (frame) within a <frameset> and each <frame> in a <frameset> can have different attributes, such as border, scrolling, the ability to resize, etc.

  Syntax: <frame>........</frame>

Attributes	Value	Description
1. frameborder	0 1	This attribute specifies whether or not to display a border around a frame.
2. longdesc	URL	This attribute specifies a page that contains a long description of the content of a frame.
3. marginheight	pixels	This attribute specifies the top and bottom margins of a frame.
4. marginwidth	pixels	This attribute specifies the left and right margins of a frame.
5. name	name	This attribute specifies the name of a frame.
6. noresize	noresize	This attribute specifies that a frame cannot be resized.
7. scrolling	yes no auto	This attribute specifies whether or not to display scrollbars in a frame.
8. src	URL	This attribute specifies the URL of the document to show in a frame.

2. <frameset> tag: [April 12]

- The <frameset> tag holds one or more frame elements. Each frame element can hold a separate document.

  o The <frameset> tag replaces the <body> element in frameset documents.

  o The <frameset> tag defines how to divide the window into frames.

  o Each frameset defines a set of rows or columns. If you define frames by using rows then horizontal frames are created. If you define frames by using columns then vertical frames are created.

  o The values of the rows/columns indicate the amount of screen area each row/column will occupy.

  o Each frame is indicated by <frame> tag and it defines what HTML document to put into the frame.

- Following are important attributes of <frameset> and should be known to you to use frameset.

  1. cols: specifies how many columns are contained in the frameset and the size of each column. We can specify the width of each column in one of four ways:

     o Absolute values in pixels. For example to create three vertical frames, use cols="100, 500,100".

- o A percentage of the browser window. For example to create three vertical frames, use cols="10%, 80%,10%".

- o Using a wildcard symbol. For example to create three vertical frames, use cols="10%, *,10%". In this case wildcard takes remainder of the window.

- o As relative widths of the browser window. For example to create three vertical frames, use cols="3*,2*,1*". This is an alternative to percentages. You can use relative widths of the browser window. Here the window is divided into sixths: the first column takes up half of the window, the second takes one third, and the third takes one sixth.

2. `rows`: attribute works just like the cols attribute and can take the same values, but it is used to specify the rows in the frameset. For example to create two horizontal frames, use rows="10%, 90%". You can specify the height of each row in the same way as explained above for columns.

3. `border`: attribute specifies the width of the border of each frame in pixels. For example border="5". A value of zero specifies that no border should be there.

4. `frameborder`: specifies whether a three-dimensional border should be displayed between frames. This attribute takes value either 1 (yes) or 0 (no). For example frameborder="0" specifies no border.

5. `framespacing`: specifies the amount of space between frames in a frameset. This can take any integer value. For example framespacing="10" means there should be 10 pixels spacing between each frames.

Example for frameset element defining rows and columns:

```
<!DOCTYPE html>
<head>
<meta name="GENERATOR" content="Microsoft FrontPage 4.0">
<meta name="ProgId" content="FrontPage.Editor.Document">
<title>Frameset Element Defining Rows and Columns</title>
</head>
<frameset rows="64,*,64">
<frame src="z:\comp.html">
<frameset cols="150,*">
<frame src="z:\about.html">
<frame src="z:\dept1.html">
</frameset>
<frame src="z:\it.html">
</frameset>
</html
```

Output:

```
<!DOCTYPE html>
<head>
<meta name="GENERATOR" content="Microsoft FrontPage 4.0">
<meta name="ProgId" content="FrontPage.Editor.Document">
<title>FrameSet Element with rows and columns</title>
</head>
<frameset cols="150,*">
<frame name="contents" scrolling= "no" noresize src="z:\comp.html">
<frameset rows="20%,*">
   <frame name="rtop" src="z:\it.html">
   <frame name="main" src="z:\etc.html">
</frameset>
</frameset>
</html>
```

Output:

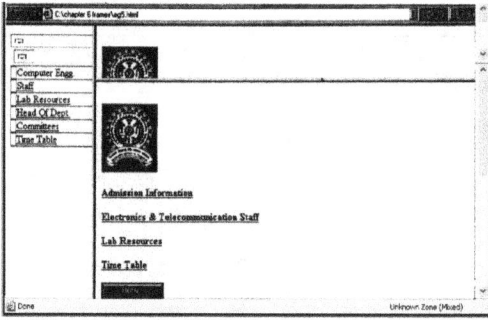

Code of frame defining src, name, noresize and scrolling attributes:

```
<!DOCTYPE html>
<head>
<meta name="GENERATOR" content="Microsoft FrontPage 4.0">
<meta name="ProgId" content="FrontPage.Editor.Document">
<title>example of frame src,name,scrolling</title></head>
<frameset rows="160,*,160">
\ <frame name="banner" scrolling="no" noresize src="z:\comp.html">
<frame name="content" scrolling=yes noresize src="z:\etc.html">
<frame scrolling="no" noresize src="z:\about.html">
</frameset>
</html>
```

Output:

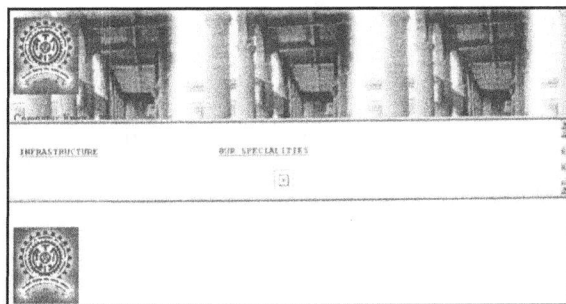

3. <noframes> Tag:

• If a user is using any old browser or any browser which does not support frames then <noframes> element should be displayed to the user.

Syntax: <noframes>............</noframes>

• The noframes element contains content that should only be rendered when frames are not displayed. noframes is typically used in a frameset document to provide alternate content for browsers that do not support frames or have frames disabled.

Example for <noframes> tag:

```
<!DOCTYPE html>
<head>
<meta name="generator" content="Microsoft FrontPage 4.0">
<meta name="ProgId" content="FrontPage.Editor.Document">
<title>a frameset document which has a noframes alternative</title>
</head>
<frameset rows="*,*">
<frame src="z:\comp.html" name=foo>
<frame src="z:\etc.html" name=bar>
<noframes>
<body>
this is the noframes alternative section.
any block-level html element may be used here.
</body>
</noframes>
</frameset>
</html>
```

Output:

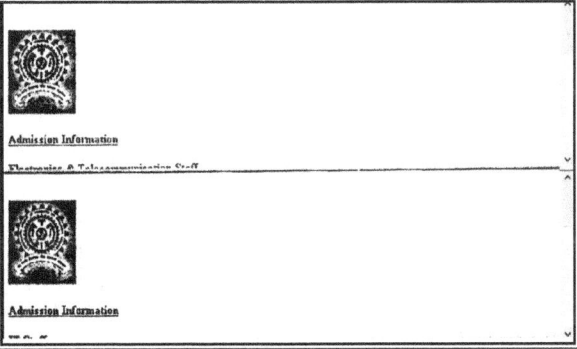

4. <iframe> Tag: [Oct. 11]

- We can define an inline frame with the <iframe> tag.
- The <iframe> tag is not used within a <frameset> tag. Instead, it appears anywhere in our document.
- The <iframe> tag defines a rectangular region within the document in which the browser displays a separate document, including scrollbars and borders.
- Use the src attribute with <iframe> to specify the URL of the document that occupies the inline frame.
- All of the other, optional attributes for the <iframe> tag, including name, class, frameborder, id, longdesc, marginheight, marginwidth, name, scrolling, style, and title behave exactly like the corresponding attributes for the <frame> tag.

Example:

```
<html>
<head>
<title>IFrames example</title>
</head>
<body>
<p>...other document content...</p>
<iframe src="/html/menu.htm" width="100" height="200" align="right">
Your browser does not support inline frames. To view this
<a href="/html/menu.htm">Menu</a> correctly, you'll need
a copy of Internet Explorer or the latest Netscape Navigator.
</iframe>
<p>...subsequent document content...</p>
</body>
</html>
```

5. Frame's name and target attributes:

- One of the most popular uses of frames is to place navigation bars in one frame and then load the pages with the content into a separate frame.

```
<!DOCTYPE html>
<head>
<title>Frames example</title>
</head>
    <frameset cols="200, *">
        <frame src="/html/menu.htm" name="menu_page" />
        <frame src="/html/main.htm" name="main_page" />
        <noframes>
        <body>
        Your browser does not support frames.
        </body>
        </noframes>
    </frameset>
</html>
```

1.5.8 Forms

- HTML forms are used to pass data to a server.

- A form is a group of controls that the user interacts with and sends the result to a specific files as designed by an application developer.

- To create an effective form, HTML provides various text based and selection controls that can handle almost any scenario. Besides these, there are action controls that actually send a signal to a script.

- A form is the central control that manages the other controls. Although the controls can send their data to a script, a form can be used to collect the values typed or selected on the controls, gather them as if they constituted one control and make these values available to a validating file on a server.

- The form element acts as a container for controls and it specifies:

  1. The layout of the form (given by the controls of the element).

  2. The program that will handle the completed and submitted form (the action attribute). The receiving program must be able to parse name/value pairs in order to make use of them.

  3. The method by which user data will be sent to the server (the method attribute).

- A form can contain input elements like text fields, checkboxes, radio-buttons, submit buttons and more. A form can also contain select lists, textarea, fieldset, legend, and label elements.

- The <form> tag is used to create an HTML form for user input, like this

  ```
  <form>
  .
  .
  .
  input elements
  .
  .
  .
  </form>
  ```

- HTML forms are required when we want to collect some data from the site visitor. For example registration information: name, email address, credit card, etc.

- A form will take input from the site visitor and then will post your back-end application such as CGI, ASP Script or PHP script etc. Then our back-end application will do required processing on that data in whatever way we like.

- A simple syntax of using <form> is as follows:

  ```
  <form action="back-end script" method="posting method">
      form elements like input, textarea etc.
  </form>
  ```

- Most frequently used form attributes are:
  1. `name`: This is the name of the form.
  2. `action`: Here you will specify any script URL which will receive uploaded data.
  3. `method`: Here you will specify method to be used to upload data. It can take various values but most frequently used are GET and POST.

     HTML documents are generally retrieved by requesting it's URL from web server using GET method. When large amount of data is to be passed to server. POST method is used. In POST, form contents are not send in URL. In POST method, form contents are send to server in the body of message.
  4. `target`: It specifies the target page where the result of the script will be displayed. It takes values like _blank, _self, _parent etc.
  5. `enctype`: We can use the enctype attribute to specify how the browser encodes the data before it sends it to the server. Possible values are like:
     - `application/x-www-form-urlencoded`: This is the standard method most forms use. It converts spaces to the plus sign and non-alphanumeric characters into the hexadecimal code for that character in ASCII text.
     - `mutlipart/form-data`: This allows the data to be sent in parts, with each consecutive part corresponding the a form control, in the order they appear in the form. Each part can have an optional content-type header of its own indicating the type of data for that form control.
- There are different types of form controls that you can use to collect data from a visitor to your site.
  - Text input controls,
  - Buttons,
  - Checkboxes and radio buttons,
  - Select boxes,
  - File select boxes,
  - Hidden controls,
  - Submit and reset button.
- We will learn these controls in 1.5.9.

1.5.9 Introduction to HTML Controls

- An HTML form is a section of a document containing normal content, markup, special elements called controls (checkboxes, radio buttons, menus, etc.), and labels on those controls. Users generally "complete" a form by modifying its controls (entering text, selecting menu items, etc.).

- Users interact with forms through named controls.

- A control's "*control name*" is given by its name attribute. The scope of the name attribute for a control within a FORM element is the FORM element.

- Each control has both an initial value and a current value, both of which are character strings. However, the initial value of a TEXTAREA element is given by its contents, and the initial value of an OBJECT element in a form is determined by the object implementation (i.e., it lies outside the scope of this specification).

- The control's "*current value*" is first set to the initial value. Thereafter, the control's current value may be modified through user interaction and scripts.

- A control's initial value does not change. Thus, when a form is reset, each control's current value is reset to its initial value. If a control does not have an initial value, the effect of a form reset on that control is undefined.

<input> Tag:

- The most important form element is the input tag.

- <input> defines an input control.

- The input tag is used to select user information.

- An input tag can vary in many ways, depending on the type attribute. An <input> tag can be of type text field, checkbox, password, radio button, submit button, and more.

- <input> tag are used within a <form> element to declare input controls that allow users to input data.

- An input field can vary in many ways, depending on the type attribute.

  Syntax: `<input type= " ">`

Attributes	Value	Description
1. `accept`	`audio/*` `video/*` `image/*` `MIME_type`	This attribute specifies the types of files that the server accepts (only for type="file").
2. `align`	`left` `right` `top` `middle` `bottom`	This attribute specifies the alignment of an image input (only for type="image").
3. `alt`	`text`	This attribute specifies an alternate text for an image (only for type="image").

contd. ...

4.	checked	checked	This attribute specifies that an <input> element should be preselected when the page loads (for type="checkbox" or type="radio").
5.	disabled	disabled	This attribute specifies that an <input> element should be disabled.
6.	maxlength	number	This attribute specifies the maximum number of characters allowed in an <input> element.
7.	name	name	This attribute specifies the name of an <input> element.
8.	readonly	readonly	This attribute specifies that an input field should be read-only.
9.	size	number	This attribute specifies the width, in characters, of an <input> element.
10.	src	URL	This attribute specifies the URL of the image to use as a submit button (only for type="image").
11.	type	button checkbox file hidden image password radio reset submit text	This attribute specifies the type of <input> element.
12.	value	text	This attribute specifies the value of an <input> element.

1. Text Field:

• Text fields are one line areas that allow the user to input text.

Syntax: `<input type = "text">`

- Following is the list of attributes for <input> tag.

  1. `type`: Indicates the type of input control you want to create. This element is also used to create other form controls such as radio buttons and checkboxes.

  2. `name`: Used to give the name part of the name/value pair that is sent to the server, representing each form control and the value the user entered.

  3. `value`: Provides an initial value for the text input control that the user will see when the form loads.

  4. `size`: Allows you to specify the width of the text-input control in terms of characters.

  5. `maxlength`: Allows you to specify the maximum number of characters a user can enter into the text box.

- Here, is a basic example of a single-line text input used to take first name and last name:

```
<!DOCTYPE html>
  <body>
<head>
<title>Concepts of Form</title>
    <form action="/cgi-bin/hello_get.cgi" method="get">
First name:
<input type="text" name="first_name" />
<br>
Last name:
<input type="text" name="last_name" />
<br>
<input type="submit" value="submit" />
</form>
  </body>
</head>
</html>
```

Output:

2. Password Field:

- Password fields are similar to text fields.

- The difference is that what is entered into a password field shows up a dots on the screen. This is, of course, to prevent others from reading the password on the screen.

Syntax: `<input type = "password">`

Attribute	Explanation
1. size=	Characters shown.
2. maxlength=	Max characters allowed.
3. name=	Name of the field.
4. value=	Initial value in the field.
5. align=	Alignment of the field.
6. tabindex=	Tab order of the field.

Example for password field.

```
<!DOCTYPE html>
<head>
<title>MyPage</title>
<head>
<body>
<form name="myform"
action="http://www.mydomain.com/myformhandler.cgi"
method="POST">
<div align="center">
Enter Password: <input type="password" size="25">
<br><br>
</div>
</form>
</body>
</html>
```

Output:

Enter Password: [   ]

3. <label> Tag:

- The <label> tag defines a label for an <input> element.

- The <label> tag does not render as anything special for the user. However, it provides a usability improvement for mouse users, because if the user clicks on the text within the <label> element, it toggles the control.

- The for attribute of the <label> tag should be equal to the id attribute of the related element to bind them together.

4. <fieldset> Tag:

*   <fieldset> Defines a border around elements in a form. The <fieldset> tag is used to group related elements in a form.
*   The <fieldset> tag draws a box around the related elements.

5. Hidden Field:

*   Hidden fields are similar to text fields. The difference is that the hidden field does not show on the page. Therefore the visitor cannot type anything into a hidden field, which leads to the purpose of the field. To submit information that is not entered by the visitor.

Syntax: `<input typ = "hidden">`

Attribute	Explanation
1. name=	Name of the field
2. value=	Value of the field

Example for hidden field:

```
<!DOCTYPE html>
<head>
<title>MyPage</title>
<head>
<body>
<form name="myform"
action="http://www.mydomain.com/myformhandler.cgi"
method="POST">
<div align="center">
<input type="text" size="25" value="Enter your name here!">
<input type="hidden" name="Language" value="English">
<br><br>
</div>
</form>
</body>
<html>
```

Output:

| Enter your name here! |

*   The hidden field does not show, but still, when the form is submitted the hidden field is sent with it.
*   In above example, the hidden field would tell the program that handles the form, that the users preferred language in English.

6. <textarea> Tag:

*   It defines a multi-line text input control. Textarea are text fields that can span several lines.
*   A textarea can hold an unlimited number of characters, and the text renders in a fixed-width font, (usually Courier).
*   The size of a text area is specified by the cols and rows attributes.

Syntax: `<textarea>.........</textarea>`

- Attributes for <textarea> tag are:
  1. `name`: The name of the control. This is used in the name/value pair that is sent to the server.
  2. `rows`: Indicates the number of rows of text area box.
  3. `cols`: Indicates the number of columns of text area box.

Example for <textarea> tag:

```
<!DOCTYPE html>
  <body>
<head>
<title>Concepts of Form</title>
    <p> This example cannot be edited because our editor uses a
textarea for input, and your browser does not allow a textarea inside
a textarea. </p>
<textarea rows="10" cols="30"> The cat was playing in the garden.
</textarea>
  </body>
</head>
</html>
```

Output:

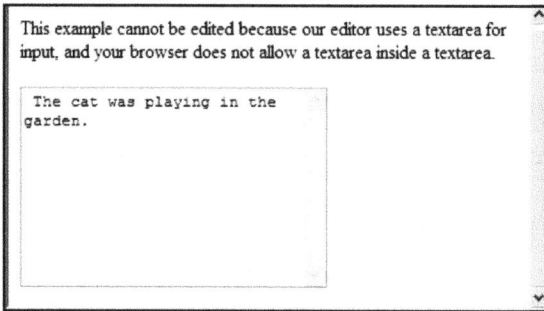

7. Radio Buttons:

- Radio buttons are used when only one option is required to be selected. They are created using <input> tag.

  Syntax: `<input type="radio">`
- Following is the list of important radiobox attributes:
  1. `type`: Indicates that you want to create a radiobox.
  2. `name`: Name of the control.
  3. `value`: Used to indicate the value that will be sent to the server if this option is selected.
  4. `checked`: Indicates that this option should be selected by default when the page loads.

Example for radio button:

```
<!DOCTYPE html>
<head>
<title>Practice HTML input radiobox tag</title>
</head>
<body>
<form action="/cgi-bin/radiobutton.cgi" method="post">
<input type="radio" name="subject" value="maths" /> Maths
<input type="radio" name="subject" value="physics" /> Physics
<input type="submit" value="Select Subject" />
</form>
</body>
</html>
```

Output:

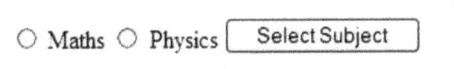

8. Checkbox Control:

* Checkboxes are used when more than one option is required to be selected. They are created using <input> tag.

  Syntax: `<input type="checkbox">`
* Following is the list of important checkbox attributes:
  1. `type`: Indicates that you want to create a checkbox.
  2. `name`: Name of the control.
  3. `value`: The value that will be used if the checkbox is selected. More than one checkbox should share the same name only if you want to allow users to select several items from the same list.
  4. `checked`: Indicates that when the page loads, the checkbox should be selected.

Example for checkboxes:

```
<!DOCTYPE html>
<head>
<title>Practice HTML input checkbox tag</title>
</head>
<body>
<p>Try  with different checkbox and different attributes</p>
<form action="" method="get">
<input type="checkbox" name="maths" value="on" /> Maths
<input type="checkbox" name="physics" value="on" /> Physics
<input type="reset" value="Select Subject" />
</form>
</body>
</html>
```

Output:

Try with different checkbox and different attributes

☐ Maths ☐ Physics   Select Subject

9. <select>Tag:

- The <select> tag is used to create a drop-down list.
- Drop-down list is used when we have many options available to be selected but only one or two will be selected.
- The <option> tags inside the <select> element define the available options in the list.

Syntax: <select>............</select>

Attributes	Value	Description
1. disabled	disabled	This attribute specifies that a drop-down list should be disabled.
2. multiple	multiple	This attribute specifies that multiple options can be selected at once.
3. name	name	This attribute defines a name for the drop-down list.
4. size	number	This attribute specifies defines the number of visible options in a drop-down list.

Example for <select> tag:

```
<!DOCTYPE html>
<head>
<title>Practice HTML input selectbox tag</title>
</head>
<body>
<p>Try  with different selectbox and different attributes</p>
<form action="" method="get">
<select name="dropdown">
<option value="Maths" selected>Maths</option>
<option value="Physics">Physics</option>
</select>
<input type="reset" value="reset" />
</form>
</body>
</html>
```

Output:

Try with different selectbox and different attributes

Maths ▼   reset

10. Creating Button:
- The `<button>` tag defines a push button.
- There are various ways in HTML to create clickable buttons. We can create clickable button using <input> tag.
- When we use the <input> element to create a button, the type of button we create is specified using the type attribute.
- The type attribute can take the following values:
  1. **submit:** This creates a button that automatically submits a form.
  2. **reset:** This creates a button that automatically resets form controls to their initial values.
  3. **button:** This creates a button that is used to trigger a client-side script when the user clicks that button.

Syntax: `<button>...............</button>`

Attributes	Value	Description
1. `disabled`	`disabled`	This attribute specifies that a button should be disabled.
2. `name`	`name`	This attribute specifies the name for a button.
3. `type`	`button` `reset` `submit`	This attribute specifies the type of button.
4. `value`	`text`	This attribute specifies the initial value for a button.

Example for <button> tag:
```
<!DOCTYPE html>
<body>
<form name="input" action="html_form_action.asp" method="get">
First name: <input type="text" name="FirstName"
                                          value="Mickey" /><br />
Last name: <input type="text" name="LastName" value="Mouse" /><br />
<input type="submit" value="Submit" />
</form>
<p>If you click the "Submit" button, the form-data will be sent to a
page called "html_form_action.asp".</p>
</body>
</html>
```

Output:

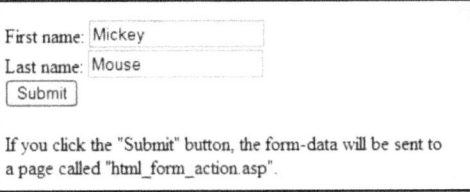

Example:
```
<!DOCTYPE html>
<body>
<form action="/cgi-bin/hello_get.cgi" method="get">
First name:
<input type="text" name="first_name" />
<br>
Last name:
<input type="text" name="last_name" />
<input type="submit" value="Submit" />
<input type="reset" value="Reset" />
</form>
</body>
</html>
```
Output:

11. <option> Tag:

- It defines an option in a select list.
- The <option> tag go inside a <select> element.

Syntax: `<option>...............</option>`

	Attributes	Value	Description
1.	`disabled`	`disabled`	This attribute specifies that an option should be disabled.
2.	`label`	`text`	This attribute specifies a shorter label for an option.
3.	`selected`	`selected`	This attribute specifies that an option should be pre-selected when the page loads.
4.	`value`	`text`	This attribute specifies the value to be sent to a server.

Example for <option> tag:
```
<!DOCTYPE html>
<body>
<form name="myform" action="nextpage.html" method="post" > <select size=1 name="mydropdown">
    <option value="milk">Fresh Milk</option><br>
    <option value="cheese">Old Cheese</option><br>
    <option value="bread">Hot Bread</option>
    </select>
    </form>
</body>
</html>
```
Output:

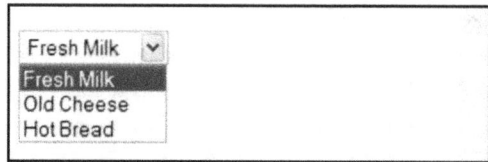

Example for form using various controls:

```
<!DOCTYPE html>
<body>
<head><h3><b> EX. FORM FOR RADIO BUTTON, CHECKBOXES & PULL DOWN
                                        MENU</b></h3>
</head>
<form action="nextpage.html" method ="post">
<h3>Enter your information:</h3>
<b><i>Enter your name:</b>
<input type=text size="25"><br>
<b><i>Your age is in between:</b><br>
<input type="radio" name="radios" value="radio1" checked>15-20
                                        yrs<br>
<input type="radio" name="radios" value="radio2">20-25 yrs<br>
<input type="radio" name="radios" value="radio3">25 yrs and
above<br>
<br><b><i>
Your Hobbies
<input type=checkbox name="option" value="read">Reading novels
<br>
<input type="checkbox" name="option" value="write" checked> Writing
<br>
<input type="checkbox" name="option" value="sing">Singing <br >
<br><br><b><i> Enter your city: </b>
<select>
<option value=pune> Pune </option>
<option value=mumbai> Mumbai</option>
<option value=a'nagar> Ahmednagar </option>
</select><br><br>
<input type="submit" name="button" value="Submit data">
</form>
</body>
</html>
```

Output:

Practice Questions

1. Define the following terms:
   (i)   Web page,
   (ii) Web publishing.
2. What are web pages?
3. How will you build a web site?
4. Distinguish between dynamic and static web pages.
5. Write and explain the steps to publish your page on the Internet.
6. Which four tags are required in every HTML page?
7. How will you use different header tags in the HTML page?
8. Write HTML code to generate the following:
   - Left alignment for the sentence
     "This is my first web page"
   - Change the font from Arial to Courier new and write the sentence.
     "Now onwards I will try to write something useful for your people".
   - Insert proper Breaklines in the code.
9. Write the HTML codes for the following:
   I have
   - One car
   - One Motorcycle
   - One Bicycle

   I also have
   - One Bookshelf
   - One Computer
   - One CD-Player
10. How can you open a link in a new browser window?
11. Develop HTML code for the following:
    Go to the bottom

    –

    –

    Text for your article

    –

    Go to the top
12. Create a Email link to write a mail to your friend to invite him/her for your Birthday party, describing the venue, out and time.
13. Develop a web page to give information about your college.
14. Develop two web pages which will include questions and answers for different subjects and link to specific part from another document.
15. How can different types of images be used in the HTML code?

16. What is meant understand by client-side image map? Give one example.

17. Write a HTML code to generate the following output.

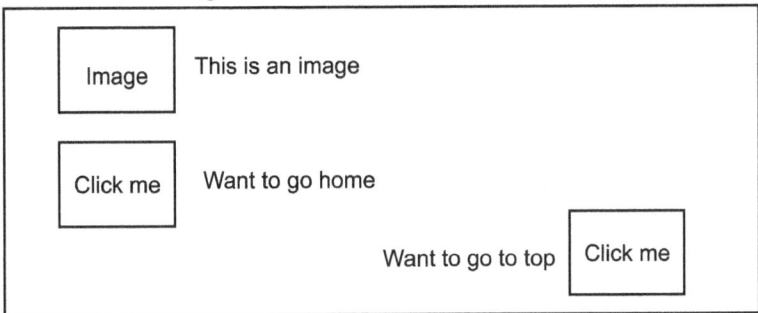

18. Explain why server-side image map is useful in HTML.

19. Write different types of image alignment and text wrapping formats.

20. What is a table? How do you build a table? What is the use of building a table?

21. Explain the different attributes that are used with <table> tag.

22. Write the HTML code to create the table shown in the following figure. (You can take any image).

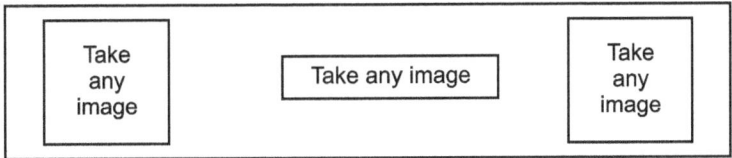

23. How do we create a frame? What is a frameset?

24. Explain different attributes that can be used with frame elements.

25. Write the HTML to list the name Mickey, Minnie, and Donald in a frame taking up the left 25 percent of the browser window. Make it so that clicking each name brings up a corresponding Web Page in the right 75 percent of the browser window.

26. What is a form?

27. How to create a form? Explain with example.

28. What are the methods used in forms.

29. Write code for following form:

Nirali Prakashan

Name of employee :   [_____]

Address :   [_____]

Phone No. :   [_____]

[Submit]

■■■

Chapter 2...

CSS

Contents ...

2.1 CSS

- CSS stands for Cascading Style Sheet.
- CSS is a language that we can use to define styles against any HTML element. These styles are set using CSS properties. For example, we can set font properties (size, colors, style etc.), background images, border styles, and so on.
- Cascading style sheets is a language used to describe the look and formatting of a document written in a markup language.
- CSS's most common use is to style web pages written in HTML. Prior to CSS, most of the presentational attributes (font colors, background styles, element alignments, borders and sizes) were contained within the HTML. All had to be explicitly described, often repeatedly, which was a nightmare for web designers.

2.1.1 Concept of CSS

- Cascading style sheets are used to specify particular styles for a character, a word, a group of words, a page or a whole web site. Although we can change almost any behavior using these styles, including some behaviors that were not possible in HTML.

- CSS does not constitute an independent or complete language, the styles are used to control the display of items or sections on a web page.
- A CSS comprises of style rules that are interpreted by the browser and then applied to the corresponding elements in our document.
- A style rule is made of three parts:
  1. **Selector:** A selector is an HTML tag at which style will be applied. This could be any tag like <h1> or <table> etc.
  2. **Property:** A property is a type of attribute of HTML tag. Put simply, all the HTML attributes are converted into CSS properties. They could be color or border etc.
  3. **Value:** Values are assigned to properties. For example color property can have value either red or #F1F1F1 etc.
- Syntax of CSS is: `selector { property: value }`
- **Example:** We can define a table border as follows:

```
table{ border:1px solid #C00; }
```

Here, table is a selector and border is a property and given value 1px solid #C00 is the value of that property.

We can define selectors in various simple ways based on your comfort. Let me put these selectors one by one.

Type Selectors: This is the same selector we have seen above. Again one more example to give a color to all level 1 headings like this:

```
h1 {
   color: #36CFFF;
}
```

1. **Universal Selectors:**

   Rather than selecting elements of a specific type, the universal selector quite simply matches the name of any element type:

```
* {
   color: #000000;
}
```

   This rule renders the content of every element in our document in black.

2. **Descendant Selectors:**

   Suppose we want to apply a style rule to a particular element only when it lies inside a particular element. As given in the following example, style rule will apply to <em> element only when it lies inside <ul> tag.

```
ul em {
   color: #000000;
}
```

3. **Class Selectors:**

We can define style rules based on the class attribute of the elements. All the elements having that class will be formatted according to the defined rule. It is denoted by . (dot).

```
.black {
   color: #000000;
}
```

This rule renders the content in black for every element with class attribute set to black in our document. We can make it a bit more particular. For example:

```
h1.black {
   color: #000000;
}
```

This rule renders the content in black for only <h1> elements with class attribute set to black.

We can apply more than one class selectors to given element. Consider the following example:

```
<p class="center bold">
This para will be styled by the classes center and bold.
</p>
```

4. **ID Selectors:**

We can define style rules based on the id attribute of the elements. All the elements having that id will be formatted according to the defined rule.

```
#black {
   color: #000000;
}
```

This rule renders the content in black for every element with id attribute set to black in our document. You can make it a bit more particular. For example:

```
h1#black {
   color: #000000;
}
```

This rule renders the content in black for only <h1> elements with id attribute set to black.

The true power of id selectors is when they are used as the foundation for descendant selectors, For example:

```
#black h2 {
   color: #000000;
}
```

In above example all level 2 headings will be displayed in black color only when those headings will lie with in tags having id attribute set to black.

5. **Child Selectors:**

We have seen descendant selectors. There is one more type of selectors which is very similar to descendants but have different functionality. Consider the following example:

```
body > p {
  color: #000000;
}
```

This rule will render all the paragraphs in black if they are direct child of <body> element. Other paragraphs put inside other elements like <div> or <td> etc. would not have any effect of this rule.

6. **Attribute Selectors:**

We can also apply styles to HTML elements with particular attributes. The style rule below will match all input elements that has a type attribute with a value of text:

```
input[type="text"]{
  color: #000000;
}
```

The advantage to this method is that the <input type="submit" /> element is unaffected, and the color applied only to the desired text fields.

There are following rules applied to attribute selector.

o **p[lang]:** Selects all paragraph elements with a lang attribute.
o **p[lang="fr"]:** Selects all paragraph elements whose lang attribute has a value of exactly "fr".
o **p[lang~="fr"]:** Selects all paragraph elements whose lang attribute contains the word "fr".
o **p[lang|="en"]:** Selects all paragraph elements whose lang attribute contains values that are exactly "en", or begin with "en-".

Multiple Style Rules:

• We may need to define multiple style rules for a single element. We can define these rules to combine multiple properties and corresponding values into a single block as defined in the following example:

```
h1 {
color: #36C;
font-weight: normal;
letter-spacing: .4em;
margin-bottom: 1em;
text-transform: lowercase;
}
```

• Here, all the property and value pairs are separated by a semi colon (;). We can keep them in a ingle line or multiple lines. For better readability we keep them into separate lines.

• For a while do not bother about the properties mentioned in the above block.

7. Grouping Selectors:

We can apply a style to many selectors if we like. Just separate the selectors with a comma as given in the following example:

```
h1, h2, h3 {
color: #36C;
font-weight: normal;
letter-spacing: .4em;
margin-bottom: 1em;
text-transform: lowercase;
}
```

This define style rule will be applicable to h1, h2 and h3 element as well. The order of the list is irrelevant. All the elements in the selector will have the corresponding declarations applied to them.

We can combine various class selectors together as shown below:

```
#content, #footer, #supplement {
position: absolute;
left: 510px;
width: 200px;
}
```

Advantages of CSS:

1. **CSS saves time:** We can write CSS once and then reuse same sheet in multiple HTML pages. We can define a style for each HTML element and apply it to as many Web pages as we want.

2. **Pages load faster:** If we are using CSS, we do not need to write HTML tag attributes every time. Just write one CSS rule of a tag and apply to all the occurrences of that tag. So less code means faster download times.

3. **Easy maintenance:** To make a global change, simply change the style, and all elements in all the web pages will be updated automatically.

4. **Superior styles to HTML:** CSS has a much wider array of attributes than HTML so you can give far better look to your HTML page in comparison of HTML attributes.

5. **Multiple Device Compatibility:** Style sheets allow content to be optimized for more than one type of device. By using the same HTML document, different versions of a website can be presented for handheld devices such as PDAs and cell phones or for printing.

6. **Global web standards:** Now HTML attributes are being deprecated and it is being recommended to use CSS. So its a good idea to start using CSS in all the HTML pages to make them compatible to future browsers.

2.2 Types of Style Sheets

- CSS can be inserted in three following ways:
  1. Inline,
  2. Embedded(Internally), and
  3. Externally.

2.2.1 Inline CSS

- An inline style loses many of the advantages of style sheets by mixing content with presentation.
- It is possible to place CSS right in the opening tag of HTML element.

  Syntax:
  ```
  <tag style="property1: value;
        property2: value;">
  </tag>
  ```

Example for inline CSS:
```
<!DOCTYPE html>
<body>
<p style="background: pink; color: blue;">
Text color is green with blue background
</p>
</body>
</html>
```

Output:

Text color is green with blue background

2.2.2 Embedded(Internal) CSS

- An internal style sheet should be used when a single document has a unique style.
- CSS can be inserted in HTML within the head section of HTML code. This is sometimes called embedding CSS in HTML.
- CSS and HTML are different, so we need to tell the browser that we are dealing with CSS. This is done using style tag followed by type attribute.

  Syntax:
  ```
  <head>
  <style type="text/css">
  selector { property: value; }
  </style>
  </head>
  ```

Example for Internal/Embedded Stylesheet:

```html
<!DOCTYPE html>
<head>
<style type="text/css">
p {
color: blue;
}
h1 {
color: red;
text-align: center;
}
body {
background-color: grey;
}
</style>
</head>
<body>
<h1>Internal CSS Example</h1>
<p> Now thats how CSS is inserted internally </p>
</body>
</html>
```

- In the above example, we inserted CSS code in the head section, using style tag. This tells the browser that the code that follows will be style sheet code.
  - **Paragraph** text will be blue in color.
  - **heading (h1)** will be center aligned and text color will be red.
  - **body** background color will be grey.

Output:

2.2.3 External CSS

- An external style sheet is ideal when the style is applied to many pages. With an external style sheet, we change the look of an entire web site by changing one file.
- Best way to insert CSS code is to write it in a different file and then refer it in HTML code.
- External CSS contains only CSS code and is saved with a ".css" file extension. This CSS file is referred from HTML file using the <link> tag.
- An external CSS is ideal when the style is applied to many web pages. Web designers can change the look of an entire Web site by changing one file.

CSS Code:

```
p {
text-align: center;
color: white;
}
body {
background-color: green;
}
```

- Save the above file as sample.css

HTML Code:

```
<!DOCTYPE html>
<head>
<link rel="stylesheet" type="text/css" href="sample.css" />
</head>
<body>
<p> This is an example for inserting CSS externally. </p>
</body>
</html>
```

Output:

This is an example for inserting CSS externally.

2.3 CSS Properties

1. Background Properties:

- The CSS background properties are used to define the background effects.
- The background properties are: background, background color, background image, background repeat, background position and background attachment.

Example for CSS background property:

```
<!DOCTYPE html>
<head>
<style type="text/css">
body { background: pink; }
</style>
</head>
<body>
This is an example for background
</body>
</html>
```

Output:

This is an example for background

(i) CSS Background color:

- We can specify a color for the background of an element using the background-color property like this `background-color: value;`
- Value could be color name, hexadecimal number or RGB color code.

Example:

```
<!DOCTYPE html>
<head>
<style type="text/css">
body { background-color: #DEB887; }
</style>
</head>
<body>
This is an example for background color with a hexadecimal number.
</body>
</html>
```

Output:

> **This is an example for background color with a hexadecimal number**

(ii) CSS Background image:

- We can set an image in the background using the background-image property.

Example:

```
<!DOCTYPE html>
<head>
<style type="text/css">
p { background-image: url(imageBG.gif); }
</style>
</head>
<body>
<p>This is a paragraph, and its background is an image.</p>
</body>
</html>
```

Output:

> This is a paragraph, and its background is an image.

(iii) CSS Background position:

- We can position an image using background-position property like this, `background-position: value;`
- Values could be top left, top center, top right, center left, center center, center right, bottom left, bottom center, bottom right, x% y% or x-pos y-pos.

Example:
```
<!DOCTYPE html>
<head>
<style type="text/css">
h1 {
background-image: url(geniusAtWork.gif);
background-position: top center;
}
h2 {
background-image: url(geniusAtWork.gif);
background-position: 30% 30%;
}
</style>
</head>
<body>
<h1>See the difference in image</h1>
<h2>See the difference in image</h2>
</body>
</html>
```

Output:

(iv) CSS Background Repeat:
- We can repeat the image set as a background using the background-repeat property like this,

      background-repeat: value;
- Value could be no-repeat, repeat, repeat-x or repeat-y.

Example:
```
<!DOCTYPE html>
<head>
<style type="text/css">
h1 {
background-image: url(geniusAtWork.gif);
background-position: repeat;
}
h2 {
background-image: url(geniusAtWork.gif);
background-repeat: repeat-y;
}
</style>
</head>
<body>
<h1>example for background repeat</h1>
<h2>example for background repeat</h2>
</body>
</html>
```

Output:

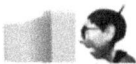

(v) CSS Background Attachment:

- We can set the image in background to scroll with the page or set it fixed when the user scrolls down the page using background-attachment property like this.

```
background-attachment: value;
```

- Value could be fixed or scroll.

Example:

```
<!DOCTYPE html>
<head>
<style type="text/css">
body
{
background-image: url('geniusAtWork.gif');
background-repeat: no-repeat;
background-attachment: fixed;
}
</style>
</head>
<body>
<p>An interesting story comes here. See example to read the story</p>
</body>
</html>
```

Output:

This story is from www. pragati.com

Visit www.**pragati.com**/stories.php for more stories.

Back in the fifteenth century

in a tiny village near Nuremberg, lived a family with eighteen children. Eighteen! In order merely to keep food on the table for this mob, the father and head of the household, a goldsmith by profession, worked almost eighteen hours a day at his trade and any other paying chore he could find in the neighborhood.

Despite their seemingly hopeless

condition, two of Albrecht Durer, the Elder's, children had a dream. They both wanted to pursue their talent for art, but they knew full well that their father would never be financially able to send either of them to Nuremberg to study at the Academy.

After many long discussions at night

2. CSS Font Properties:

- We can change the text size, color, style, make it bold or light etc using CSS font properties.
- The font properties are: font-family, font-size, font-weight, font-style and font-variant.

(i) CSS font family

- We can set the font to be serif, sans-serif, verdana, cursive etc using font-family property like this, `font-family: value;`

Example:

```
<!DOCTYPE html>
<head>
<style type="text/css">
h1 { font-family: serif; }
h2 { font-family: sans-serif; }
h3 { font-family: cursive; }
</style>
</head>
<body>
<h1>This is serif </h1>
<h2>This is sans-serif </h2>
<h3>This is cursive </h3>
</body>
</html>
```

Output:

This is serif

This is sans-serif

This is cursive

(ii) CSS font size:

- We can set the font size using font-size property like this `font-size: value;`
- The value could be xx-large, px (pixel>, x-large, larger, large, medium, small, smaller, x-small, xx-small, length or %.

Example:

```
<!DOCTYPE html>
<head>
<style type="text/css">
p.first { font-size: 150%; }
p.second { font-size: 30px; }
p.third { font-size: small; }
</style>
</head>
<body>
<p class="first">This font is 150% </p>
<p class="second">This font is 30 pixels</p>
<p class="third">This font is small</p>
</body>
</html>
```

Output:

This font is 150%

This font is 30 pixels

This font is small

(iii) CSS font weight:

- We can make font thick or bold using the font-weight property like this

  ```
  font-weight: value;
  ```

- The value could be normal, bold, bolder, lighter or any number(usually multiples of 100 are used).

Example:

```
<!DOCTYPE html>
<head>
<style type="text/css">
p.first { font-weight: normal; }
p.second { font-weight: bolder; }
p.third { font-weight: 900; }
</style>
</head>
<body>
<p class="first">This font is normal </p>
<p class="second">This font is bolder </p>
<p class="third">This font weight is 900</p>
</body>
</html>
```

Output:

This font is normal

This font is bolder

This font weight is 900

(iv) CSS font style:

- We can set font style using the font-style property like this `font-style: value;`
- The value could be normal, italic or oblique.

Example:

```
<!DOCTYPE html>
<head>
<style type="text/css">
p.first { font-style: normal; }
p.second { font-style: italic; }
p.third { font-style: oblique; }
</style>
</head>
<body>
<p class="first">This font is normal </p>
<p class="second">This font is italic </p>
<p class="third">This font is oblique</p>
</body>
</html>
```

Output:

> This font is normal
>
> *This font is italic*
>
> *This font is oblique*

(v) CSS font variant:

- We can set font variant using the font-variant property like this,

    ```
    font-variant: value;
    ```

- The value could be normal or small-caps.

Example:

```
<!DOCTYPE html>
<head>
<style type="text/css">
p.first { font-variant: normal; }
p.second { font-variant: small-caps; }
</style>
</head>
<body>
<p class="first">This font is normal</p>
<p class="second">THIS FONT IS SMALLCAPS </p>
</body>
</html>
```

Output:

> This font is normal
>
> THIS FONT IS SMALLCAPS

3. CSS text Properties:

- Using CSS text properties we can control the text spacing, decoration, alignment or transform the text to upper or lowercase.
- The text properties are letter spacing, text decoration, text align, text transform, word spacing, text indent.

(i) CSS letter spacing:

- We can adjust the space between letters using letter spacing property.

    Syntax: `letter-spacing: value;`

    value could be normal or length (0.2ex, 0.3ex, 5ex, 1px etc).

Example:
```
<!DOCTYPE html>
<head>
<style type="text/css">
p.first { letter-spacing: 5ex; }
p.second{ letter-spacing: normal; }
p.third { letter-spacing: 2px; }
</style>
</head>
<body>
<p class="first">Letter spacing is 5ex</p>
<p class="second">Letter spacing is normal </p>
<p class="third">Letter spacing is 2px </p>
</body>
</html>
```

Output:

```
L    e    t    t    e    r         s    p    a    c    i    n    g         i    s
5     e    x

Letter spacing is normal

Letter spacing is 2px
```

(ii) CSS text decoration:

• We can decorate the text using text decoration property.

Syntax: `text-decoration: value;`

value could be underline, overline, line through or blink

Example:
```
<!DOCTYPE html>
<head>
<style type="text/css">
p.first { text-decoration: underline; }
p.second{ text-decoration: line-through; }
p.third { text-decoration: overline; }
</style>
</head>
<body>
<p class="first">Text is underlined</p>
<p class="second">Text is lined-through </p>
<p class="third">Text is overlined </p>
</body>
</html>
```

Output:

```
Text is underlined

Text is lined-through

Text is overlined
```

(iii) CSS text align:

- We can align the text using text align property.

  Syntax: `text-align: value;`

  value could be left, right, center or justify.

Example:

```
<!DOCTYPE html>
<head>
<style type="text/css">
p.first { text-align: center; }
p.second{ text-align: right; }
p.third { text-align: left; }
p.fourth{ text-align: justify; }
</style>
</head>
<body>
<p class="first">Text is centered</p>
<p class="second">Text is right aligned </p>
<p class="third">Text is left aligned </p>
<p class="fourth">Text is justified </p>
</body>
</html>
```

Output:

(iv) CSS text transform:

- We can transform the text to lowercase, uppercase or capitalize. using text transform property.

  Syntax: `text-transform: value;`

  value could be capitalize, uppercase, or lowercase.

Example:

```
<!DOCTYPE html>
<head>
<style type="text/css">
p.first { text-transform: capitalize; }
p.second{ text-transform: uppercase; }
p.third { text-transform: lowercase; }
</style>
</head>
<body>
<p class="first">This Text Is Capitalize</p>
<p class="second">this text uppercase </p>
<p class="third">THIS TEXT IS LOWERCASE </p>
</body>
</html>
```

Output:

This Text Is Capitalize

THIS TEXT UPPERCASE

this text is lowercase

(v) CSS word spacing:

* We can adjust the spaces between words using word spacing property.

Syntax: `word-spacing: value;`

value could be normal, or value (0.2ex, 0.3ex, 5ex, 1px etc).

Example:

```
<!DOCTYPE html>
<head>
<style type="text/css">
h1 { word-spacing: normal; }
p{ word-spacing: 8px; }
</style>
</head>
<body>
<h1>Heading is normal</h1>
<p>This text has 8px space between words </p>
</body>
</html>
```

Output:

Heading is normal

This text has 8px space between words

(vi) CSS text indent:

* We can indent the text using text indent property.

Syntax: `text-indent: value;`

value could be length like 1ex 2ex 5px etc, or percentage like 20%, 30% etc.

Example:

```
<!DOCTYPE html>
<head>
<style type="text/css">
h1 { text-indent: 50%; }
p{ text-indent: 50px; }
</style>
</head>
<body>
<h1>Heading is 50% intended</h1>
<p>You've got to start with the customer experience and work back
towards the technology
- not the other way around.</p>
</body>
</html>
```

Output:

> # Heading is 50% intended
>
> You've got to start with the customer experience and work back towards the technology - not the other way around.

4. CSS border properties:

- CSS border properties allow us to customize the borders.
- The border properties are: border style, border color, border width, border top, border bottom, border left and border right.

(i) CSS border style:

- We can style the borders of HTML elements using the border-style property.

    Syntax: `border-style: value;`

    value could be dashed, dotted, double, groove, hidden, inset, outset, ridge or solid,

Example:

```
<!DOCTYPE html>
<head>
<style type="text/css">
table.first { border-style: solid; }
table.second { border-style: dotted; }
table.third { border-style: inset; }
</style>
</head>
<body>
<table class="first">
<tr><td> Table is solid </td></tr>
</table><br/>
<table class="second">
<tr><td> Table is dotted </td></tr>
</table><br/>
<table class="third">
<tr><td> Table is inset </td></tr>
</table><br/>
</body>
</html>
```

Output:

Table is solid

Table is dotted

Table is inset

(ii) CSS border color:

- We can set the color of borders using the border-color property.

    Syntax: `border-color: value;`

    value could be color name, hexadecimal number, RGB color code or transparent

Example:

```
<!DOCTYPE html>
<head>
<style type="text/css">
table.first{
border-color: rgb( 100, 200, 300);
border-style: dotted;
}
table.second{
border-color: #786786;
border-style: solid;
}
p.first{
border-color: red;
border-style: outset;
}
p.second{
border-color: transparent;
border-style: dashed;
}
</style>
</head>
<body>
<p class="first">This is a paragraph</p>
<p class="second">This is a paragraph</p>
<table class="first">
<tr><td>Table 1</tr></td>
</table><br/>
<table class="second">
<tr><td>Table 2</tr></td>
</table>
</body>
</html>
```

Output:

This is a paragraph

This is a paragraph

Table 1

Table 2

(iii) CSS border width:

- We can set the width of borders using the border-width property.

    Syntax: `border-width: value;`

    value could be medium, thin, thick or length

Example:
```
<!DOCTYPE html>
<head>
<style type="text/css">
p.first{
border-width: thin;
border-style: dotted;
}
p.second{
border-width: 3px;
border-style: solid;
}
</style>
</head>
<body>
<p class="first">width is thin</p>
<p class="second">width is 3px</p>
</body>
</html>
```

Output:

(iv) CSS border sides:

- We can position the border sides using the border-top, border-bottom, border-left and border-right properties.

Example:
```
<!DOCTYPE html>
<head>
<style type="text/css">
table.first{
border-top-color: green;
border-top-style: groove;
border-top-width: 3px;
}
```

```
table.second{
border-bottom-color: green;
border-bottom-style: groove;
border-bottom-width: 3px;
}
table.third{
border-left-color: green;
border-left-style: groove;
border-left-width: 3px;
}
table.fourth{
border-right-color: green;
border-right-style: groove;
border-right-width: 3px;
}
</style>
</head>
<body>
<table class="first">
<tr><td>FIRST TABLE</td></td>
</table><br/>
<table class="second">
<tr><td>SECOND TABLE</td></td>
</table><br/>
<table class="third">
<tr><td>THIRD TABLE</td></td>
</table><br/>
<table class="fourth">
<tr><td>FOURTH TABLE</td></td>
</table>
</body>
</html>
```

Output:

5. CSS list styles properties:

- The appearance of ordered and unordered lists can be controlled using the list style properties.
- The list style properties are: list style type, list style image and list style position.

(i) CSS list style type.

- We can add circles, squares, romans etc to ordered and unordered lists using the list-style-type property.

  Syntax: `list-style-type: value;`

  value could be disc, circle, square, decimal, lower-roman, upper-roman, lower-alpha or upper-alpha.

Example:

```
<!DOCTYPE html>
<head>
<style type="text/css">
ol { list-style-type: square; }
ul { list-style-type: upper-alpha; }
</style>
</head>
<body>
<ol>
<li>Facebook</li>
<li>Twitter</li>
<li>Google+</li>
<li>Myspace</li>
</ol>
<ul>
<li>Facebook</li>
<li>Twitter</li>
<li>Google+</li>
<li>Myspace</li>
</ul>
</body>
</html>
```

Output:

```
   ■ Facebook
   ■ Twitter
   ■ Google+
   ■ Myspace

   A. Facebook
   B. Twitter
   C. Google+
   D. Myspace
```

(ii) CSS list style image:

- We can add images to ordered and unordered lists using the list-style-image property.

  Syntax: `list-style-image: url(image-path);`

Example:

```
<!DOCTYPE html>
<head>
<style type="text/css">
ol { list-style-image:url("arrow1.gif"); }
ul { list-style-image: url("star1.jpg"); }
</style>
</head>
<body>
<ol>
<li>Facebook</li>
<li>Twitter</li>
<li>Google+</li>
<li>Myspace</li>
</ol>
<ul>
<li>Facebook</li>
<li>Twitter</li>
<li>Google+</li>
<li>Myspace</li>
</ul>
</body>
</html>
```

Output:

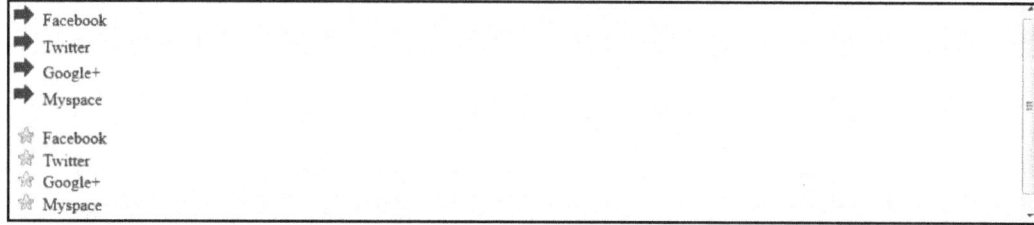

(iii) CSS list style position:

- We can control the position of ordered and unordered lists using the list-style-position property.

  Syntax: `list-style-position: value;`

  value could be inside or outside.

Example:

```
<!DOCTYPE html>
<head>
<style type="text/css">
ol { list-style-position: inside; }
ul { list-style-position: outside; }
</style>
</head>
<body>
<p>This list is positioned inside</p>
<ol>
<li>Facebook</li>
<li>Twitter</li>
<li>Google+</li>
<li>Myspace</li>
</ol>
<p>This list is positioned outside</p>
<ul>
<li>Facebook</li>
<li>Twitter</li>
<li>Google+</li>
<li>Myspace</li>
</ul>
</body>
</html>
```

Output:

This list is positioned inside

1. Facebook
2. Twitter
3. Google+
4. Myspace

This list is positioned outside

• Facebook
• Twitter
• Google+
• Myspace

6. CSS Links:

- Using link properties we can set colors for visited links, unvisited links, active links etc.
- The link properties are: a:link (for unvisited links), a:visited (for visited links), a:hover (for mouseover links), a:active (changes color as the link is pressed), a:focus (for keyboard tabs).

Example:

```
<!DOCTYPE html>
<head>
<style type="text/css">
a:link { color: green; }
a:visited { color: blue; }
a:active { color: red; }
a:hover { color: yellow; }
a:focus { color: black; }
</style>
</head>
<body>
<h1><a href="#"> Click me </a><br/></h1>
</body>
</html>
```

Output:

> Click me

7. Positioning with Style Sheet:

- The position property changes how elements are positioned on our webpage.

  Syntax: `position: value;`

  Values are static, relative, absolute and fix.

(i) Static:

State positioning is by default the way an element will appear in the normal flow of our HTML file. It is not necessary to declare a position of static. Doing so, is no different than not declaring it at all.

Syntax: `position: static;`

(ii) Relative:

- Positioning an element relatively places the element in the normal flow of our HTML file and then offsets it by some amount using the properties left, right, top and bottom. This may cause the element to overlap other elements that are on the page, which of course may be the effect that is required.

  Syntax: `position: relative;`

(iii) Absolute:

Positioning an element absolutely, removes the element from the normal flow of our HTML file and positions it to the top left of it's nearest parent element that has a position declared other than static. If no parent element with a position other than static exists then it will be positioned from the top left of the browser window.

Syntax: `position: absolute;`

(iv) Fixed:

Positioning an element with the fixed value, is the same as absolute except the parent element is always the browser window. It makes no difference if the fixed element is nested inside other positioned elements.

Furthermore, an element that is positioned with a fixed value, will not scroll with the document. It will remain in its position regardless of the scroll position of the page.

Syntax: `position: fixed;`

When positioning element with relative, absolute or fixed values the following properties are used to offset the element: top, left, right and bottom.

Syntax: `position: absolute; top: 10px; right: 10px;`

8. CSS Margins:

* As we may have guessed, the margin property declares the margin between an HTML element and the elements around it.

* The margin property can be set for the top, left, right and bottom of an element, like this:

```
margin-top: length percentage or auto;

margin-left: length percentage or auto;

margin-right: length percentage or auto;

margin-bottom: length percentage or auto;
```

* As we can also see in the above example we have three choices or values for the margin property i.e. length, percentage and auto.

* We can also declare all the margins of an element in a single property as follows:

```
margin: 10px 10px 10px 10px;
```

* If we declare all four values as we have above, the order is as follows:

  1. top
  2. right
  3. bottom
  4. left

* If only one value is declared, it sets the margin on all sides.

```
margin: 10px;
```

* If we only declare two or three values, the undeclared values are taken from the opposing side.

```
margin: 10px 10px; /* 2 values */

margin: 10px 10px 10px; /* 3 values */
```

- We can set the margin property to negative values. If we do not declare the margin value of an element, the margin is 0 (zero).

```
margin: -10 px;
```

- Elements like paragraphs have default margins in some browsers, to combat this set the margin to 0 (zero).

```
p(margin; 0;)
```

- We can see in the example below, the elements for this site are set to by 20px (pixels) from the body,

```
body
{
    margin: 20 px;
    background: #eeeeee;
    font-size: small;
    font-family: Tahoma, Arial, "Trebuchet MS", Helvetica, sans-serif;
    text-align: left;
}
```

9. CSS Padding:

- Padding is the distance between the border of an HTML element and the content within it.
- Most of the rules for margins also apply to padding, except there is no "auto" value and negative values cannot be declared for padding.

```
padding-top: length percentage;
padding-left: length percentage;
padding-right: length percentage;
padding-bottom: length percentage;
```

- As we can also see in the above example we have 2 choices of values for the padding property,
  - length
  - percentage
- We can also declare all the padding of an element in a single property as follows:

```
padding: 10px 10px 10px 10px;
```

- If we declare all 4 values as we have above, the order is as follows:
  1. top
  2. right
  3. bottom
  4. left

- If only one value is declared, it sets the padding on all sides.

    ```
    padding: 10px;
    ```

- If we only declare two or three values, the undeclared values are taken from the opposing side, like this.

    ```
    padding: 10px 10px; /* 2 values */

    padding: 10px 10px 10px; /* 3 values */
    ```

- If we do not declare the padding value of an element, the padding is 0 (zero).

- We can see in the example below, the main container for this site has 30px (pixels) of padding between the border and the text.

    ```
    #container

    {

        width: 70%;

        margin: auto;

        padding: 30 px;

        border: 1px solid #666;

        background: #ffffff;

    }

    {

        padding: 20px;

        border: 1px solid #666;

        background: #ffffff;

    }
    ```

2.4 <div> and <span> Tags

1. **CSS Divisions:**

- Divisions are a block level HTML element used to define sections of an HTML file.
- A division can contain all the parts that make up our website. Including additional divisions, spans, images, text and so on.
- We define a division within an HTML file by placing the following between the <body> </body> tags.

    Syntax: `<div>`

    ```
            Site contents go here ............

            </div>
    ```

- Though, most likely we will want to add some style to it. We can do that in the following fashion:

```
<div id="container">
Site contents go here ...........
</div>
```

- The CSS file contains this:

```
#container{
    width: 70%;
    margin: auto;
    padding: 20 px;
    border: 1px solid #666;
    background: #ffffff;
}
```

- Now everything within that division will be styled by the "container" style rule, we defined within my CSS file. A division creates a linebreak by default. We can use both classes and IDs with a division tag to style sections of we website.

2. CSS Spans:

- Spans are very similar to divisions except they are an inline element versus a block level.

- No linebreak is created when a span is declared.

- We can use the span tag to style certain areas of text, as shown below:

    Syntax: `<span class="italic"> This text is italic</span>`

- Add the follwoing in my CSS file:

```
.italic{
    font-style: italic;
}
```

Output:

```
This text is italic.
```

2.5 Uses of Classes in CSS

- Using a class is easy, we need to specify a class extension in HTML and that extension should be added in CSS code. Confused? Don't worry go on, the code given below will make it easy to understand.

- A class selector begin with dot (.).

CSS Code:

```
h1.right{ color: green; text-align: right;}
h1.left{ color: blue; text-align: left;}
h1.center{ color: red; text-align: center;}
```

HTML Code:

```
<!DOCTYPE html>
<body>
<h1 class="right">h1 heading in green </h1>
<h1 class="left">h1 heading in blue </h1>
<h1 class="center">h1 heading in red </h1>
</body>
</html>
```

- In HTML code, we specified class extension in <h1> tags using values right, left and center.

- In CSS code, we added class extension.

Output:

CSS ID:

- CSS Ids is similar to CSS classes, but they are applied to a unique identifier of an HTML elements.

- Id is defined in the HTML, and each Id must be unique on the page.

- There are two ways to add ids in CSS code.

  1. Hash (#) followed by Id name.

  2. HTML element followed by Hash and Id name.

CSS Code:

```
#para{
text-align: center;
color: green;
}
```

HTML Code:

```
<!DOCTYPE html>
<body>
<p id="para">
A user friendly computer first requires a friendly user.
</p>
<p>
This is a normal paragraph. The only way to do great work is to love
what you do.
</p>
</body>
</html>
```

- In the above example, paragraph is given a unique id para in the HTML code. In the CSS code we added hash (#) followed by Id name.

Output:

A user friendly computer first requires a friendly user.

This is a normal paragraph. The only way to do great thing is to love what you do.

2.6 Introduction to CSS3

History

- The development of **style sheet** was to make the markup language more impressive. It was discovered around 1980s in the beginning of the **SGML**.
- The third level of **CSS** was started to develop around 1998. And till 2009, it was under development. The first working draft of **CSS3** came in 19-01-2001. And since the first introduction still it is under construction.
- There were some certain shortcomings in **CSS2** and due to its unlikeness the developer introduced **CSS3**. It is divided into different modules according to its specifications. Though the first working draft of **CSS3** came on 19-01-2001, but it was initially declared early in the June 1999.
- Cascading Style Sheets (CSS) is a style sheet language used for describing the look and formatting of a document written in a markup language.CSS3 is a latest standard of css earlier versions(CSS2).
- The main difference between css2 and css3 is follows:
  - o Media Queries
  - o Namespaces
  - o Selectors Level 3
  - o Color

CSS3 Modules

- CSS3 has been split into "modules". It contains the "old CSS specification" (which has been split into smaller pieces). In addition, new modules are added.
- Some of the most important CSS3 modules are:
  - Selectors
  - Box Model
  - Backgrounds and Borders
  - Image Values and Replaced Content
  - Text Effects
  - 2D/3D Transformations
  - Animations
  - Multiple Column Layout
  - User Interface

  Most of the new CSS3 properties are implemented in modern browsers.

2.6.1 Gradients

- CSS3 gradients allow you display even transitions between two or more specified colors.
- Earlier, you had to use images for these effects. However, by using CSS3 gradients you can reduce download time and bandwidth usage. In addition, elements with gradients look better when zoomed, because the gradient is generated by the browser.
- CSS3 defines two types of gradients:
  - **Linear Gradients (goes down/up/left/right/diagonally)**
  - **Radial Gradients (defined by their center)**

2.6.1.1 Linear Gradient

- To create a linear gradient you must define at least two color stops. Color stops are the colors you want to render smooth transitions among. You can also set a starting point and a direction (or an angle) along with the gradient effect.

  Syntax: `background: linear-gradient(direction, color-stop1,`
  `                                      color-stop2, ...);`

2.6.1.2 Linear Gradient - Top to Bottom (this is default)

- The following example shows a linear gradient that starts at the top. It starts red, transitioning to yellow:

CSS Code:

```
#gradTopBottom {
    height: 200px;
    background: blue;

/* For browsers that do not support gradients */
    background: -webkit-linear-gradient(left, blue, pink);

/* For Safari 5.1 to 6.0 */
    background: -o-linear-gradient(right, blue, pink);

/* For Opera 11.1 to 12.0 */
    background: -moz-linear-gradient(right, blue,pink);

 /* For Firefox 3.6 to 15 */
    background: linear-gradient(to right,blue, pink);
}
```

Linear Gradient - Left to Right

- The following example shows a linear gradient that starts from the left. It starts red, transitioning to yellow:

CSS Code:

```
#gradLetToRight {
    height: 200px;
    background: red;

  /* For browsers that do not support gradients */
    background: -webkit-linear-gradient(left, red , yellow);

/* For Safari 5.1 to 6.0 */
    background: -o-linear-gradient(right, red, yellow);

/* For Opera 11.1 to 12.0 */
    background: -moz-linear-gradient(right, red, yellow);

/* For Firefox 3.6 to 15 */
    background: linear-gradient(to right, red , yellow);
}
```

Linear Gradient - Diagonal

- You can make a gradient diagonally by specifying both the horizontal and vertical starting positions.

- The following example shows a linear gradient that starts at top left (and goes to bottom right). It starts red, transitioning to yellow:

CSS Code:

```
#gradDiagonal {

    height: 200px;

    background: red; /* For browsers that do not support gradients */

    background: -webkit-linear-gradient(left top, red, yellow); /*
For Safari 5.1 to 6.0 */

    background: -o-linear-gradient(bottom right, red, yellow); /* For
Opera 11.1 to 12.0 */

    background: -moz-linear-gradient(bottom right, red, yellow); /*
For Firefox 3.6 to 15 */

    background: linear-gradient(to bottom right, red, yellow); /*
Standard syntax (must be last) */

}
```

Using Angles

- If you want more control over the direction of the gradient, you can define an angle, instead of the predefined directions (to bottom, to top, to right, to left, to bottom right, etc.).

  Syntax: `background: linear-gradient(angle, color-stop1, color-stop2);`

Using Multiple Color Stops

- You can use multiple colors

  Syntax: `background: linear-gradient(red, yellow, green);`

Using Transparency

- CSS3 gradients also support transparency, which can be used to create fading effects.
- To add transparency, we use the rgba() function to define the color stops. The last parameter in the rgba() function can be a value from 0 to 1, and it defines the transparency of the color: 0 indicates full transparency, 1 indicates full color (no transparency).

  Syntax: `background: linear-gradient(to right, rgba(255,0,0,0),`

  `rgba(255,0,0,1));`

Repeating a linear-gradient

- The repeating-linear-gradient() function is used to repeat linear gradients

  Syntax: `background: repeating-linear-gradient(red, yellow 10%, green 20%);`

Set Shape

- The shape parameter defines the shape. It can take the value circle or ellipse. The default value is ellipse.

  Syntax: `background: radial-gradient(circle, red, yellow, green);`

Use of Different Size Keywords

- The size parameter defines the size of the gradient. It can take four values:
  - **closest-side:**

    `background: radial-gradient(closest-side at 60% 55%, red, yellow, black);`
  - **farthest-side**

    `background: radial-gradient(farthest-side at 60% 55%, red, yellow, black);`
  - **closest-corner**

    `background: radial-gradient(closest-corner at 60% 55%, red, yellow, black);`
  - **farthest-corner**

    `background: radial-gradient(farthest-corner at 60% 55%, red, yellow, black);`

Repeating a radial-gradient

- The repeating-radial-gradient() function is used to repeat radial gradients

  Syntax: `background: repeating-radial-gradient(red, yellow 10%, green 15%);`

2.6.2 Transitions

- CSS3 transitions allows you to change property values smoothly (from one value to another), over a given duration.

Example:

Mouse over the element below to see a CSS3 transition effect:

- To create a transition effect, you must specify two things:
  - the CSS property you want to add an effect to
  - the duration of the effect

  Note: If the duration part is not specified, the transition will have no effect, because the default value is 0.

- The following example shows a 100px * 100px red <div> element. The <div> element has also specified a transition effect for the width property, with a duration of 2 seconds:

CSS Code:

```
div {

    width: 100px;

    height: 100px;

    background: red;

    -webkit-transition: width 2s; /* Safari */

    transition: width 2s;

}
```

- The transition effect will start when the specified CSS property (width) changes value.
- Now, let us specify a new value for the width property when a user mouses over the <div> element:

```
div:hover {

    width: 350px;

}
```

when the cursor mouses out of the element, it will gradually change back to its original style.

Properties of Transition

- **Transition Property:** The transition property is a shorthand property for the four transition properties:

  transition-property, transition-duration, transition-timing-function, and transition-delay.

  Syntax: `transition: property duration timing-function`

  `delay|initial|inherit;`

- The transition property can have the following values:

Transition Property	Values
transition-property	Specifies the name of the CSS property the transition effect is for.
transition-duration	Specifies how many seconds or milliseconds the transition effect takes to complete.
transition-timing-function	Specifies the speed curve of the transition effect.
transition-delay	Defines when the transition effect will start.
initial	Sets this property to its default value. Read about initial.
inherit	Inherits this property from its parent element. Read about inherit.

Example:

When an <input type="text"> gets focus, gradually change the width from 100px to 250px:

```
input[type=text] {
    width: 100px;
    -webkit-transition: ease-in-out, width .35s ease-in-out; /* Safari
    3.1 to 6.0 */
    transition: ease-in-out, width .35s ease-in-out;
}
input[type=text]:focus {
    width: 250px;
}
```

Transition-property Property

- The transition-property property specifies the name of the CSS property the transition effect is for (the transition effect will start when the specified CSS property changes).

  Syntax: `transition-property: none|all|property|initial|inherit;`

The transition-property property can have the following values:

Transition-Property Property	Values
none	No property will get a transition effect.
all	Default value. All properties will get a transition effect.
property	Defines a comma separated list of CSS property names the transition effect is for.
initial	Sets this property to its default value.
inherit	Inherits this property from its parent element.

CSS Code:

Hover over a <div> element, and change the width with a smooth transition effect:

```
div {
    -webkit-transition-property: width; /* Safari */
    transition-property: width;
}
div:hover {
width: 250px;
}
```

Transition Duration:

• The transition-duration property specifies how many seconds (s) or milliseconds (ms) a transition effect takes to complete.

Syntax: `transition-duration: time|initial|inherit;`

• The transition duration property can have the following values:

Transition Duration Property	Values
time	Specifies how many seconds or milliseconds a transition effect takes to complete. Default value is 0s, meaning there will be no effect.
initial	Sets this property to its default value.
inherit	Inherits this property from its parent element.

CSS Code:

Transition effect last for 7 seconds:

```
div {
    -webkit-transition-duration: 7s; /* Safari */
    transition-duration: 7s;
}
```

Transition-timing-function:

- The transition-timing-function property specifies the speed curve of the transition effect.

  Syntax: `transition-timing-function: ease|linear|ease-in|ease-out|ease-in-out|cubic-bezier()|initial|inherit;`

- The transition-timing-function property can have the following values:

Transition-Timing-Function-Property	Values
ease	Specifies a transition effect with a slow start, then fast, then end slowly (this is default).
linear	Specifies a transition effect with the same speed from start to end.
ease-in	Specifies a transition effect with a slow start.
ease-out	Specifies a transition effect with a slow end.
ease-in-out	Specifies a transition effect with a slow start and end.
cubic-bezier(n,n,n,n)	Lets you define your own values in a cubic-bezier function,

CSS Code:

- To better understand the different function values: Here are five different div elements with five different values:

```
/* For Safari 3.1 to 6.0 */
#div1 {-webkit-transition-timing-function: linear;}
#div2 {-webkit-transition-timing-function: ease;}
#div3 {-webkit-transition-timing-function: ease-in;}
#div4 {-webkit-transition-timing-function: ease-out;}
#div5 {-webkit-transition-timing-function: ease-in-out;}

/* Standard syntax */
#div1 {transition-timing-function: linear;}
#div2 {transition-timing-function: ease;}
#div3 {transition-timing-function: ease-in;}
#div4 {transition-timing-function: ease-out;}
#div5 {transition-timing-function: ease-in-out;}
```

Transition-Delay:

- The transition-delay property specifies when the transition effect will start.The transition-delay value is defined in seconds (s) or milliseconds (ms).

  Syntax: `transition-delay: time|initial|inherit;`

- The transition duration property can have the following values:

Transition Duration Property	Values
time	Specifies how many seconds or milliseconds a transition effect takes to complete. Default value is 0s, meaning there will be no effect.
initial	Sets this property to its default value.
inherit	Inherits this property from its parent element.

CSS Code:

```
div {
    -webkit-transition-delay: 1s; /* Safari */
    transition-delay: 1s;
}
```

2.7.3 Animations

- The animation property is a shorthand property for eight of the animation properties:
  - animation-name
  - animation-duration
  - animation-timing-function
  - animation-delay
  - animation-iteration-count
  - animation-direction
  - animation-fill-mode
  - animation-play-state

  Syntax: `animation: name duration timing-function delay iteration-count direction fill-mode play-state;`

Animation-name Property:

- The animation-name property specifies a name for the @keyframes animation.

  Syntax: `animation-name: keyframename|none|initial|inherit;`

- The animation-name property can have the following values:

Animation-name Property	Values
keyframename	Specifies the name of the keyframe you want to bind to the selector.
none	Default value. Specifies that there will be no animation (can be used to override animations coming from the cascade).
initial	Sets this property to its default value.
inherit	Inherits this property from its parent element.

CSS Code:

Specify a name for the @keyframes animation:

```
div {
    -webkit-animation-name: mymove; /* Chrome, Safari, Opera */
    animation-name: mymove;
}
```

Animation-duration Property:

- The animation-duration property defines how many seconds or milliseconds an animation takes to complete one cycle.

  Syntax: `animation-duration: time|initial|inherit;`

- The animation-duration property can have the following values:

Animation-duration Property	Values
time	Specifies the length an animation takes to finish. Default value is 0, meaning there will be no animation.
initial	Sets this property to its default value.
inherit	Inherits this property from its parent element.

CSS Code:

Make the animation complete in two seconds:

```
div {
    -webkit-animation-duration: 2s; /* Chrome, Safari, Opera */
    animation-duration: 2s;
}
```

Animation-timing-function Property:

- The animation-timing-function specifies the speed curve of an animation.
- The speed curve defines the TIME an animation uses to change from one set of CSS styles to another.
- The speed curve is used to make the changes smoothly.

  Syntax: `animation-timing-function: linear|ease|ease-in|ease-out|cubic-bezier(n,n,n,n)|initial|inherit;`

- The animation-timing-function property can have the following values:

Animation-Timing-Function-Property	Values
linear	The animation has the same speed from start to end.
ease	Default value. The animation has a slow start, then fast, before it ends slowly.
ease-in	The animation has a slow start.
ease-out	The animation has a slow end.

contd. ...

ease-in-out	The animation has both a slow start and a slow end.
cubic-bezier(n,n,n,n)	Define your own values in the cubic-bezier function Possible values are numeric values from 0 to 1.
initial	Sets this property to its default value. Read about initial.
inherit	Inherits this property from its parent element. Read about inherit.

CSS Code:

Play an animation with the same speed from beginning to end:

```
div {

    -webkit-animation-timing-function: linear;

                                        /* Chrome, Safari, Opera */

    animation-timing-function: linear;

}
```

Animation-delay Property:

- The animation-delay property specifies a delay for the start of an animation.
- The animation-delay value is defined in seconds (s) or milliseconds (ms).

   Syntax: `animation-delay: time|initial|inherit;`

- The animation-delay property can have the following values:

Animation-delay Property	Values
time	Optional. Defines the number of seconds (s) or milliseconds (ms) to wait before the animation will start. Default value is 0. Negative values are allowed.
initial	Sets this property to its default value.
inherit	Inherits this property from its parent element.

CSS Code:

Wait two seconds, then start the animation:

```
div {
    -webkit-animation-delay: 2s; /* Chrome, Safari, Opera */
    animation-delay: 2s;
}
```

Animation-iteration-count Property:

- The animation-iteration-count property specifies the number of times an animation should be played.

   Syntax: `animation-iteration-count: number|infinite|initial|inherit;`

- The animation-iteration-count property can have the following values:

Animation-Iteration-Count Property	Values
number	A number that defines how many times an animation should be played. Default value is 1.
infinite	Specifies that the animation should be played infinite times (for ever).
initial	Sets this property to its default value.
inherit	Inherits this property from its parent element.

CSS Code:

Play the animation three times:

```
div {
    -webkit-animation-iteration-count: 3; /* Chrome, Safari, Opera */
    animation-iteration-count: 3;
}
```

Animation-direction Property:

- The animation-direction property defines whether an animation should play in reverse direction or in alternate cycles.

  Syntax: `animation-direction: normal|reverse|alternate|alternate reverse|initial|inherit;`

- The animation-direction property can have the following values:

Animation-direction Property	Values
normal	Default value. The animation should be played as normal.
reverse	The animation should play in reverse direction.
alternate	The animation will be played as normal every odd time (1,3,5,etc..) and in reverse direction every even time (2,4,6,etc...).
alternate-reverse	The animation will be played in reverse direction every odd time (1,3,5,etc..) and in a normal direction every even time (2,4,6,etc...)
initial	Sets this property to its default value.
inherit	Inherits this property from its parent element.

CSS Code:

Do the animation once, then do the animation backwards:

```
div {
    -webkit-animation-direction: alternate; /* Chrome, Safari, Opera */
    animation-direction: alternate;
}
```

Animation-fill-mode Property:

- The animation-fill-mode property specifies a style for the element when the animation is not playing (when it is finished, or when it has a delay).
- By default, CSS animations do not affect the element until the first keyframe is "played", and then stops once the last keyframe has completed. The animation-fill-mode property can override this behavior.

  Syntax: `animation-fill-mode: none|forwards|backwards|both|initial|inherit;`
- The animation-fill-mode property can have the following values:

Animation-fill-mode Property	Values
none	Default value. The animation will not apply any styles to the target element before or after it is executing.
forwards	After the animation ends (determined by animation-iteration-count), the animation will apply the property values for the time the animation ended
backwards	The animation will apply the property values defined in the keyframe that will start the first iteration of the animation, during the period defined by animation-delay.
both	The animation will follow the rules for both forwards and backwards. That is, it will extend the animation properties in both directions.
initial	Sets this property to its default value.
inherit	Inherits this property from its parent element.

CSS Code:

Animate something moving from one place to another and have it stay there:

```
div {
    -webkit-animation-fill-mode: forwards; /*  Chrome,  Safari,  Opera
*/
    animation-fill-mode: forwards;
}
```

Animation-play-state Property:

- The animation-play-state property specifies whether the animation is running or paused.

  Syntax: `animation-play-state: paused|running|initial|inherit;`
- The animation-play-state property can have the following values:

Animation-play-state Property	Values
paused	Specifies that the animation is paused.
running	Default value. Specifies that the animation is running.
initial	Sets this property to its default value.
inherit	Inherits this property from its parent element.

CSS Code:

Pause an animation:

```
div {
    -webkit-animation-play-state: paused; /* Chrome, Safari, Opera */
    animation-play-state: paused;
}
```

2.6.4 Multiple Columns

- The CSS3 multi-column layout allows easy definition of multiple columns of text - just like in newspapers:

- multi column layout module allows content to run from one column to another and makes it easily adaptable for different viewing devices and dynamic data.

- Supported Browsers

  o IE10+

  o Firefox 5+

  o Chrome 12+

  o Safari 3.2+

  o Opera 11.1+

- Following are the multi-column properties:

Column-count

- The column-count property specifies the number of columns an element should be divided into.

  Syntax: `column-count: number|auto|initial|inherit;`

CSS Code:

Divide the text in the <div> element into three columns:

```
div {
    -webkit-column-count: 3; /* Chrome, Safari, Opera */
    -moz-column-count: 3; /* Firefox */
    column-count: 3;
}
```

Column-gap:

The column-gap property specifies the gap between the columns.

Syntax: `column-gap: length|normal|initial|inherit;`

CSS Code:

Specify a 40 pixels gap between the columns:

```
div {
    -webkit-column-gap: 40px; /* Chrome, Safari, Opera */
    -moz-column-gap: 40px; /* Firefox */
    column-gap: 40px;
}
```

Column-rule-style:

• The column-rule-style property specifies the style of the rule between columns.

Syntax: `column-rule-style: none|hidden|dotted|dashed|solid|double|`
`|groove|ridge|inset|outset|initial|inherit;`

• The column-rule-style property can have the following values:

Column-rule-style Property	Values
none	Default value. Defines no rule.
hidden	Defines a hidden rule.
dotted	Defines a dotted rule.
dashed	Defines a dashed rule.
solid	Defines a solid rule.
double	Defines a double rule.
groove	Specifies a 3D grooved rule. The effect depends on the width and color values.
ridge	Specifies a 3D ridged rule. The effect depends on the width and color values
inset	Specifies a 3D inset rule. The effect depends on the width and color values.
outset	Specifies a 3D outset rule. The effect depends on the width and color values.
initial	Sets this property to its default value.
inherit	Inherits this property from its parent element.

Example:

Specify the style of the rule between columns:

```
div {
    -webkit-column-rule-style: dotted; /* Chrome, Safari, Opera */
    -moz-column-rule-style: dotted; /* Firefox */
    column-rule-style: dotted;
}
```

Column-rule-width:

• The column-rule-width property specifies the width of the rule between columns.

Syntax: `column-rule-width: medium|thin|thick|length|initial|inherit;`

- The column-rule-width property can have the following values:

Column-rule-width Property	Values
medium	Default value. Defines a medium rule
thin	Defines a thin rule.
thick	Defines a thick rule.
length	Specifies the width of the rule.
initial	Sets this property to its default value.
inherit	Inherits this property from its parent element.

CSS Code:

Specify the width of the rule between columns:

```
div {
    -webkit-column-rule-width: 1px; /* Chrome, Safari, Opera */
    -moz-column-rule-width: 1px; /* Firefox */
    column-rule-width: 1px;
}
```

Column-rule-color:

- The column-rule-color property specifies the color of the rule between columns.

    Syntax: `column-rule-color: color|initial|inherit;`

CSS Code:

Specify the color of the rule between columns:

```
div {
    -webkit-column-rule-color: #ff0000; /* Chrome, Safari, Opera */
    -moz-column-rule-color: #ff0000; /* Firefox */
    column-rule-color: #ff0000;
}
```

Column-rule:

- The column-rule property is a shorthand property for setting all the column-rule-* properties.
- The column-rule property sets the width, style, and color of the rule between columns.

    Syntax: `column-rule: column-rule-width column-rule-style column-rule-color|initial|inherit;`

- The column-rule property can have the following values:

Column-rule Property	Values
column-rule-width	Sets the width of the rule between columns. Default value is medium.
column-rule-style	Sets the style of the rule between columns. Default value is none.
column-rule-color	Sets the color of the rule between columns. Default value is the color of the element.
initial	Sets this property to its default value.
inherit	Inherits this property from its parent element.

CSS Code:

Specify the width, style and color of the rule between columns:

```
div {
    -webkit-column-rule: 4px outset #ff00ff; /* Chrome, Safari, Opera */
    -moz-column-rule: 4px outset #ff00ff; /* Firefox */
    column-rule: 4px outset #ff00ff;
}
```

Column-span:

The column-span property specifies how many columns an element should span across.

Syntax: `column-span: 1|all|initial|inherit;`

• The column-span property can have the following values:

Column-span Property	Values
1	Default value. The element should span across one column.
all	The element should span across all columns.
initial	Sets this property to its default value.
inherit	Inherits this property from its parent element.

CSS Code:

Let the <h2> element span across all columns:

```
h2 {
    -webkit-column-span: all; /* Chrome, Safari, Opera */
    column-span: all;
}
```

Column-width:

Syntax: `column-width: auto|length|initial|inherit;`

• The column-width property can have the following values:

Column-width Property	Values
auto	Default value. The column width will be determined by the browser.
length	A length that specifies the width of the columns.
initial	Sets this property to its default value.
inherit	Inherits this property from its parent element.

CSS Code:

Specify a suggested, optimal width for the columns:

```
div {
    -webkit-column-width: 100px; /* Chrome, Safari, Opera */
    -moz-column-width: 100px; /* Firefox */
    column-width: 100px;
}
```

Practice Questions

1. What is CSS? Give its syntax.

2. Explain CSS ID in detail.

3. Describe the following tags:

   (i) <span> (ii) <div>

4. Enlist various border properties of CSS.

5. Enlist various text properties of CSS.

6. Enlist various font properties of CSS.

7. Enlist various margin properties of CSS.

8. Write short note on: CSS classes.

9. What are the types of CSS?

10. Explain embedded style sheet with example.

11. What is inline stylesheet? Explain in detail.

12. What is CSS3? Give its syntax.

13. Write a short note on:

    (i)   Gradient

    (ii) Animations

    (iii) Transition Property

14. Define Multiple Column in CSS3 with suitable example.

■■■

Chapter 3...

JAVASCRIPT

Contents ...

3.1 Concept of Script and Types of Scripts

- Script means list of actions for the something to perform.
- Scripting languages are usually interpreted rather than compiled.
- That means that a software routine, an interpreter, must translate a program's statements into machine code, code understandable by a particular type of computer, before executing them every time the program in run.
- Compiled languages, one the other hand are translated into machine code and stored for later execution. When the compiled program is run, it executes immediately without further need of interpretation; it was interpreted into machine code when it was compiled.
- Because programs written in interpreted languages must be translated into machine code every time they are run, they are typically slower than compiled programs.
- However, this does not usually present a problem for the small applications for which scripting languages are generally used.
- HTML is a simple text mark up language, it cannot respond to the user, make decisions, or automatic repetitive tasks. Interactive tasks like these require a more complex language, a programming language or a scripting language.
- Scripting languages are generally simple. They have a simple syntax, can perform tasks with a minimum of commands and are easy to learn.
- Web scripting languages allow we to combine scripting with HTML to create interactive web pages.

What is a Scripting Language?

- Scripting language is a programming language only it is smaller and to some extent less powerful.
- A scripting language is a light weight programming language.
- Scripting languages are of two types:
  1. Client-side scripting languages, and
  2. Server-side scripting languages.
- Client-server script runs at user's end i.e. the browser executes the scripts. Where as server-side scripting language is executed on a web server.
- When a user requests a program coded in client-server scripting language, server will send it to the browser, executes the script and displays it to the user.
- When a user requests a program coded in server-side scripting language, server will execute the script and send the result to the user, which can be viewed using a browser.

Advantages of Scripting Languages:

1. Being interpreted does have its advantages. One is platform independence. Because an interpreter performs the translation, we can write our program once and run it on variety of platforms.
2. All we need is the correct interpreter. In the case of Javascript, the interpreter is built into web browsers. Browsers were available for a variety of platforms and operating systems.
3. Another advantage is the scripting languages are often loosely typed and more forgiving than compiled languages.

1. Client Side Scripting: [April 12]

- Client side scripting is the class of computer programs on the web that are executed client side, by the user's web browser, instead of server-side.

- This type of programming is an important part of the Dynamic HTML concept, enabling web pages to be scripted; that is, to have different and changing content depending on user input, environmental conditions like time of day or other variables.

- Web authors or writers write client-side scripts and languages like JavaScript (client-side JavaScript) or VBScript, which are based on several standards such as :

  (i) HTML scripting,

  (ii) HTTP, and

  (iii) Document Object Model (DOM).

- This type of scripts are often embedded within a HTML document, but they may be also be contained in a separate file, which is referenced by the document or documents that use it.

2. Server Side Scripting: [April 12]

- This type of scripting is a web server technology in which a user's request is fulfilled by running a script directly on the web server to generate Dynamic HTML (DHTML) pages.

- It is usually used to provide interactive (dynamic) web sites that interface to databases or other data stores.

Basic Concepts:

1. <script> Tag:

- One of the most usual ways we will use JavaScript is to display text, as if we were using HTML. Indeed, added just a few instructions, we can use any of the HTML tags and make them part of our script.

- To set the instructions of a script, the section that has the script must start with the <script> tag and end with the </script> tag, as follows :

  Syntax: `<script>............</script>`

- Because a script is written in a particular language that is not HTML and because there are various scripting languages, to use a script, we should let the browser know what scripting language we are using.

- To let the browser know, type the word Language, followed by the = sign, followed by the name of the script language included in double-quotes. For example, to use JavaScript in a page, start the section with

  ```
  <script language="JavaScript">
  ```

  and end it with the closing tag. Therefore the scripting section can be delimited with:

  ```
  <script Language="JavaScript>
  </script>
  ```

2. Scripting Languages:

(i) JavaScript:

- JavaScript was developed by Netscape Communication Corporation, the makers of the popular Netscape Navigator Web Browser.

- JavaScript was the first Web scripting language to be introduced, and it is so far the most popular. JavaScript is almost as easy to learn as HTML and it can be included directly in HTML documents.

- Here, are a few things we can do with JavaScript.

    1. Add scrolling or changing messages to the browser's status line.
    2. Validate the contents of a form and make calculations.
    3. Display messages to the user, either as part of a Web page or in alert boxes.
    4. Animate images or create images that change when we move the mouse over them.
    5. Detect the browser in use and display different content for different browsers.
    6. Detect installed plug-ins and notify the user if a plug-in is required.

(ii) VBScript:

- VBScript, or by its full name, the Microsoft Visual Basic Scripting Edition language, is a simplified version of the Visual Basic. It is also considered to be closely related to the basic programming language.

- VBScript is a scripting language or more precisely a "scripting environment", which can enhance HTML web pages by making them active, as compared to a simple static display.

- Specifically, VBScript was created by Microsoft to use either as a client-side scripting language for the Microsoft Internet Explorer (versions 3.0 and later) or as a server-side scripting language with the Microsoft Internet Information (versions 3.0 and later).

- A primary advantage for using the server-side approach is that the VBScript is processed by the server before it is transmitted to the client. Therefore, the client only receives an HTML page and we do not have to concern ourselves as to whether, the browser can interpret the VBScript.

3.2 Introduction to JavaScript

- JavaScript is the most popular scripting language on the internet and works in all major browsers, such as Internet Explorer, Firefox, Chrome, Opera and Safari.

- JavaScript usually runs on the client-side (the browser's side), as opposed to server-side (on the web server). One benefit of doing this is performance. On the client side, JavaScript is loaded into the browser and can run as soon as it is called. Without running on the client side, the page would need to refresh each time we needed a script to run.

- JavaScript is a scripting language used to make webpages "smarter" by adding interactions between the webpages and the user.

- Scripting languages are programming languages that are generally easy to learn, easy to use, excellent for small routines and applications and developed to serve a particular purpose.

- For instance, PERL (Practical Extraction and Report Language) began its life as a scripting language written for the express purpose of extracting and manipulating data and writing reports.

- JavaScript was written for the express purpose of adding interactivity to Web pages.

- JavaScript is interpreted programming language with object-oriented capabilities that allows us to build interactivity into otherwise static HTML pages.

- JavaScript is usually embedded directly into HTML pages and it is an interpreted language (means that scripts execute without preliminary compilation).

- JavaScript is an object-based scripting language modeled after C++.

- JavaScript was created by Brendan Eich of Netscape Communications and was first made available in 1995 as a part of Netscape Navigator 2.0, the first JavaScript-enabled web browser.

- Originally, called LiveScript, JavaScript owes the Java part of its name to the popularity of Java, the cross-platform, object-oriented programming language created by Sun Microsystems.

- JavaScript was designed for the specific purpose of extending the capabilities of Web browsers and providing web developers with an easy means of adding interactivity to their web sites.

- There are actually three flavors of JavaScript: Core JavaScript, Client-Side JavaScript and Server-Side JavaScript.

  1. **Core JavaScript** is the basic JavaScript language and it includes the operators, control structures, built-in functions and object that make JavaScript a programming language.

  2. **Client-Side JavaScript (CSJS)** extends the Core JavaScript to provide access to browser and Web document objects via the Document Object Model (DOM) supported by a particular browser.

  3. **Client-Side JavaScript** is, by far, the most popular form of JavaScript.

- Most of Client-Side JavaScript's objects come from things found in Web pages such as images, forms and form elements. That's one of the reasons JavaScript is considered an object-based language.

What can a JavaScript do?

  1. **JavaScript gives HTML designers a programming tool:** HTML authors are normally not programmers, but JavaScript is a scripting language with a very simple syntax! Almost anyone can put small "snippets" of code into their HIML pages.

2. **JavaScript can put dynamic text into an HTML page:** A JavaScript statement like document.write("<h1>" + name + "</h1>") can write a variable text into an HTML page.

3. **JavaScript can react to events:** A JavaScript can be set to execute when something happens, like when a page has finished loading or when a user clicks on an HTML element.

4. **JavaScript can read and write HTML elements:** A JavaScript can read and change the content of an HTML element.

5. **JavaScript can be used to validate data:** A JavaScript can be used to validate form data before it is submitted to a server. This saves the server from extra processing.

6. **JavaScript can be used to detect the visitor's browser:** A JavaScript can be used to detect the visitor's browser and depending on the browser load another page specifically designed for that browser.

7. **JavaScript can be used to create cookies:** A JavaScript can be used to store to retrieve information on the visitor's computer.

First Example:

- The HTML<script> tag is used to insert a JavaScript into an HTML page.
- Browser will not know where javascript has started. So, in order to tell it where javascript has started we use a special HTML tag, <script>.

  Syntax of javascript:

  ```
  <script type="text/javascript">
  javascript comes here ………
  </script>
  ```

- <script> and </script> informs browser that everything in between is a scripting language. The attribute type, is given a value "text/javascript", specifying that the scripting language is javascript.

Embedding Javascript:

- Javascript can be added in the <body> or in the <head> sections of an HTML code.

Example of embedding javascript in <head> tag:

```
<html>
<head>
<title>Javascript Example </title>
<script type="text/javascript">
document.write("My first Javascript");
</script>
</head>
</html>
```

Output:

```
My first Javascript
```

Example shows embedded javascript in <body > tag.

```
<html>
<body>
<script type="text/javascript">
document.write("Hello World!");
</script>
</body>
</html>
```

Output:

```
Hello World!
```

- Document is the part of browser where we see webpage content, document.write will write the text in parentheses (round brackets) to the browser document. In our case, the text "My First Javascript" will be written. The double quotes are important when we want to print/write the text in is. And every statement in javascript ends with a semi-colon(;).

Embedding a JavaScript using external file:

```
<!DOCTYPE html>
<html>
<body>
<h1>My Web Page</h1>
<p id="demo">A Paragraph.</p>
<button type="button" onclick="myFunction()">Nirali Prakashan</button>
<p><strong>Note:</strong> The actual script is in an external script file
                                       called "myScript.js".</p>
<script type="text/javascript" src="myScript.js"></script>
</body>
</html>
```

Advantages of JavaScript:

1. **Less server interaction:** We can validate user input before sending the page off to the server. This saves server traffic, which means less load on our server.
2. **Immediate feedback to the visitors:** They do not have to wait for a page reload to see if they have forgotten to enter something.
3. **Increased interactivity:** We can create interfaces that react when the user hovers over them with a mouse or activates them via the keyboard.
4. **Richer interfaces:** We can use JavaScript to include such items as drag-and-drop components and sliders to give a Rich Interface to our site visitors.

Limitations with JavaScript:

1. Client-side JavaScript does not allow the reading or writing of files. This has been kept for security reason.
2. JavaScript can not be used for Networking applications because there is no such support available.
3. JavaScript does not have any multithreading or multiprocess capabilities.

Javascript comments:

- We can use comments to explain our code, so that we can understand it better when we view it in future.
- Comments are ignored by a browser.
- In javascript we have single line comment and multi-line comments.

1. **Single line comments:** Single line comments can be added in javascript using double forward slash //.

Example:

```
<html>
<head>
<title> Javascript Example </title>
<script type="text/javascript">
//comments are ignored
document.write("Nirali Prakashan");
</script>
</head>
</html>
```

Output:

```
Nirali Prakashan
```

2. **Multiline comments:** To start a multi line comment in javascript, a forward slash and an asterisk (/*) is used. To end a multi line comment an asterisk and a forward slab (*/) is used.

Example:

```
<html>
<head>
<title> Javascript Example </title>
<script type="text/javascript">
/* This is a multi line comment, and will be ignored by the browser */
document.write("Nirali Prakashan");
</script>
</head>
</html>
```

Output:

```
Nirali Prakashan
```

3.3 JavaScript Concepts

3.3.1 Variables

- Variables are "containers" for storing information.
- JavaScript variables are used to hold values (a = 5) or expressions (x = y + z) in them.
  Syntax: `var variable_name = value;`
- We define variables in javascript using a keyword (a pre-defined word) var. variable_name is name of the variable which holds some value. We are using an assignment operator (= sign) to assign a value to a variable.

Example:

```
var x = 10;
```

- In the above statement, we assigned value "10" to a variable. And we have named the variable as "x". Normally we say "x is equal to 10", but its "x holds a number whose value is 10".

- There are some rules for variable names in javascript:

    1. A variable must start with an alphabet or an underscore.

    2. The subsequent characters can be digits (0-9) or alphabets or an underscore.

    3. As javascript is case-sensitive, number is not same as Number.

- Some valid examples of variable names in javascript are given below:

```
simple_Interest, _name, number1
```

- Some invalid examples of variable names are given below

```
23Amar, &MyName, Mega%tron
```

Example for variable:

```
<!DOCTYPE html>
<html>
<body>
<p>Click the button to create a variable, and display the result.</p>
<button onclick="myFunction()">Nirali Prakashan</button>
<p id="demo"></p>
<script>
function myFunction()
{
var carname="Alto";
document.getElementById("demo").innerHTML=carname;
}
</script>
</body>
</html>
```

1. Variable Scope:

- The scope of a variable is the region of our program in which it is defined.

- JavaScript variable will have only two scopes:

    (i) Global variables: A global variable has global scope which means it is defined everywhere in our JavaScript code.

    (ii) Local variables: A local variable will be visible only within a function where it is defined. Function parameters are always local to that function.

- Global variables are accessible from anywhere in the program. On other hand, Local variables are accessible only in the function they are defined.

Example for global variable:

```
<html>
<head>
<title>Javascript Global Variable Example</title>
</head>
<body>
<script type="text/javascript">
var area = 10; //global variable
function test(){
document.write(area); //access inside function
document.write("<br/>");
}
test();
document.write(area); //acces outside function
</script>
</body>
</html>
```

Output:

```
10
10
```

- We declared area=10; outside the function, hence its a global variable, and can be accessed from anywhere in the program. In the above example, we accessed it from inside the function and as well as outside the function using document.write(area); statement. In the output 10 will be displayed twice.

Example of Local variable:

```
<html>
<head>
<title>Javascript Global Variable Example</title>
</head>
<body>
<script type="text/javascript">
function test(){
var area = 10; //local variable
document.write(area); //access inside function
document.write("<br/>");
}
test();
document.write(area); //acces outside function
</script>
</body>
</html>
```

Output:

```
10
```

- We declared area=10; inside the function, hence its a local variable, and can be accessed only within the function. In the above example, we accessed it from inside the function and as well as outside the function using document.write(area); statement. In the output 10 will be displayed only once.

2. JavaScript Data Types:

(i) Strings:

- A string is a variable which stores a series of characters like "Amar Salunkhe".

- A string can be any text inside quotes and can use simple or double quotes, like this

```
var carname="Ritz XC60";

var carname='Ritz XC60';
```

(ii) Numbers:

- JavaScript has only one type of numbers. Numbers can be written with, or without decimals, like

```
var x1=40.00;       //Written with decimals

var x2=40;          //Written without decimals
```

(iii) Booleans:

- Booleans can only have two values i.e. true or false, like:

```
var x=true

var y=false
```

3.3.2 Identifiers

- An identifier is a symbol that represents, names a piece of data.

- An identifier can represent a function or a variable.

- JavaScript identifiers are used to name the JavaScript language entities like variable, object, function and to provide labels for certain loops in JavaScript code.

- JavaScript identifiers must start with character followed by subsequent characters can be letter, a digit, an underscore; Dollar sign ($) also allow.

- With some versions of JavaScript, dollar signs are not legal in identifiers. The best practice of defining JavaScript identifiers is to avoid the use of dollar signs.

- We cannot use JavaScript reserved keywords as a JavaScript identifiers like:

```
var intNum = 82     //intNum is JavaScript Identifiers

var PI = 3.14       //PI is JavaScript Identifiers

var strInfo="This is a string" // strInfo is JavaScript Identifiers

var strGreet='Hello!'; //strGreet is JavaScript Identifiers

var arrAnimal={"cat","dog") //arrAnimal in JavaScript Identifiers
```

3.3.3 Constants

- JavaScript is a programming language used to provide interactivity in web sites. JavaScript is a scripting language, which means the source code is interpreted on the fly by a web browser.
- Like other scripting languages, JavaScript has syntax for declaring variables and constants. A variable is an identifier to some piece of data that can be changed.
- A constant is similar in concept, but its value cannot be changed.
- Constants are useful for static values that do not change.
- We can define constant in JavaScript using const keyword, like const hoursInDay=24;

Example for constant:

```
<html>
<body>
<script type="text/JavaScript">
const hoursInDay=24;
document.write(hoursInDay);
</script>
</body>
</html>
```

Output:

```
24
```

1. **JavaScript Statements:**
- JavaScript is a sequence of statements to be executed by the browser.
- A JavaScript statement is a command to a browser. The purpose of the command is to tell the browser what to do.
- The JavaScript statement tells the browser to write "Hello Amar" to the web page:
  ```
  document.write("Hello Amar);
  ```
- It is normal to add a semicolon (;) at the end of each executable statement.

2. **JavaScript Code:**
- JavaScript code, (or just JavaScript) is a sequence of JavaScript statements. Each statement is executed by the browser in the sequence they are written.
  Example:
  ```
  <script type="text/javascript)
  document.write("<h1>This is a heading 1</h1>");
  document.write("<p>This is a paragraph for Web(</p">);
  document.write("<p>This is another paragraph also for Web(</p>");
  ```

3. **Blocks:**
- JavaScript statements can be grouped together in blocks.
- Blocks start with a left curly bracket { and ends with a rightly curly bracket }.
- The purpose of a block is to make the sequence of statement execute together.

Example:

```
<script type="text/javascript">
{
document.write("<h1>This is a heading 1</h1>");
document.write("<p>This is a paragraph for Web(</p">);
document.write("<p>This is another paragraph also for Web(</p>");
}
</script>
```

3.4 JavaScript Operators

- An operator is used to transform one or more values into a single resultant values and the values to which the operator is applied is referred as operands.
- JavaScript operators are used to perform an operation. There are different types of operators for different uses.
- Simple example, answer can be given using expression 4 + 5 is equal to 9. Here 4 and 5 are called operands and + is called operator.
- JavaScript language supports following type of operators.
    1. Arithmetic operators.
    2. Comparision operators,
    3. Logical (or Relational) operators,
    4. Assignment operators, and
    5. Conditional (or ternary) operators.

1. Arithmetic Operators:
- Arithmetic operators are used to perform arithmetic between variables and/or values.
- The standard arithmetic operators in javascript are addition (+), subtraction (−), multiplication (*), division (/) and modulus (%). These operators work as in standard algebra.
- Following table shows arithmetic operators supported by JavaScript language. Assume variable A holds 10 and variable B holds 20 then:

Operator	Description	Example
+ (Addition operator)	Adds two operands.	A + B = 30
− (Subtraction operator)	Subtracts second operand from the first.	A − B = −10
* (Multiplication operator)	Multiply both operands.	A * B = 200
/ (Division operator)	Divide numerator by denumerator.	B / A = 2
% (Modulus operator)	Modulus operator and remainder of after an integer division.	B % A = 0
++ (Increment operator)	Increases integer value by one.	A++ = 11
-- (Decrement operator)	Decreases integer value by one.	A-- = 9

Example:

```
<!DOCTYPE html>
<head>
<title> Arithmetic Operators Example</title>
<script type="text/javascript">
var x = 16;
var y = 5;
var sum = x + y;
var sub = x - y;
var mul = x * y;
var div = x / y;
var mod = x % y;
document.write("addition is "+sum);
document.write("subtraction is "+sub);
document.write("multiplication is "+mul);
document.write("division is "+div);
document.write("remainder is "+mod);
</script>
</head>
</html>
```

Output:

addition is 21subtraction is 11multiplication is 80division is 3.2remainder is 1

2. Comparison Operators:

- Comparison operators are used in logical statements to determine equality or difference between variables or values.
- Comparison operators are used to compare a condition and are always inside conditional statements. A comparison evaluate to their true or false. This true and false values are called Booleans.
- Following table shows comparison operators supported by JavaScript and assume variable A holds 10 and B holds 20.

Operator	Description	Example
== (Equal to Operator)	This operator checks if the value of two operands are equal or not, if yes then condition becomes true.	(A == B) is not true.
!= (Not Equal to Operator)	This operator checks if the value of two operands are equal or not, if values are not equal then condition becomes true.	(A != B) is true.
> (Greater Than Operator)	This operator checks if the value of left operand is greater than the value of right operand, if yes then condition becomes true.	(A > B) is not true.

contd. ...

< (Less Than Operator)	This operator checks if the value of left operand is less than the value of right operand, if yes then condition becomes true.	(A < B) is true.
>= (Less Than or Equal To Operator)	This operator checks if the value of left operand is greater than or equal to the value of right operand, if yes then condition becomes true.	(A >= B) is not true.
<= (Greater Than or Equal To Operator)	This operator checks if the value of left operand is less than or equal to the value of right operand, if yes then condition becomes true.	(A <= B) is true.

3. Logical Operators:

- Logical operators are used to determine the logic between variables or values.
- Using logical operators, we can test two or more conditions in one line code.
- There are following logical operators supported by JavaScript and assume variable A holds 10 and variable B holds 20 then:

Operator	Description	Example
&& (Logical AND Operator)	If both the operands are non zero then then condition becomes true.	(A && B) is true.
|| (Logical OR Operator)	If any of the two operands are non zero then then condition becomes true.	(A || B) is true.
! (Logical NOT Operator)	Use to reverses the logical state of its operand. If a condition is true then Logical NOT operator will make false.	!(A && B) is false.

4. Bitwise Operators:

- Bitwise operators act upon the individual bits of their operands.
- Following table gives bitwise operators supported by JavaScript and assume variable A holds 2 and variable B holds 3 then:

Operator		Description	Example
&	(Bitwise AND operator)	It performs a Boolean AND operation on each bit of its integer arguments.	(A & B) is 2.
|	(Bitwise OR Operator)	It performs a Boolean OR operation on each bit of its integer arguments.	(A | B) is 3.
^	(Bitwise XOR Operator)	It performs a Boolean exclusive OR operation on each bit of its integer arguments. Exclusive OR means that either operand one is true or operand two is true, but not both.	(A ^ B) is 1.

contd. ...

~	(Bitwise NOT Operator)	It is a is a unary operator and operates by reversing all bits in the operand.	(~B) is -4 .
<<	(Bitwise Shift Left Operator)	It moves all bits in its first operand to the left by the number of places specified in the second operand. New bits are filled with zeros. Shifting a value left by one position is equivalent to multiplying by 2, shifting two positions is equivalent to multiplying by 4, etc.	(A << 1) is 4.
>>	(Bitwise Shift Right with Sign Operator)	It moves all bits in its first operand to the right by the number of places specified in the second operand. The bits filled in on the left depend on the sign bit of the original operand, in order to preserve the sign of the result. If the first operand is positive, the result has zeros placed in the high bits; if the first operand is negative, the result has ones placed in the high bits. Shifting a value right one place is equivalent to dividing by 2 (discarding the remainder), shifting right two places is equivalent to integer division by 4, and so on.	(A >> 1) is 1.
>>>	(Bitwise Shift Right with Zero Operator)	This operator is just like the >> operator, except that the bits shifted in on the left are always zero.	(A >>> 1) is 1.

5. Assignment Operators:

- Assignment operators are used to assign values to JavaScript variables.
- There are following assignment operators supported by JavaScript.

Operator		Description	Example
=	(Simple assignment operator)	Assigns values from right side operands to left side operand.	C = A + B will assignee value of A + B into C
+=	(Add AND assignment operator)	It adds right operand to the left operand and assign the result to left operand.	C += A is equivalent to C = C + A
-=	(Subtract AND assignment operator)	It subtracts right operand from the left operand and assign the result to left operand.	C -= A is equivalent to C = C - A
*=	(Multiply AND assignment operator)	It multiplies right operand with the left operand and assign the result to left operand.	C *= A is equivalent to C = C * A
/=	(Divide AND assignment operator)	It divides left operand with the right operand and assign the result to left operand.	C /= A is equivalent to C = C / A
%=	(Modulus AND assignment operator)	It takes modulus using two operands and assign the result to left operand.	C %= A is equivalent to C = C % A

6. Conditional Operators (?:):

- There is an operator called conditional operator. This first evaluates an expression for a true or false value and then execute one of the two given statements depending upon the result of the evaluation.
- The conditional operator has following syntax:

Operator	Description	Example
? :	Conditional Expression	If Condition is true ? Then value X : Otherwise value Y.

7. typeof Operator:

- The typeof is a unary operator that is placed before its single operand, which can be of any type. Its value is a string indicating the data type of the operand.
- The typeof operator evaluates to "number", "string", or "boolean" if its operand is a number, string, or boolean value and returns true or false based on the evaluation.
- Here, is the list of return values for the typeof Operator :

Type	String Returned by typeof
Number	"number"
String	"string"
Boolean	"boolean"
Object	"object"
Function	"function"
Undefined	"undefined"
Null	"object"

Example for typeof operator:

```
<!DOCTYPE html>
<body>
<script type="text/javascript">
<!--
var a = 10;
var b = "String";
var linebreak = "<br />";
result = (typeof b == "string" ? "B is String" : "B is Numeric");
document.write("Result => ");
document.write(result);
document.write(linebreak);
result = (typeof a == "string" ? "A is String" : "A is Numeric");
document.write("Result => ");
document.write(result);
document.write(linebreak);
//-->
</script>
<p>Set the variables to different values and different operators and
then try...</p>
</body>
</html>
```

Example for Logical Operators:

```
<!DOCTYPE html>
<body>
<script type="text/javascript">
<!--
var a = true;
var b = false;
var linebreak = "<br />";
document.write("(a &&  b) => ");
result = (a && b);
document.write(result);
document.write(linebreak);
document.write("(a || b) => ");
result = (a || b);
document.write(result);
document.write(linebreak);
document.write("!(a && b) => ");
result = (!(a && b));
document.write(result);
document.write(linebreak);
//-->
</script>
<p>Set the variables to different values and different operators and
then try...</p>
</body>
</html>
```

Example of Comparison Operators:

```
<!DOCTYPE html>
<body>
<script type="text/javascript">
<!--
var a = 20;
var b = 30;
var linebreak = "<br />";
document.write("(a == b) => ");
result = (a == b);
document.write(result);
document.write(linebreak);
document.write("(a < b) => ");
result = (a < b);
```

```
document.write(result);
document.write(linebreak);
document.write("(a > b) => ");
result = (a > b);
document.write(result);
document.write(linebreak);
document.write("(a != b) => ");
result = (a != b);
document.write(result);
document.write(linebreak);
document.write("(a >= b) => ");
result = (a >= b);
document.write(result);
document.write(linebreak);
document.write("(a <= b) => ");
result = (a <= b);
document.write(result);
document.write(linebreak);
//-->
</script>
<p>Set the variables to different values and different operators and
then try...</p>
</body>
</html>
```

Example of Bitwise Operators:

```
<html>
<body>
<script type="text/javascript">
<!--
var a = 3;  // Bit presentation 11
var b = 4;  // Bit presentation 12
var linebreak = "<br />";
document.write("(a &  b) => ");
result = (a & b);
document.write(result);
document.write(linebreak);
document.write("(a | b) => ");
result = (a | b);
document.write(result);
document.write(linebreak);
```

```
document.write("(a ^ b) => ");
result = (a ^ b);
document.write(result);
document.write(linebreak);
document.write("(~b) => ");
result = (~b);
document.write(result);
document.write(linebreak);
document.write("(a << b) => ");
result = (a << b);
document.write(result);
document.write(linebreak);
document.write("(a >> b) => ");
result = (a >> b);
document.write(result);
document.write(linebreak);
//-->
</script>
<p>Set the variables to different values and different operators and
then try...</p>
</body>
</html>
```

Example for Assignment Operator:

```
<html>
<body>
<script type="text/javascript">
<!--
var a = 44;
var b = 10;
var linebreak = "<br />";
document.write("Value of a => (a = b) => ");
result = (a = b);
document.write(result);
document.write(linebreak);
document.write("Value of a => (a += b) => ");
result = (a += b);
document.write(result);
document.write(linebreak);
document.write("Value of a => (a -= b) => ");
result = (a -= b);
```

```
    document.write(result);
    document.write(linebreak);
    document.write("Value of a => (a *=  b) => ");
    result = (a *= b);
    document.write(result);
    document.write(linebreak);
    document.write("Value of a => (a /= b) => ");
    result = (a /= b);
    document.write(result);
    document.write(linebreak);
    document.write("Value of a => (a %= b) => ");
    result = (a %= b);
    document.write(result);
    document.write(linebreak);
    //-->
    </script>
    <p>Set the variables to different values and different operators and
    then try...</p>
    </body>
    </html>
```

Example for Conditional Operator:

```
    <html>
    <body>
    <script type="text/javascript">
    <!--
    var a = 10;
    var b = 20;
    var linebreak = "<br />";
    document.write("((a > b) ? 100 : 200) => ");
    result = (a > b) ? 100 : 200;
    document.write(result);
    document.write(linebreak);
    document.write("((a < b) ? 100 : 200) => ");
    result = (a < b) ? 100 : 200;
    document.write(result);
    document.write(linebreak);
    //-->
    </script>
    <p>Set the variables to different values and different operators and
    then try...</p>
    </body>
    </html>
```

3.5 Control and Looping Structure

- While writing a program, there may be a situation when we need to adopt one path out of the given two paths. So we need to make use of conditional statements that allow our program to make correct decisions and perform right actions.

- JavaScript supports conditional statements which are used to perform different actions based on different conditions.

- Very often when we write code, we want to perform different actions for different decisions. We can use conditional statements in our code to do this.

- Examples of some daily life decisions are:

  1. If it's a weekend, do not get up early.

  2. If trailer is good, watch the movie, else do not.

- In JavaScript we have the following conditional statements:

  1. **if statement:** Use this statement to execute some code only if a specified condition is true.

  2. **if...else statement:** Use this statement to execute some code if the condition is true and another code if the condition is false.

  3. **if...else if....else statement:** Use this statement to select one of many blocks of code to be executed

  4. **switch statement:** Use this statement to select one of many blocks of code to be executed.

3.5.1 if Statement

- The if statement is the fundamental control statement that allows JavaScript to make decisions and execute statements conditionally.

- We can use the if statement to execute some code only if a specified condition is true.

Syntax:

```
if(condition)
{
execute this statement;
}
```

- The keyword if specifies that what follows is a decision control instruction.

- The condition to be checked is always enclosed in round brackets ().
  The statements to be executed, if the condition is true, are added in flower brackets {}, normally called an if block.

Example 1:

```
<!DOCTYPE html>
<head><title>If statement</title></head>
<body>
<script type="text/javascript">
var x = 7;
var y = 7;
if(x==y)
{
document.write("Both are equal");
}
</script>
</body>
</html>
```

Output:

Both are equal

- Notice that in above example the condition we are checking is x == y. Double equal sign is a comparison operator. Single equal (=) is not used to compare, as javascript uses it to assign values to variables.

Example 2:

```
<!DOCTYPE html>
<body>
<script type="text/javascript">
<!--
var age = 20;
if( age > 18 ){
    document.write("<b>Qualifies for driving</b>");
}
//-->
</script>
<p>Set the variable to different value and then try...</p>
</body>
</html>
```

3.5.2 if...else Statement

- The if...else statement is the next form of control statement that allows JavaScript to execute statements in more controlled way.
- We can use the if....else statement to execute some code if a condition is true and another code if the condition is not true.
- The keyword if executes a statement only if the condition is true. It does not do anything if the condition is false.

Syntax:

```
if(condition)
{
execute this statement;
}
else
{
execute this statement;
}
```

- In above syntax, if the condition is true, the statement in the if block is executed, and the statement in else block is skipped. If the condition is false, the statement in else block is executed, and the statement in if block is skipped.

Example 1:

```
<!DOCTYPE html>
<body>
<script type="text/javascript">
var age = 14;
if(age >= 18)
{
document.write("Get a drivers license.");
document.write("Drive dads car");
}
else
{
document.write("Anuja, ride a bicycle.");
document.write("You are only 14");
}
</script>
</body>
</html>
```

Output:

```
Anuja, ride a bicycleYou are only 14
```

Example 2:

```
<!DOCTYPE html>
<body>
<p>Click the button to get a time-based greeting.</p>
<button onclick="myFunction()">Nirali Prakashan</button>
<p id="demo"></p>
<script>
```

```
function myFunction()
{
var x="";
var time=new Date().getHours();
if (time<20)
  {
  x="Good day";
  }
else
  {
  x="Good evening";
  }
document.getElementById("demo").innerHTML=x;
}
</script>
</body>
</html>
```

3.5.3 if...elseif...else Statement

- We use the if....else if...else statement to select one of several blocks of code to be executed.

- The if...else if... statement is the one level advance form of control statement that allows JavaScript to make correct decision out of several conditions.

Syntax:

```
if(condition) {
execute this statement;
}
else if(condition) {
execute this statement;
}
else {
execute this statement;
}
```

Example 1:

```
<!DOCTYPE html>
<body>
<script type="text/javascript">
var your_age = 14;
var friends_age = 16;
```

```
if(your_age >= 18)
{
document.write("Get a drivers license");
}
else if(friends_age >= 18) {
document.write("Let our friend drive the car");
}
else {
document.write("Kids, stick to bicycle");
}
</script>
</body>
</html>
```

Output:

```
Kids, stick to bicycle
```

Example 2:

```
<!DOCTYPE html>
<body>
<p>Click the button to get a time-based greeting.</p>
<button onclick="myFunction()">Nirali Prakashan</button>
<p id="demo"></p>
<script>
function myFunction()
{
var x="";
var time=new Date().getHours();
if (time<10)
  {
  x="Good morning";
  }
else if (time<20)
  {
  x="Good day";
  }
else
  {
  x="Good evening";
  }
document.getElementById("demo").innerHTML=x;
}
</script>
</body>
</html>
```

3.5.4 switch Statement

- Switch statement is used to execute one of the statements from many blocks of statements.
- Use the switch statement to select one of many blocks of code to be executed.
- Multiple if-else if-else statements can be used, but code gets confusing, and is not often the best choice.
- Switch statement is like enhanced if-else if-else statement, only less confusing and more easy and simple to use.

Syntax:

```
switch (value/expression)
{
case "value1":
execute this statement1;
break;
case "value2":
execute this statement2;
break;
---
---
---

default:
executes this statement;
}
```

- The switch statement begin with keyword "switch", and round brackets that contain an expression or value.
- This expression/value is matched against the value following each "case" (in our case, value is matched against value1/value2 and so on) and if there is a match, it executes the code contained inside that case.
- The break statement indicates the end of that particular case. If we omit break, it will continue executing the statements in each of the following cases. If no match is found, it executes the default statement.

Example for switch statement:

```
<!DOCTYPE html>
<body>
<p>Click the button to display what day it is today.</p>
<button onclick="myFunction()">Click it</button>
<p id="demofor Day"></p>
<script>
```

```
function myFunction()
{
var x;
var d=new Date().getDay();
switch (d)
  {
  case 0:
    x="Today it's Sunday";
    break;
  case 1:
    x="Today it's Monday";
    break;
  case 2:
    x="Today it's Tuesday";
    break;
  case 3:
    x="Today it's Wednesday";
    break;
  case 4:
    x="Today it's Thursday";
    break;
  case 5:
    x="Today it's Friday";
    break;
  case 6:
    x="Today it's Saturday";
    break;
  }
document.getElementById("demoforDays").innerHTML=x;
}
</script>
</body>
</html>
```

default Keyword:

- We use the default keyword to specify what to do if there is no match.

Example:

```
<!DOCTYPE html>
<body>
<p>Click the button to display a message based on what day it is
today.</p>
<button onclick="myFunction()">Click it</button>
<p id="demo1"></p>
<script>
function myFunction()
{
var x;
var d=new Date().getDay();
```

```
switch (d)
  {
  case 6:
    x="Today it's Saturday";
    break;
  case 0:
    x="Today it's Sunday";
    break;
  default:
    x="Looking forward to the Weekend";
  }
document.getElementById("demo1").innerHTML=x;
}
</script>
</body>
</html>
```

3.5.5 break Statement

- break statement indicates the end of that particular case.
- break statement was used to "jump out" of a switch() statement.
- The break statement can also be used to jump out of a loop.
- The break statement breaks the loop and continues executing the code after the loop (if any).

  Syntax: `break;`

Example for break statement:

```
<!DOCTYPE html>
<body>
<p>Click the button to do a loop with a break.</p>
<button onclick="myFunction()">Click it</button>
<p id="demo"></p>
<script>
function myFunction()
{
var x="",i=0;
for (i=0;i<10;i++)
  {
  if (i==3)
    {
    break;
    }
  x=x + "The number is " + i + "<br>";
  }
document.getElementById("demo").innerHTML=x;
}
</script>
</body>
</html>
```

3.5.6 continue Statement

- The continue statement breaks one iteration (in the loop), if a specified condition occurs, and continues with the next iteration in the loop.

   Syntax: `continue;`

Example:

```
<!DOCTYPE html>
<body>
<p>Click the button to do a loop which will skip the step where
i=3.</p>
<button onclick="myFunction()">Try it</button>
<p id="demo"></p>
<script>
function myFunction()
{
var x="",i=0;
for (i=0;i<10;i++)
  {
  if (i==3)
    {
    continue;
    }
  x=x + "The number is " + i + "<br>";
  }
document.getElementById("demo").innerHTML=x;
}
</script>
</body>
</html>
```

Labels:

- JavaScript statements can be labeled. To label JavaScript statements we proceed the statements with a colon(:).

   ```
   label:
   statements
   ```

- The break and the continue statements are the only JavaScript statements that can "jump out of" a code block.

   Syntax:

   ```
   break labelname;
   continue labelname;
   ```

- The continue statement (with or without a label reference) can only be used inside a loop.
- The break statement, without a label reference, can only be used inside a loop or a switch.
- With a label reference, it can be used to "jump out of" any JavaScript code block.

Example:

```
<!DOCTYPE html>
<body>
<script>
cars=["Ritz","Alto","Bravo","Ford"];
list:
{
document.write(cars[0] + "<br>");
document.write(cars[1] + "<br>");
document.write(cars[2] + "<br>");
break list;
document.write(cars[3] + "<br>");
document.write(cars[4] + "<br>");
document.write(cars[5] + "<br>");
}
</script>
</body>
</html>
```

3.5.7 Loops

- It is often the case that we want to do something fixed number of times or until a particular condition has been met. In javascript, this repetitive operation is done using loops.

- Loops can execute a block of code a number of times.

- Loops are handy, if we want to run the same code over and over again, each time with a different value.

- JavaScript supports following kinds of loops:

  1. for: loops through a block of code a number of times.

  2. for/in: loops through the properties of an object.

  3. while: loops through a block of code while a specified condition is true.

  4. do/while: loops through a block of code while a specified condition is true.

3.5.7.1 for Loop

- The for loop is often the tool we will use when we want to create a loop.

- The for loop is the most compact form of looping and includes the following three important parts:

  (i) The loop initialization where we initialize our counter to a starting value. The initialization statement is executed before the loop begins.

(ii) The test statement which will test if the given condition is true or not. If condition is true then code given inside the loop will be executed otherwise loop will come out.

(iii) The iteration statement where we can increase or decrease our counter.

- We can put all the three parts in a single line separated by a semicolon.

Syntax:

```
for(initilize; condition; increment)
{
execute statements;
}
```

Example for 'for' loop:

```
<!DOCTYPE html>
<head>
<script type="text/javascript">
for(var x=6; x<=10; x++)
{
document.write("The number is: " +x);
document.write("<br/>");
}
</script>
</head>
</html>
```

Output:

```
The number is: 6
The number is: 7
The number is: 8
The number is: 9
The number is: 10
```

- In above program when the for is executed for the first time, the value of x is 6. Now the condition x<=10 is checked. Since x is 6, the condition is true and the statements inside the for loop gets executed.
- When control reaches the closing brackets of for loop, the control goes back to the beginning of for loop. There the value of x gets incremented by 1. Now the value of x is 7.
- Again the condition is checked and the whole process is continued until the condition is false.

3.5.7.2 for/in Loop

- There is one more loop supported by JavaScript and it is called for/in loop.
- for/in loop is used to loop through an object's properties.
- In other words the JavaScript for/in statement loops through the properties of an object.

Syntax:

```
for (variablename in object){
    statement or block to execute
}
```

- In each iteration one property from object is assigned to variablename and this loop continues till all the properties of the object are exhausted.

Example:

```
<!DOCTYPE html>
<body>
<p>Click the button to loop through the properties of an object named
                                              "person".</p>
<button onclick="myFunction()">Click it</button>
<p id="demo"></p>
<script>
function myFunction()
{
var x;
var txt="";
var person={fname:"John",lname:"Doe",age:25};
for (x in person)
{
txt=txt + person[x];
}
document.getElementById("demo").innerHTML=txt;
}
</script>
</body>
</html>
```

3.5.7.3 while Loop

- The purpose of a while loop is to execute a statement or code block repeatedly as long as expression is true. Once expression becomes false, the loop will be exited.
- The while loop loops through a block of code as long as a specified condition is true.
- The keyword while creates a loop that tests an expression, and if it is true, executes a block of statements. And the loop repeats, as long as the specified condition is true.

Syntax:

```
initialize;
while (condition)
{
execute statement;
inoromont;
}
```

Example for while loop:

```
<!DOCTYPE html>
<head>
<script type="text/javascript">
var number = 3;
while (number <= 10)
{
document.write("The number is: " +number);
document.write("<br/>");
number++;
}
</script>
</head>
</html>
```

Output:

```
The number is: 3
The number is: 4
The number is: 5
The number is: 6
The number is: 7
The number is: 8
The number is: 9
The number is: 10
```

- In the statement: var number = 3, we are assigning a value 3 to a variable "number".
- In the statement: while(number <=10), we are testing a condition, i.e. testing if 3 <= 10. This condition is true, hence the while loop gets executed.
- Since, 3 <= 10, the document.write() statements gets executed. The second document.write() statement is just for a line break.
- Remember at this point the number is holding value 3. When the statement number++ is executed, it holds value 4.
- Now the condition 4 <= 10 will be checked. Since 4 <= 10, the document.write() statements are executed. After that number increments to 5. This happens until the condition (num<=10) is false.

Example:

```
<!DOCTYPE html>
<body>
<p>Click the button to loop through a block of as long as <em>i</em>
                                        is less than 5.</p>
<button onclick="myFunction()">Click it</button>
<p id="demo4"></p>
<script>
function myFunction()
{
var x="",i=0;
```

```
while (i<5)
   {
   x=x + "The number is " + i + "<br>";
   i++;
   }
document.getElementById("demo4").innerHTML=x;
}
</script>
</body>
</html>
```

3.5.7.4 do/while Loop

*   Sometimes, we want some statements to be executed atleast once even if the condition is false for the first time. To do this we use a do-while loop.
*   The do/while loop is a variant of the while loop.
*   This loop will execute the code block once, before checking if the condition is true, then it will repeat the loop as long as the condition is true.
*   The do...while loop is similar to the while loop except that the condition check happens at the end of the loop. This means that the loop will always be executed at least once, even if the condition is false.

Syntax:

```
do{
     Statements to be executed;
} while (expression);
```

Example for do/while loop:

```
<!DOCTYPE html>
<body>
<p>Click the button to loop through a block of as long as <em>i</em>
                                        is less than 5.</p>
<button onclick="myFunction()">Click it</button>
<p id="demo5"></p>
<script>
function myFunction()
{
var x="",i=0;
do
   {
   x=x + "The number is " + i + "<br>";
   i++;
   }
while (i<5)
document.getElementById("demo5").innerHTML=x;
}
</script>
</body>
</html>
```

3.6 Concept of Array   [April 10]

- Array is used to store a set of values in a single variable name.
- Arrays are a fundamental part of most programming languages and scripting languages. Arrays are simply an ordered stack of data items with the same data type.
- Using arrays, we can store multiple values under a single name. Instead of using a separate variable for each item, we can use one array to hold all of them.
- An array is a special variable, which can hold more than one value at a time.

Creating arrays in JavaScript:

- Most programming languages use similar syntax to create arrays. JavaScript arrays are created by first assigning an array object to a variable name.
- Array are objects which can store multiple values of same type, unlike variables which only store a single value at a time.
- Since, array is an object, its syntax is same as synatx used in creating a new object.

  Syntax: `var variableName = new Array(val1, val2, ....... valn );`

- Accessing an array value is quite easy. We use array index to access a value.
- If we want to access val1 from the above syntax, we use Array[0]. So,

```
Array[0] holds val1
Array[1] holds val2
Array[3] holds val3
......
Array[n] holds valn
```

For example:

```
Array InJ hold valn
var faq = new Array(3)
faq[0] = "What are JavaScript arrays"
faq[1] = "How to create arrays in JavaScript?"
faq[2] = "What are two dimensional arrays?"
```

- Whereas, one dimensional arrays can be visualized as a stack of elements, two dimensional arrays can be visualized as a multicolumn table or grid.
- For example, we could create a two dimensional array that holds three columns of data; a question, an answer, and a topic.

Two Dimensional Array			
0	Arrays	What is an array?	An ordered stack of data.
1	Arrays	How to create arrays?	Assign variable name to array object, then assign values to the array.
2	Arrays	What are two dimensional arrays?	An ordered grid of data.

Creating two dimensional arrays:

- Generally, creating two dimensional arrays is very similar to creating one dimensional arrays. Some languages allow us to create two dimensional arrays simply by adding an index item, however JavaScript doesn't support two dimensional arrays.

- JavaScript, does however, allow us to simulate a two dimensional array. We can do this by creating an "array of an array".

- To do this, we create an array, loop through the array, and for each element, we create another array. Then, we simply add an index for each column of our grid. In JavaSript this would look something like this:

```
var faq = new Array(3)
for (i=0; i &lt;3; i++)
faq[i]=new Array(3)
faq[0][1] = "Arrays"
faq[0][2] = "What is an array?"
faq[0][3] = "An ordered stack of data"
faq[1][1] = "Arrays"
faq[1][2] = "How to create arrays?"
faq[1][3] = "Assign variable name to array object, then assign values
to the array."
faq[2][1] = "Arrays"
faq[2][2] = "What are two dimensional arrays?"
faq[2][3] = "An ordered grid of data"
```

Array properties:

Property	Description
1. constructor	This property returns a reference to the array function that created the object.
2. index	This property represents the zero-based index of the match in the string.
3. input	This property is only present in arrays created by regular expression matches.
4. length	This property reflects the number of elements in an array.
5. prototype	This property allows we to add properties and methods to an object.

Array Methods:

Method	Description
1. concat()	This method returns a new array comprised of this array joined with other arrays and/or values.
2. every()	This method returns true if every element in this array satisfies the provided testing function.
3. filter()	This method creates a new array with all of the elements of this array for which the provided filtering function returns true.
4. forEach()	This method calls a function for each element in the array.
5. indexOf()	This method returns the first (least) index of an element within the array equal to the specified value, or -1 if none is found.
6. join()	This method joins all elements of an array into a string.
7. lastIndexOf()	This method returns the last (greatest) index of an element within the array equal to the specified value, or -1 if none is found.
8. map()	This method creates a new array with the results of calling a provided function on every element in this array.
9. pop()	This method removes the last element from an array and returns that element.
10. push()	This method adds one or more elements to the end of an array and returns the new length of the array.
11. reduce()	This method apply a function simultaneously against two values of the array (from left-to-right) as to reduce it to a single value.
12. reduceRight()	This method apply a function simultaneously against two values of the array (from right-to-left) as to reduce it to a single value.
13. reverse()	This method reverses the order of the elements of an array -- the first becomes the last, and the last becomes the first.
14. shift()	This method removes the first element from an array and returns that element.
15. slice()	This method extracts a section of an array and returns a new array.
16. some()	This method returns true if at least one element in this array satisfies the provided testing function.
17. toSource()	This method represents the source code of an object.
18. sort()	This method sorts the elements of an array.
19. splice()	This method adds and/or removes elements from an array.
20. toString()	This method returns a string representing the array and its elements.
21. unshift()	This method adds one or more elements to the front of an array and returns the new length of the array.

1. **Example for concat() array method:**

```html
<!DOCTYPE html>
<head>
<title>JavaScript Array concat() Method</title>
</head>
<body>
<script type="text/javascript">
    var alpha = ["x", "y", "z"];
    var numeric = [1, 2, 3];
    var alphaNumeric = alpha.concat(numeric);
    document.write("alphaNumeric : " + alphaNumeric );
</script>
</body>
</html>
```

2. **Example of sort() method:**

```html
<!DOCTYPE html>
<head>
<title>JavaScript Array sort() Method</title>
</head>
<body>
<script type="text/javascript">
var arr = new Array("orange", "mango", "banana", "apple");
var sorted = arr.sort();
document.write("Returned string is : " + sorted );
</script>
</body>
</html>
```

3.7 Event Handling in JavaScript

- Events are actions that can be detected by JavaScript.
- Events are signals generated when specific action occur.
- JavaScript is aware of these signals are scripts can be built to react to these events.

Event Handler:

- Event handlers are scripts, in the form of attributes of specific HTML tags, which we as the programmer can write.
- The general form of an event handler is:
  ```
  <html_tag other_attributes eventhandler = "JavaScript program">
  ```
- Event handler is actually a call to a function defined in the header of the document or a single JavaScript command. While any JavaScript statements, methods or functions can appear inside the quotation marks of event handler.

Creating an Event Handler:

- We do not need the <script> tag to define an event handler. Instead, we add an event attribute to an individual HTML tag.

- For example, here is a link that includes an OnMouseOver event handler.

```
<a href=http://www.pragati.com/" OnMouseOver="Window.alert ("We moved
over the link");Click here </a>
```

- Here, <a> is tag, which specifies a statement to be used as OnMouseOver event handler for the link and this statement displays an alert message when the mouse moves over the link.

- We can use JavaScript statements like the previous one in an event handler, but if we need more than one statement, its good idea to use a function as the event handler like this:

```
<a href = "#bottom" OnMouseOver = "DoIt();">
```

- Move the mouse over this link </a>

- This example calls a function called DoIt() when the user moves the mouse over the link.

Event Handlers with JavaScript:

- Instead of specifying an event handler is an HTML document, we can use JavaScript to assign a function as an event handler. This allows us to set event handlers.

- To define event handler in this way, first define a function and then assign it is an event handler.

For example:

```
<!DOCTYPE html>
<head><title> Events</title>
<script>
function react()
{
alert("Please enter any value");
}
</script></head>
<body>
document.onMousedown=react;
</body>
</html>
```

- Events are occurrences generated by the browser, such as loading a document or by the user such as moving the mouse.

- They are the user and browser activities to which we may respond dynamically with a scripting language like JavaScript.

1. onclick Event:

- onclick is the most frequently used event type which occurs when a user clicks mouse left button.

- We can put our validation, warning and so on against this event type.

Example:
```
<!DOCTYPE html>
<head>
<script type="text/javascript">
<!--
function sayHello() {
    alert("Hello JavaScript World!")
}
//-->
</script>
</head>
<body>
<script type="text/javascript">
<!--
document.write("Hello JavaScript World!")
//-->
</script>
<input type="button" onclick="sayHello()" value="Say Hello" />
</body>
</html>
```

2. onsubmit Event:

* onsubmit is another most important event type.
* This event occurs when we try to submit a form. So we can put our form validation against this event type.
* Following is a simple example showing its usage. Here, we are calling a validate() function before submitting a form data to the webserver. If validate() function returns true the form will be submitted otherwise it will not submit the data.

Example:
```
<!DOCTYPE html>
<head>
<script type="text/javascript">
<!--
function validation() {
    all validation goes here
    . . . . . . . . .
    return either true or false
}
//-->
</script>
</head>
<body>
<form method="POST" action="t.cgi" onsubmit="return validate()">
. . . . . . .
<input type="submit" value="Submit" />
</form>
</body>
</html>
```

3. onmouseover and onmouseout:

* These two event types will help us to create nice effects with images or even with text as well.
* The onMouseover event occurs when we bring our mouse over any element and the onMouseout occurs when we take our mouse out from that element.

Example:

```
<!DOCTYPE html>
<head>
<script type="text/javascript">
<!--
function over() {
    alert("Mouse Over");
}
function out() {
    alert("Mouse Out");
}
//-->
</script>
</head>
<body>
<p>Bring our mouse inside the division to see the result:</p>
<div onmouseover="over()" onmouseout="out()">
<h2> This is inside the division </h2>
</div>
</body>
</html>
```

4. onload and onunload Events:

* These two events are triggered when the user enters or leaves the page.
* The onload event can be used to check the visitor's browser type and browser version, and load the proper version of the web page based on the information.
* The onload and onunload events can be used to deal with cookies.

Example:

```
<!DOCTYPE html>
<body onload="checkCookies()">
<script>
function checkCookies()
{
if (navigator.cookieEnabled==true)
    {
    alert("Cookies are enabled")
    }
else
    {
    alert("Cookies are not enabled")
    }
}
</script>
<p>An alert box should tell we if our browser has enabled cookies or
                                                      not.</p>
</body>
</html>
```

5. onchange Event:

- This event are often used in combination with validation of input fields.
- Following is an example of how to use the onchange. The upperCase() function will be called when a user changes the content of an input field.

Example:

```html
<!DOCTYPE html>
<head>
<script>
function myFunction()
{
var x=document.getElementById("fname");
x.value=x.value.toUpperCase();
}
</script>
</head>
<body>
Enter our name: <input type="text" id="fname" onchange="myFunction()">
<p>When we leave the input field, a function is triggered which
                        transforms the input text to upper case.</p>
</body>
</html>
```

6. onmousedown, onmouseup and onclick Events:

- These three events are all parts of a mouse-click.
- First when a mouse-button is clicked, the onmousedown event is triggered, then, when the mouse-button is released, the onmouseup event is triggered, finally, when the mouse-click is completed, the onclick event is triggered.

Example:

```html
<!DOCTYPE html>
<body>
<div onmousedown="mDown(this)" onmouseup="mUp(this)"
                    style="background color:#D94A38;width:90px;height:
                                20px;padding:40px;">Click Me</div>
<script>
function mDown(obj)
{
obj.style.backgroundColor="#1ec5e5";
obj.innerHTML="Release Me"
}
function mUp(obj)
{
obj.style.backgroundColor="#D94A38";
obj.innerHTML="Thank You"
}
</script>
</body>
</html>
```

3.8 Math Object

- The math object provides properties and methods for mathematical constants and functions.

- Unlike the other global objects, Math is not a constructor. All properties and methods of Math are static and can be called by using Math as an object without creating it.

- Thus, we refer to the constant pi as Math.PI and we call the sine function as Math.sin(x), where x is the method's argument.

    Syntax:

    ```
    var pi_val = Math.PI;

    var sine_val = Math.sin(30);
    ```

Math Properties:

Property	Description
1. E	Euler's constant and the base of natural logarithms, (approximately 2.718).
2. LN2	Natural logarithm of 2, (approximately 0.693).
3. LN10	Natural logarithm of 10, (approximately 2.302).
4. LOG2E	Base 2 logarithm of E, (approximately 1.442).
5. LOG10E	Base 10 logarithm of E, (approximately 0.434).
6. PI	Ratio of the circumference of a circle to its diameter, (approximately 3.14159).
7. SQRT1_2	Square root of 1/2; equivalently, 1 over the square root of 2, (approximately 0.707).
8. SQRT2	Square root of 2, (approximately 1.414).

Math Methods:

Method	Description
1. abs()	This method returns the absolute value of a number.
2. acos()	This method returns the arccosine (in radians) of a number.
3. asin()	This method returns the arcsine (in radians) of a number.
4. atan()	This method returns the arctangent (in radians) of a number.
5. atan2()	This method returns the arctangent of the quotient of its arguments.
6. ceil()	This method returns the smallest integer greater than or equal to a number.
7. cos()	This method returns the cosine of a number.
8. exp()	This method returns E^N, where N is the argument, and E is Euler's constant, the base of the natural logarithm.

contd. ...

9. floor()	This method returns the largest integer less than or equal to a number.
10. log()	This method returns the natural logarithm (base E) of a number.
11. max()	This method returns the largest of zero or more numbers.
12. min()	This method returns the smallest of zero or more numbers.
13. pow()	This method returns base to the exponent power, that is, base exponent.
14. random()	This method returns a pseudo-random number between 0 and 1.
15. round()	This method returns the value of a number rounded to the nearest integer.
16. sin()	This method returns the sine of a number.
17. sqrt()	This method returns the square root of a number.
18. tan()	This method returns the tangent of a number.
19. toSource()	This method returns the string "Math".

3.9 Date Object

- The Date object is a datatype built into the JavaScript language. Date objects are created with the new Date( ).
- Once, a Date object is created, a number of methods allow us to operate on it. Most methods simply allow us to get and set the year, month, day, hour, minute, second, and millisecond fields of the object, using either local time or UTC (universal, or GMT) time.
- The ECMAScript standard requires the Date object to be able to represent any date and time, to millisecond precision, within 100 million days before or after 1/1/1970. This is a range of plus or minus 273,785 years, so the JavaScript is able to represent date and time till year 275755.

    Syntax: Following are the different variant of Data() constructor.
    1. new Date( )
    2. new Date(milliseconds)
    3. new Date(datestring)
    4. new Date(year,month,date[,hour,minute,second,millisecond])

- Here, is the description of the parameters of Date objects syntax a:
    o **No Argument:** With no arguments, the Date( ) constructor creates a Date object set to the current date and time.
    o **milliseconds:** When one numeric argument is passed, it is taken as the internal numeric representation of the date in milliseconds, as returned by the getTime( ) method. For example, passing the argument 5000 creates a date that represents five seconds past midnight on 1/1/70.
    o **datestring:** When one string argument is passed, it is a string representation of a date, in the format accepted by the Date.parse( ) method.

- o **Seven agruments:** To use the last form of constructor given above, Here is the description of each argument:
  - **(i)** **year:** Integer value representing the year.
  - **(ii)** **month:** Integer value representing the month, beginning with 0 for January to 11 for December.
  - **(iii)** **date:** Integer value representing the day of the month.
  - **(iv)** **hour:** Integer value representing the hour of the day (24-hour scale).
  - **(v)** **minute:** Integer value representing the minute segment of a time reading.
  - **(vi)** **second:** Integer value representing the second segment of a time reading.
  - **(vii)** **millisecond:** Integer value representing the millisecond segment of a time reading.

Date Properties:

Property	Description
1. constructor	This property specifies the function that creates an object's prototype.
2. prototype	This property allows us to add properties and methods to an object.

Date Methods:

Method	Description
1. Date()	This method returns today's date and time.
2. getDate()	This method returns the day of the month for the specified date according to local time.
3. getDay()	This method returns the day of the week for the specified date according to local time.
4. getFullYear()	This method returns the year of the specified date according to local time.
5. getHours()	This method returns the hour in the specified date according to local time.
6. getMilliseconds()	This method returns the milliseconds in the specified date according to local time.
7. getMinutes()	This method returns the minutes in the specified date according to local time.
8. getMonth()	This method returns the month in the specified date according to local time.
9. getSeconds()	This method returns the seconds in the specified date according to local time.
10. getTime()	This method returns the numeric value of the specified date as the number of milliseconds since January 1, 1970, 00:00:00 UTC.
11. getTimezoneOffset()	This method returns the time-zone offset in minutes for the current locale.

contd. ...

12. getUTCDate()	This method returns the day (date) of the month in the specified date according to universal time.
13. getUTCDay()	This method returns the day of the week in the specified date according to universal time.
14. getUTCFullYear()	This method returns the year in the specified date according to universal time.
15. getUTCHours()	This method returns the hours in the specified date according to universal time.
16. getUTCMilliseconds()	This method returns the milliseconds in the specified date according to universal time.
17. getUTCMinutes()	This method returns the minutes in the specified date according to universal time.
18. getUTCMonth()	This method returns the month in the specified date according to universal time.
19. getUTCSeconds()	This method returns the seconds in the specified date according to universal time.
20. getYear()	This method returns the year in the specified date according to local time and use getFullYear instead.
21. setDate()	This method sets the day of the month for a specified date according to local time.
22. setFullYear()	This method sets the full year for a specified date according to local time.
23. setHours()	This method sets the hours for a specified date according to local time.
24. setMilliseconds()	This method sets the milliseconds for a specified date according to local time.
25. setMinutes()	This method sets the minutes for a specified date according to local time.
26. setMonth()	This method sets the month for a specified date according to local time.
27. setSeconds()	This method sets the seconds for a specified date according to local time.
28. setTime()	This method sets the Date object to the time represented by a number of milliseconds since January 1, 1970, 00:00:00 UTC.
29. setUTCDate()	This method sets the day of the month for a specified date according to universal time.
30. setUTCFullYear()	This method sets the full year for a specified date according to universal time.
31. setUTCHours()	This method sets the hour for a specified date according to universal time.

contd. ...

32. `setUTCMilliseconds()`	This method sets the milliseconds for a specified date according to universal time.
33. `setUTCMinutes()`	This method sets the minutes for a specified date according to universal time.
34. `setUTCMonth()`	This method sets the month for a specified date according to universal time.
35. `setUTCSeconds()`	This method sets the seconds for a specified date according to universal time.
36. `setYear()`	This method sets the year for a specified date according to local time. Use setFullYear instead.
37. `toDateString()`	This method returns the "date" portion of the Date as a human-readable string.
38. `toGMTString()`	This method converts a date to a string, using the Internet GMT conventions and use toUTCString instead.
39. `toLocaleDateString()`	This method returns the "date" portion of the Date as a string, using the current locale's conventions.
40. `toLocaleFormat()`	This method converts a date to a string, using a format string.
41. `toLocaleString()`	This method converts a date to a string, using the current locale's conventions.
42. `toLocaleTimeString()`	This method returns the "time" portion of the Date as a string, using the current locale's conventions.
43. `toSource()`	This method returns a string representing the source for an equivalent Date object; we can use this value to create a new object.
44. `toString()`	This method returns a string representing the specified Date object.
45. `toTimeString()`	This method returns the "time" portion of the Date as a human-readable string.
46. `toUTCString()`	This method converts a date to a string, using the universal time convention.
47. `valueOf()`	This method returns the primitive value of a Date object.

Date Static Methods:

Method	Description
1. `Date.parse( )`	This method parses a string representation of a date and time and returns the internal millisecond representation of that date.
2. `Date.UTC( )`	This method returns the millisecond representation of the specified UTC date and time.

3.10 String Object

- The string object is used for storing and manipulating text.
- A string simply stores a series of characters like "Amar and Akbar".
- A string can be any text inside quotes and we can use simple or double quotes as:
  ```
  var carname="Alto XC60";
  var carname='Alto XC60';
  ```
- The string object let's us work with a series of characters and wraps Javascript's string primitive data type with a number of helper methods.
- Because Javascript automatically converts between string primitives and String objects, we can call any of the helper methods of the String object on a string primitive.

  Syntax: Creating a String object use following syntax :
  ```
  var val = new String(string);
  ```
- The string parameter is series of characters that has been properly encoded.

String Properties:

Property	Description
1. constructor	This property returns a reference to the String function that created the object.
2. length	This property returns the length of the string.
3. prototype	This property allows we to add properties and methods to an object.

String Methods:

Method	Description
1. charAt()	This method returns the character at the specified index.
2. charCodeAt()	This method returns a number indicating the Unicode value of the character at the given index.
3. concat()	This method combines the text of two strings and returns a new string.
4. indexOf()	This method returns the index within the calling String object of the first occurrence of the specified value, or −1 if not found.
5. lastIndexOf()	This method returns the index within the calling String object of the last occurrence of the specified value, or −1 if not found.
6. localeCompare()	This method returns a number indicating whether a reference string comes before or after or is the same as the given string in sort order.
7. match()	This method used to match a regular expression against a string.

contd. ...

8. `replace()`	This method used to find a match between a regular expression and a string, and to replace the matched substring with a new substring.
9. `search()`	This method executes the search for a match between a regular expression and a specified string.
10. `slice()`	This method extracts a section of a string and returns a new string.
11. `split()`	This method Splits a String object into an array of strings by separating the string into substrings.
12. `substr()`	This method returns the characters in a string beginning at the specified location through the specified number of characters.
13. `substring()`	This method returns the characters in a string between two indexes into the string.
14. `toLocaleLowerCase()`	This method returns the characters within a string are converted to lower case while respecting the current locale.
15. `toLocaleUpperCase()`	This method returns the characters within a string are converted to upper case while respecting the current locale.
16. `toLowerCase()`	This method returns the calling string value converted to lower case.
17. `toString()`	This method returns a string representing the specified object.
18. `toUpperCase()`	This method returns the calling string value converted to uppercase.
19. `valueOf()`	This method returns the primitive value of the specified object.

1. The length of a string (a String object) is found in the built in property **length()**.

```
<!DOCTYPE html>
<body>
<script>
var txt = "Hello JavaScript World!";
document.write("<p>" + txt.length + "</p>");
var txt="Amar and Akbar";
document.write("<p>" + txt.length + "</p>");
</script>
</body>
</html>
```

2. The **indexOf()** method returns the position (as a number) of the first found occurrence of a specified text inside a string.

```
<!DOCTYPE html>
<body>
<p id="p1">Click the button to locate where "locate" first occurs.</p>
<p id="p2">0</p>
<button onclick="myFunction()">Click it</button>
<script>
function myFunction()
{
var str=document.getElementById("p1").innerHTML;
var n=str.indexOf("locate");
document.getElementById("p2").innerHTML=n+1;
}
</script>
</body>
</html>
```

3. The **match()** method can be used to search for a matching content in a string.

```
<!DOCTYPE html>
<body>
<script>
var str="Hello JavaScript world!";
document.write(str.match("world") + "<br>");
document.write(str.match("World") + "<br>");
document.write(str.match("world!"));
</script>
</body>
</html>
```

4. The **replace()** method replaces a specified value with another value in a string.

```
<!DOCTYPE html>
<body>
<p>Click the button to replace "Nirali Prakashan" with "Pragati" in
the paragraph below:</p>
<p id="demo">Please visit Nirali Prakashan!</p>
<button onclick="myFunction()">Click it</button>
<script>
```

```
function myFunction()
{
var str=document.getElementById("demo").innerHTML;
var n=str.replace("Nirali Prakashan ","Pragati");
document.getElementById("demo").innerHTML=n;
}
</script>
</body>
</html>
```

5. A string is converted to upper/lower case with the methods **toUpperCase()** / **toLowerCase()**:

```
<!DOCTYPE html>
<body>
<script>
var txt="Hello JavaScript World!";
document.write("<p>" + txt.toUpperCase() + "</p>");
document.write("<p>" + txt.toLowerCase() + "</p>");
document.write("<p>" + txt + "</p>");
</script>
<p>
The methods returns a new string.
The original string is not changed.
</p>
</body>
</html>
```

3.10.1 Functions

- Like any other advance programming language, JavaScript also supports all the features necessary to write modular code using functions.
- A function is a block of code that will be executed when "someone" calls it:
- Function is a block of statements that performs certain task.
- Functions are building blocks of any programming language.
- Functions are of two types pre-defined/built-in functions and user-defined functions.
- Built-in functions are the functions that are already defined in the javascript. Examples are write(), alert(), prompt() etc.
- User-defined functions are defined by a user. Sometimes, this functions are simple, and sometimes they are quite complex.

Function Definition:

- Before we use a function we need to define that function.
- The most common way to define a function in JavaScript is by using the function keyword, followed by a unique function name, a list of parameters (that might be empty), and a statement block surrounded by curly braces.

  Syntax:

```
<script type="text/javascript">
<!--
function function_name(parameter-list)
{
   statements
}
//-->
</script>
```

- A simple function that takes no parameters called sayHelloJavaScript is defined here:

```
<script type="text/JavaScript">
<!--
function sayHelloJavaScript()
{
    alert("Hello JavaScript");
}
//-->
</script>
```

Calling a Function:

- Calling a function is using the defined function. A function can be called from any section of our code.

  Syntax: `functionName();`

  Syntax is simple, just functionName with empty brackets and a semi-colon.

Example:

```
<!DOCTYPE html>
<head>
<title>Javascript Function Example </title>
</head>
<body>
<script type="text/javascript">
function test(){          //defining function
var a = 40;
document.write(a);
}
test();               //calling function
</script>
</body>
</html>
```

Output:

```
40
```

- We have defined a function test using keyword function. In the function block we have assigned a value 40 to variable a. The next line is document.write() statement.

- This function test() will not print 40 to the screen all by itself. It has to be called, which we are doing using the statement test();

Function Parameters:

- In the previous point, we defined a function test() without any values in the round brackets.

- In practical situations, we might need to add some values (parameters) in the round brackets.

Syntax:

```
function functionName(para_1, para_2...para_n) {

statements to be executed;

}
```

Example:

```
<!DOCTYPE html>
<head>
<title>Javascript Function Parameters</title>
</head>
<body>
<script type="text/javascript">
function add(x,y){
result = x+y;
document.write("addition is: "+result);
document.write("<br/>");
}
add(10,10);
add(23,12);
</script>
</body>
</html>
```

Output:

```
addition is: 20
addition is: 35
```

- Notice how we are passing parameter values to the function. The function add() is called twice.

- Everytime we want to add two numbers, we need not write the code for it every single time. We can write the code once, and call it as many times as we want.

return Statement:

- Sometimes, we want the functions to perform some calculations and return the result, so that we can use that result outside the function. We use return statement to return a value.

- A JavaScript function can have an optional return statement. This is required if we want to return a value from a function. This statement should be the last statement in a function.

- For example, we can pass two numbers in a function and then we can expect from the function to return their multiplication in our calling program.

   Syntax: `return value;`

Example:

```
<!DOCTYPE html>
<head>
<title>Javascript Return statement</title>
</head>
<body>
<script type="text/javascript">
function areaRect(L,B){
var area = L*B;
return area;
}
x=areaRect(6,8);
document.write(x);
</script>
</body>
</html>
```

Output:

```
48
```

- areaRect(6,8); calls the function and passes values 6 and 8.
- The function calculates the area, and returns it (in our case, 48).
- Now, after the function has returned a value, areaRect(6,8) is 48. This value 48, is assigned to x.
- The statement document.write(x) will print 48 in the webpage.

3.11 Document Object Model (DOM)

- The Document Object Model represents possibilities.
- Unfortunately, there's currently only a smattering of agreement among the major browser vendors, Netscape, Microsoft and Opera as to what possibilities to support and how to access them.

- The situation is improving with each new browser release as the major browser vendors adopt more of the current World Wide Web Consortium (W3C) DOM standard as well as the W3C's HTML and Cascading Style Sheets (CSS) standards.

- Pressure from standards support groups like the Web Standard Project (WaSP) have helped encourage browser vendors to comply with W3C standards.

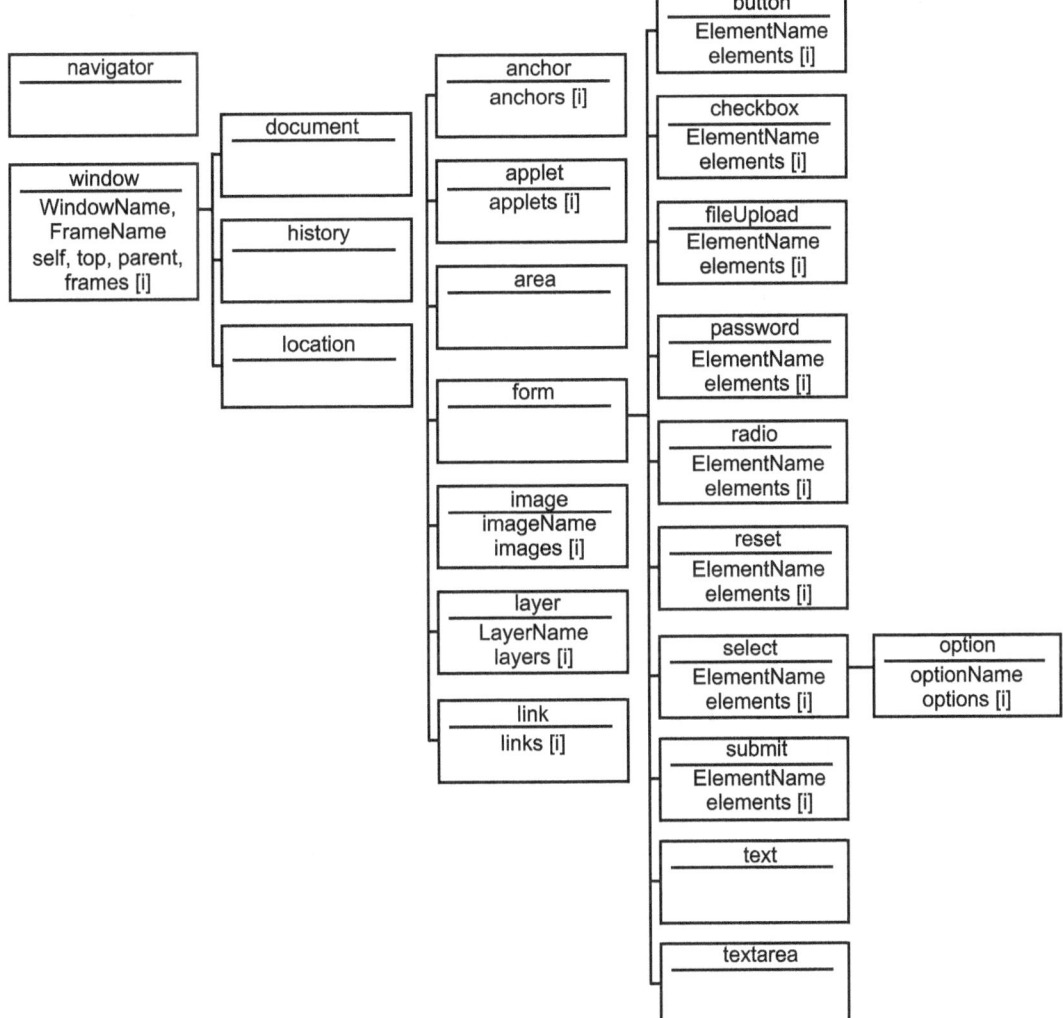

Fig. 3.1: Cross-browser DOM (JavaScript 1.1)

- The above DOM illustration (See Fig. 3.1) represents the DOM common to all three major browsers i.e. Netscape Navigator, Microsoft Internet Explorer and Opera. The newest browsers each support many more objects than those shown here, but they do so independently of or inconsistently with the other browser companies.

When are Objects Created?

- The items contained in a Web document become objects in the browser's memory as the browser loads and interprets the HTML code that defines them. Notice that the DOM is arranged in a hierarchical way with window as the highest-level object.

- If we think about it a moment, we will realize that every web document is displayed or contained within a browser window. In essence, every object in a web document is contained within some other object, with the exception of the `window` and `navigator` `objects`.

- The window object is the topmost or outermost, container, and the `navigator` `object`, which represents the browser, is on the same level. Netscape characterizes this an "**instance hierarchy**".

- Netscape originally called its DOM an "instance hierarchy" because its objects come into being the instant that the HTML code or JavaScript code that defines them is read and interpreted by the browser. Each web document, therefore, creates a different and unique instance hierarchy.

- While the Document Object Model supported by a particular browser provides possibilities, the instance hierarchy specifies the actual objects that are created in the browser's memory when a particular.

- Web document loads. If we stop a Web document's loading halfway through, only those objects already read and interpreted by the browser will be represented in its instance hierarchy.

- Let's take a look at a simple HTML document, listed in the first column and the instance hierarchy the browser creates in memory as it loads the document. We will use the DOM in Fig. 3.2 as our guide.

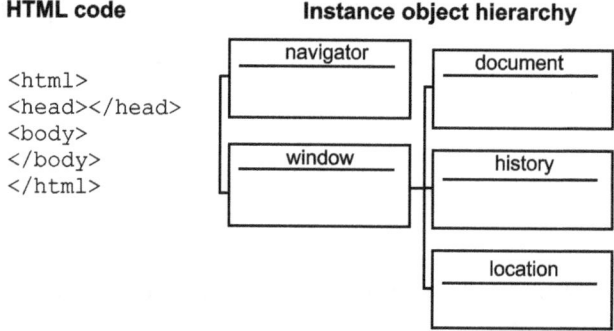

Fig. 3.2: Illustration of instance hierarchy

- Above web document does not really contain anything. If we preview it in our browser, we will see only a blank page. Still, notice that this document does have an instance hierarchy. It is turned on its side to make it easy to see the associated dot notation.

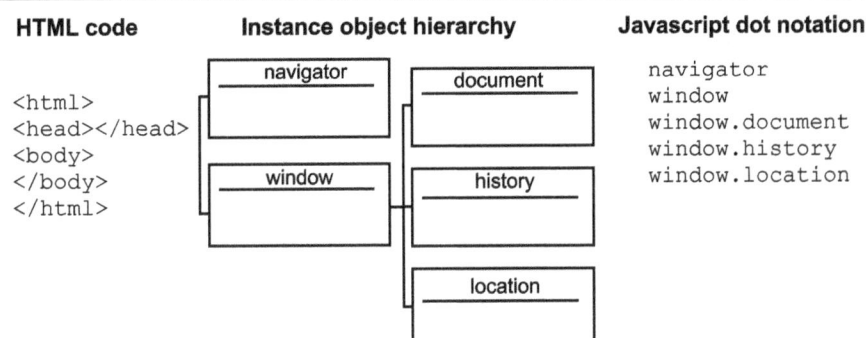

HTML code   **Instance object hierarchy**   **Javascript dot notation**

```
<html>
<head></head>
<body>
</body>
</html>
```

navigator
window
window.document
window.history
window.location

navigator | document

window | history

location

Fig. 3.3: Illustration of instance hierarchy with dot notation

- Dot notation indicates that we write the object name, followed by a dot and the object's property. Read the instance object hierarchy diagram above, left to right, inserting dots as needed and we get the dot notation listed in the last column.
- The `navigator` object represents the browser and is one of two top-level objects, its name is rather Netscape biased, "browser" would be a non-biased name, but then Netscape was the company that created the JavaScript language, so we think that entitles them to some liberties. The `window` object is the other top-level object.
- The `document` object is itself a property of the window object. This makes sense, because all documents in a Web browser are displayed in a window.
- The `history` object, also a property of the `window` objects, represents the history list in the window.
- The history list contains the most recent pages we have visited during the current browser session, those that we can get to with the Back and Forward buttons.
- The `location` object, also a property of the window, represents the location of the current document (usually shown in the location bar, also known as the address bar) in the browser window.

JavaScript DOM Objects:

1. The anchors array:

- The anchors array is an array of anchor objects and it is a property of the document object.
- This objects are reflections of a elements that have a name attribute:

```
<a name="anchorName">anchorText</a>
```

2. The button Object:

- It is a reflection of an input element with a type attribute of "button".

```
<input type="button">
```

- Button objects are members of the containing form object's elements array.

3. The checkbox Object:

- This object is a reflection of an input element with a type attribute of "checkbox".

```
<input type="checkbox">
```

- Checkbox objects are members of the containing form's elements array.

4. The document Object:

- This object contains information about the currently displayed document and its properties are derived from the document's body element.

  ```
  <body>document contents</body>
  ```

The elements Array:

- It contains references to input elements in a form.

- We cannot add elements to this array, replace elements in the array or remove elements from the array. The elements array is a form object property.

5. The form Object:

- This object collects input from the user and may send the input to a server and it is a reflection of a form element:

  ```
  <form>form contents</form>
  ```

- Each and every form object is a member of the containing document object's forms array.

The forms Array:

- It is a property of the containing document object and contains references to all of the form objects in the document, in source order.

- We cannot add a form to the array, replace a form in the array, or remove a form from the array.

6. The frame Object:

- This object is a reflection of a frame element:

  ```
  <frame>
  ```

The frames Array:

- A frames array contains the non-empty frames within a frame or a window.

7. The hidden Object:

- This object is a reflection of an input element with a type attribute of "hidden".

  ```
  <input type="hidden">
  ```

8. The link Object:

- This object is a reflection of an a element that has an href attribute.

  ```
  <a href=url>anchorText</a>
  ```

- All links are members of the document's links array in source order.

The links Array:

- It contains references to all the links in the document, in source order.

- We cannot remove a link from the array or replace a link in the array and we can create another links with the string object's link() method.

9. The password Object:

- This object is a reflection of an input element with a type attribute of "password".

```
<input type="password">
```

The data entered by the user is not visible to the display each and every character appears as an asterisk (*) and it is not visible programmatically.

Password objects are members of the containing form object's elements array.

10. The radio Object:

- This object represents a set of input elements of type "radio" with the same name attribute:

```
<input type="radio" name=radioName>
```

Each button is a radio object is a member of the containing form object's elements array.

11. The reset Object:

- This object is a reflection of an input tag with a type attribute of "reset".

```
<input type="reset">
```

Reset objects are members of the containing form object's elements array.

12. The select Object:

- This object is a reflection of a SELECT element of form.

```
<select><option>...</select>
```

Select objects are members of the containing form object's elements array.

The options Array:

- This is a property of select objects and it allows we to manipulate the options of the select object. Individual options objects are reflections of option elements.

```
<option>, text to be displayed ...........
```

13. The submit Object:

- This object is a reflection of an input element with a type attribute of "submit".

```
<input type="submit">
```

Submit objects are members of the containing form object's elements array.

14. The text Object:

- This object is a reflection of an input element with a type attribute of "text".

```
<input type="text">
```

Text object are members of the containing form object's elements array.

15. The textarea Object:

- This object is a reflection of textarea element like:

```
<textarea> text to be displayed........</textarea>
```

3.11.1 DOM Objects

3.11.1.1 Window Object

- The window object represents an open window in a browser.
- If a document contains frames (<frame>or<iframe>tags), the browser creates one window object for the HTML document and one additional window object for each frame.

Window Object Properties:

Property	Description
1. closed	This property returns a Boolean value indicating whether a window has been closed or not.
2. defaultStatus	This property sets or returns the default text in the statusbar of a window.
3. document	This property returns the Document object for the window.
4. frames	This property returns an array of all the frames (including iframes) in the current window.
5. history	This property returns turns the History object for the window.
6. innerHeight	This property sets or returns the inner height of a window's content area.
7. innerWidth	This property sets or returns the inner width of a window's content area.
8. length	This property returns the number of frames (including iframes) in a window.
9. location	This property returns the Location object for the window.
10. name	This property sets or returns the name of a window.
11. navigator	This property returns the Navigator object for the window.
12. opener	This property returns reference to the window that created the window.
13. outerHeight	This property sets or returns the outer height of a window, including toolbars/scrollbars.
14. outerWidth	This property sets or returns the outer width of a window, including toolbars/scrollbars.
15. pageXOffset	This property returns the pixels the current document has been scrolled (horizontally) from the upper left corner of the window.
16. pageYOffset	This property returns the pixels the current document has been scrolled (vertically) from the upper left corner of the window.

contd. ...

17. parent	This property returns the parent window of the current window.
18. screen	This property returns the Screen object for the window.
19. screenLeft	This property returns the x coordinate of the window relative to the screen.
20. screenTop	This property returns y coordinate of the window relative to the screen.
21. screenX	This property returns the x coordinate of the window relative to the screen.
22. screenY	This property returns y coordinate of the window relative to the screen.
23. self	This property returns the current window.
24. status	This property sets the text in the statusbar of a window.
25. top	This property returns the topmost browser window.

Window Object Methods:

Method	Description
1. alert()	This method displays an alert box with a message and an OK button.
2. blur()	This method removes focus from the current window.
3. clearInterval()	This method clears a timer set with setInterval().
4. clearTimeout()	This method clears a timer set with setTimeout().
5. close()	This method closes the current window.
6. confirm()	This method displays a dialog box with a message and an OK and a Cancel button.
7. createPopup()	This method creates a pop-up window.
8. focus()	This method sets focus to the current window.
9. moveBy()	This method moves a window relative to its current position.
10. moveTo()	This method moves a window to the specified position.
11. open()	This method opens a new browser window.
12. print()	This method prints the content of the current window.
13. prompt()	This method displays a dialog box that prompts the visitor for input.
14. resizeBy()	This method resizes the window by the specified pixels.
15. resizeTo()	This method resizes the window to the specified width and height.
16. scrollBy()	This method scrolls the content by the specified number of pixels.
17. scrollTo()	This method scrolls the content to the specified coordinates.
18. setInterval()	This method calls a function or evaluates an expression at specified intervals (in milliseconds).
19. setTimeOut()	This method calls a function or evaluates an expression after a specified number of milliseconds.

3.11.1.2 Navigator Object

- The JavaScript navigator object is the object representation of the client Internet browser or web navigator program that is being used.
- Navigator object is the top level object to all others.
- The navigator object contains information about the browser.

Navigator Object Properties:

Property	Description
1. appCodeName	This property returns the code name of the browser.
2. appName	This property returns the name of the browser.
3. appVersion	This property returns the version information of the browser.
4. cookieEnabled	This property determines whether cookies are enabled in the browser.
5. platform	This property returns for which platform the browser is compiled.
6. userAgent	This property returns the user-agent header sent by the browser to the server.

Navigator Object Methods:

Method	Description
1. javaEnabled()	This method specifies whether or not the browser has Java enabled.
2. taintEnabled()	This method specifies whether or not the browser has data tainting enabled.

3.11.1.3 History Object

- The history object is automatically created by the JavaScript runtime engine and consists of an array of URLs.
- These URLs are the URLs the user has visited within a browser window.
- The history object is part of the Window object and is accessed through the window.history property.

(i) History Object Properties:

Property	Description
1. length	This property returns the number of elements in the history list.

(ii) History Object Methods:

Method	Description
1. back()	This method loads the previous URL in the history list.
2. forward()	This method loads the next URL in the history list.
3. go()	This method loads a specific page in the history list.

3.11.1.4 Location Object

- The location object is actually a JavaScript object, not an HTML DOM object.
- The location object is automatically created by the JavaScript run-time engine and contains information about the current URL.
- The location object is part of the Window object and is accessed through the window.location property.

Location Object Properties:

Property	Description
1. `hash`	This property sets or returns the URL from the hash sign (#).
2. `host`	This property sets or returns the hostname and port number of the current URL.
3. `hostname`	This property sets or returns the hostname of the current URL.
4. `href`	This property sets or returns the entire URL.
5. `pathname`	This property sets or returns the path of the current URL.
6. `port`	This property sets or returns the port number of the current URL.
7. `protocol`	This property sets or returns the protocol of the current URL.
8. `search`	This property sets or returns the URL from the question mark (?).

Location Object Methods:

Method	Description
1. `assign()`	This method loads a new document.
2. `reload()`	This method reloads the current document.
3. `replace()`	This method replaces the current document with a new one.

3.12 Validation and Forms in JavaScript

Accessing forms in a JavaScript:

- Javascript is very useful in validating forms.
- We validate forms to check the user has entered genuine/real information before he/her can submit it.
- Validation is the process of checking that a form has been filled correctly.
- For example, we do not want the user to leave mandatory fields empty or we want the user to enter a valid format email id etc.

- Form validation used to occur at the server, after the client had entered all necessary data and then pressed the Submit button. If some of the data that had been entered by the client had been in the wrong form or was simply missing, the server would have to send all the data back to the client and request that the form be resubmitted with correct information.

- Validation was really a lengthy process and over burdening server.

- JavaScript, provides a way to validate form's data on the client's computer before sending it to the web server.

- Form validation generally performs two functions.

   1. **Basic Validation:** First of all, the form must be checked to make sure data was entered into each form field that required it. This would need just loop through each field in the form and check for data.

   2. **Data Format Validation:** Secondly, the data that is entered must be checked for correct form and value. This would need to put more logic to test correctness of data.

- To validate an HTML form, we need to access it first.

- Forms are objects and it has a property forms, which is a javascript array.

- Lets create two different forms in HTML

```
<form name="first_form">
First Name: <input type="text" name="fname"/>
Last Name: <input type="text" name="lname"/>
<input type="submit" value="Submit" />
</form>
<form name="second_form">
Phone: <input type="text" name="phone"/>
<input type="submit" value="Submit" />
</form>
```

- We created two forms named "first_form" and "second_form". In first_form, we have three elements, first name, last name and submit button. In second_form we have two elements, phone and submit button.

- We can access them, using forms in two ways. Using a form index and using the form name.

```
var name = document.forms[0]; //first form
        or
var name = document.forms["first_form"];
```

- In the below given example, we access both the forms and print out the number of elements each form has using a property length.

```
<!DOCTYPE html>
<body>
<form name="first_form">
First Name: <input type="text" name="fname"/>
Last Name: <input type="text" name="lname"/>
<input type="submit" value="Submit" />
</form>
<form name="second_form">
Phone: <input type="text" name="phone"/>
<input type="submit" value="Submit" />
</form>
<script type="text/javascript">
var num1 = document.forms[0].length;
var num2 = document.forms["second_form"].length;
document.write(num1);
document.write("<br/>");
document.write(num2);
</script>
</body>
</html>
```

Output:

3
2

- We are accessing first form using index value, i.e. forms[0] and the second form using form name "second_form".

Accessing Form Elements:

- In the previous point, we accessed forms. In this we will learn to access form elements.
- We can access form elements using, getElementById. Lets create an HTML form.

```
<form name="form1">
First Name: <input type="text" id="fname"/>
Last Name: <input type="text" id="lname"/>
<input type="submit" value="Submit" />
</form>
```

- We must give a unique id to the form elements we want to access, as shown above. Lets assume, we want to access, first element (First Name) from the form.
- When we want to access the element, we can access it using its "id". See the code given below.

```
var variableName = document.getElementById('fname');
```

```
<!DOCTYPE html>
<head>
<script type="text/javascript">
function validate()
{
var result = document.getElementById('fname').value;
alert("Hi "+result);
}
</script>
</head>
<body>
<form name="form1" onsubmit="validate()">
First Name: <input type="text" id="fname"/><br/>
Last Name: <input type="text" id="lname"/><br/>
<input type="submit" value="Submit"/>
</form>
</body>
</html>
```

- In form tag we have onsubmit attribute. When "Submit" button is clicked, it calls function validate, which is in the head section of html.
- First Name is accessed using its id fname, using the statement document.getElementId('fname').
- The value user enters, is accessed using value. So, the sentence document.getElementById('fname').value, hold the data entered by user in First Name field. If user doesn't enter data, it is empty.
- We are assigning the data entered by user to result. And we are displaying the result in an alert box.

First Name: Last Name: Submit

- Let's build a simple form with one textbox called "Name", and a submit button. We will validate it to ensure that the user enters his name before the form is submitted.

Code for textbox validation

```
<script type="text/javascript">
function nameValidate( ) {
valid = true;
if (document.getElementById('name').value == "" )
{
alert ( "Please enter our Name" );
valid = false;
}
return valid;
}
</script>
<form name="form1" method="post" action="" onsubmit="return
                                        nameValidate( );">
Name: <input type="text" id="name" />
<input type="submit" value="Click" />
</form>
```

- We have created a form named "form1". It has an attribute onsubmit. When submit button is clicked, the function nameValidate() is called. nameValidate() function which has variable valid is set to true.
- In the if statement, we are accessing the form element Name using document.getElementById('name').value (check the previous topic).
- In plain english, the if condition and block translates to this "if the value is empty, display an alert box asking the user to enter name in the field". If the field is empty, valid is set to false. If the field is filled, valid is true.

Code for Validating Checkboxes:

```
<!DOCTYPE html>
<head>
<script type="text/javascript">
function formValidate()
{
var choice1=document.getElementById("banana").checked;
var choice2=document.getElementById("apple").checked;
  if ((choice1=="")&&(choice2==""))
  {
  alert("Choose a fruit");
  return false;
  }
return true;
}
</script>
</head>
<body>
<form name="form1" onsubmit="return formValidate()">
<input type="checkbox" id="banana">Orange
<input type="checkbox" id="apple">Apple
<input type="submit" value="Submit"  />
<input type="reset" value="Reset" />
</form>
</body>
</html>
```

Code for validating radio buttons:

```
<!DOCTYPE html>
<head>
<script type="text/javascript">
function validate(){
var r1 = document.getElementById('male').checked;
var r2 = document.getElementById('female').checked;
  if((r1=="") && (r2=="")){
  alert("Select either Male or Female");
  return false;
  }
  return true;
  }
```

```
</script>
</head>
<body>
We are?
<form name="form1" method="post">
<input type="radio" id="male" value="male">Male
<input type="radio" id="female" value="female">Female
<input type="submit" onclick="return validate();">
</form>
</body>
</html>
```

Code for validating dropdown list:

```
<script type='text/javascript'>
function validateDropdown(){
var s1 = document.getElementById('selection');
    if(s1.value == "select movie"){
          alert("Please select a movie");
          return false;
    }else{
          return true;
    }
}
</script>
<form name="form1" method="post">
Favorite Movie: <select id='selection'>
<option value = "select movie">select movie</option>
<option>Munnabhai MBBS</option>
<option>Gagani</option>
<option>Golmal</option>
</select>
<input type='button' onclick="return validateDropdown()"
    value="Submit"/>
</form>
```

Practice Questions

1. Who developed JavaScript?
2. What is JavaScript?
3. What are the data types used in JavaScript?
4. What is a function? How to create it?
5. Enlist various operators in JavaScript.
6. Explain number function with syntax.

7. Describe navigation object with example.

8. What is meant by array? How to define an array.

9. What is event? Explain event handling in JavaScript.

10. Explain JavaScript Window object with example.

11. Create a personal home page named home.html with the following content:

    (a) Your name written in the <title> and an <h1> tag at the top.

    (b) A picture of yourself after or next to the heading. If we do not have a digital picture of yourself, use clip art or a favorite landscape.

    (c) Add the following sections using the tags listed:

        (i)   <h2>My Assignments</h2>—leave space underneath for later input.

        (ii) <h2>About Me</h2>—again leave space for later input.

        (iii) <h2>Bio</h2>—complete this section with some biographical information in paragraphs <p> ... </p>.

        (iv) <h2>My Hobbies</h2>—leave blank for later input.

        (v)   <h2>MyWork/Job</h2>—leave blank for later input.

        (vi) <h2>My Browser</h2>leave blank for later input.

        (vii) <address>Contract Info</address>—leave blank for now.

        (viii) <p><b>Last Update:</b> </p>we'll add more later.

12. Create a home page named toy Store.html for a company that sells toys. Include images of balls, jacks, whistles, skateboards, dolls, and other items that the toy company sells. We should be able to find the images we need from an online clip art library.

13. Write a program to display even and odd number between 1 to 20.

14. Explain various control statement statement with example.

15. What is a loop? What are its types? Explain with example.

16. Write short notes on: (i) math object, (ii) date object.

17. What is function? How to create and call it? Explain with example.

18. Write a program for finding prime numbers.

19. What is form and validation? Explain with example.

20. Explain DOM object in detail.

■■■

Chapter 4...

ASP

Contents ...

4.1 Introduction to ASP

• ASP stands for Active Server Pages (ASPs) .Active Server Pages are Web pages that contain server-side scripts in addition to the usual mixture of text and HTML (Hypertext Markup Language) tags. When you type a URL in the Address box or click a link on a Web page, you're asking a Web hosting server to send a file to the Web browser (sometimes called a "client") on your computer. If that file is a normal HTML file, it looks exactly the same when your Web browser receives it as it did before the Web server sent it.

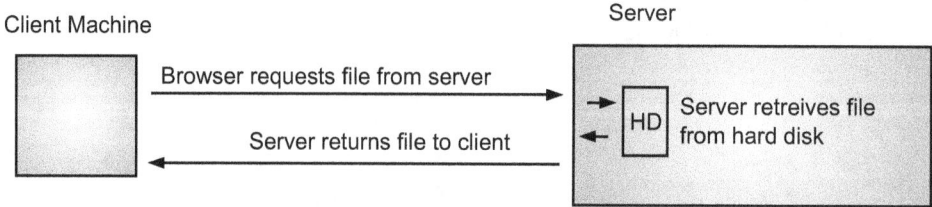

Fig. 4.1: Standard HTML Pages

• After receiving the file, your Web browser displays its contents as a combination of text, images, and sounds.

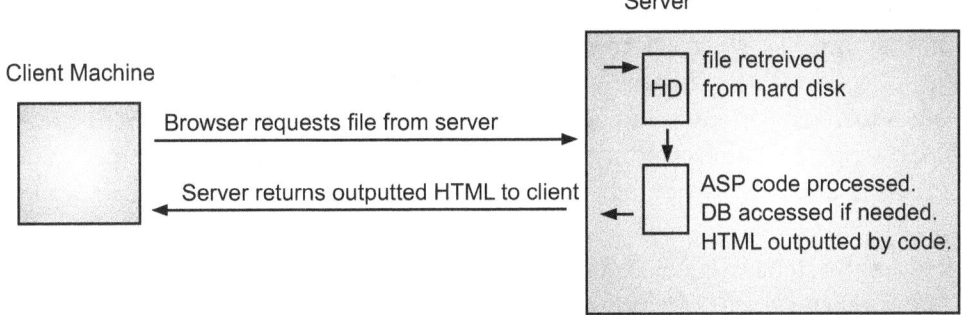

Fig. 4.2: Active Server Pages

- In the case of an Active Server Page, the process is similar, except there's an extra processing step that takes place just before the Web server sends the file.

- Before the Web server sends the Active Server Page to the Web browser, it runs all server-side scripts contained in the page.

- To distinguish them from normal HTML pages, ASP's are given the ".asp" extension.

- There are many things you can do with Active Server Pages.

  o You can display date, time, and other information in different ways.

  o You can make a survey form and ask people who visit your site to fill it out, send emails, save the information to a file, etc

Differences between ASP and HTML:

- HTML is a client-side language, whereas ASP is a server-side language.

- ASP is used to design user-interactive pages or dynamic pages, whereas HTML is used to design static pages.

- ASP can use any scripting languages.

- ASP is used to embed programming and server side directives into an HTML web page.

- HTML page can not connect to the database, but ASP and ASP.NET Pages can.

Why should we use Active Server Pages?

Following are some reasons for using Active Server Page technology:

- Active Server Pages are browser independent.

- Easy to create and use.

- Offers choice of scripting languages.

- No extra software costs

4.2 How to Install IIS

- To run ASP scripts, Personal Web Server (PWS) or Internet Information Services (IIS) must be installed on Windows. A PWS is intended for Windows 95 or 98 or NT. The IIS is intended for latest versions of Windows.

- This installation sets up your computer to act as a server when it is executing the ASP code that you will write. Of course, when your computer's browser is requesting the page, it acts as a client. Installing any one of the Web servers mentioned above, should create a folder called inetpub and a subfolder called wwwroot on the hard-drive. All of the ASP scripts must be saved with an .asp file extension under the wwwroot folder or in a subfolder under wwwroot, as long as you remember to set IIS to the folder in which your ASP code exists.

- Below are the steps to install IIS on Windows XP

  1. Configuring the IP settings on your Web Server

  1.1 Open Control Panels.

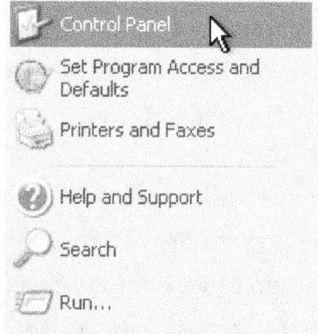

Fig. 4.3

1.2 Click on Network and Internet Connections.

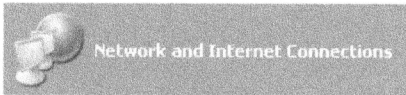

Fig. 4.4

1.3 Click on Network Connections.

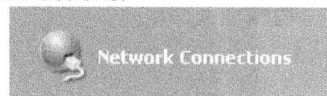

Fig. 4.5

1.4 Right-click on your Local Area Connection icon, and choose Properties

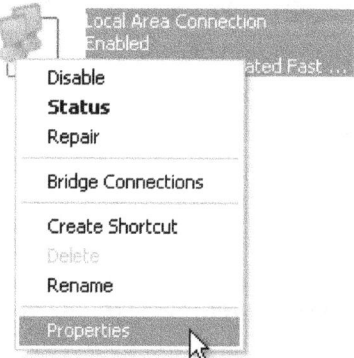

Fig. 4.6

1.5 Select Internet Protocol (TCP/IP).

This connection uses the following items:

- ☑ 🖳 Client for Microsoft Networks
- ☑ 🖳 File and Printer Sharing for Microsoft Networks
- ☑ 🖳 QoS Packet Scheduler
- ☑ 📶 Internet Protocol (TCP/IP)

[Install...]   [Uninstall]   [Properties]

Fig. 4.7

Click on the Properties button.

1.6 Click to Use the following IP address, and enter an IP address and DNS address compatible with your network.

You can get IP settings assigned automatically if your network supports this capability. Otherwise, you need to ask your network administrator for the appropriate IP settings.

- ○ Obtain an IP address automatically
- ◉ Use the following IP address:

IP address:	10 . 38 . 1 . 30
Subnet mask:	255 . 255 . 255 . 0
Default gateway:	10 . 38 . 1 . 1

- ○ Obtain DNS server address automatically
- ◉ Use the following DNS server addresses:

| Preferred DNS server: | 153 . 107 . 37 . 21 |
| Alternate DNS server: | 153 . 107 . 37 . 22 |

[Advanced...]

Fig. 4.8

NSW DET schools should use 10.x.x.30 (or 28, or 29) Click on OK.

1.7 You can check that the computer is connecting to the network by running a "ping" test to a known local IP address from Run in the Start menu.

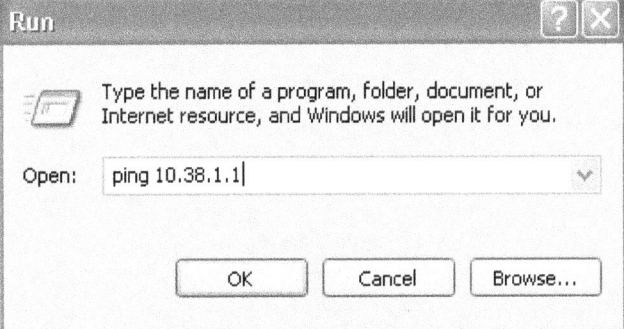

Fig. 4.9

1.8 You can also repeat the ping test from another network computer back to your web server's IP address.

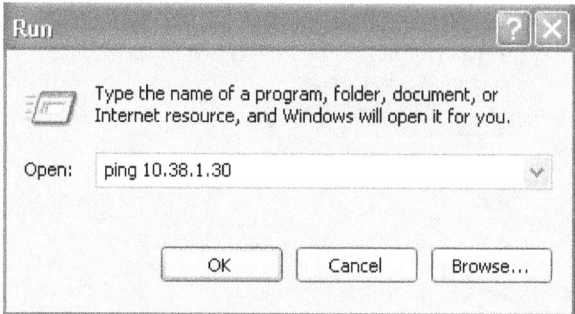

Fig. 4.10

If your are unable to ping the server address, and your network is intact, check that the Firewall on the web server is not enabled to block incoming requests on Port 80 (Network connections > Properties > Advanced).

2. Set-up IIS

2.1 Open Control Panels.

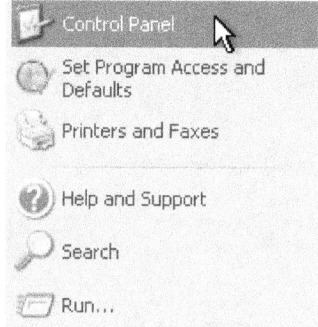

Fig. 4.11

2.2 Click on Add or Remove Programs

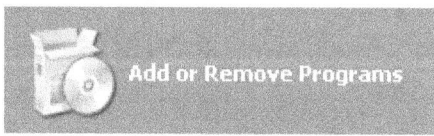

Fig. 4.12

2.3 Click on Add/Remove Windows Components.

Fig. 4.13

2.4 You will see the Windows Components Wizard. Tick the box next to Internet Information Services (IIS).

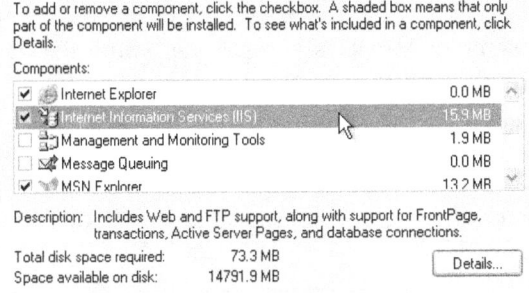

Fig. 4.14

Click on the Next button.

2.5 You will be asked to insert your Windows XP installer disk.

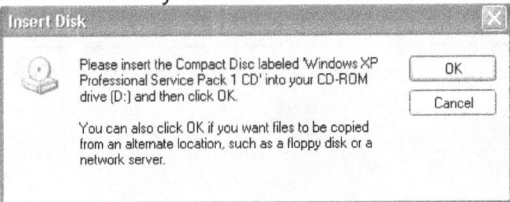

Fig. 4.15

2.6 The setup Wizard will copy and install the necessary files from the CD.

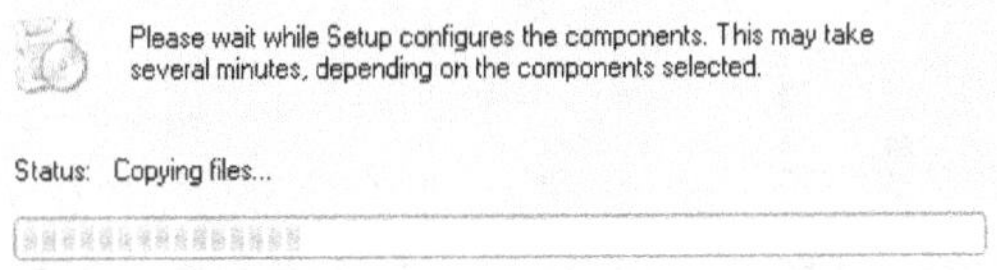

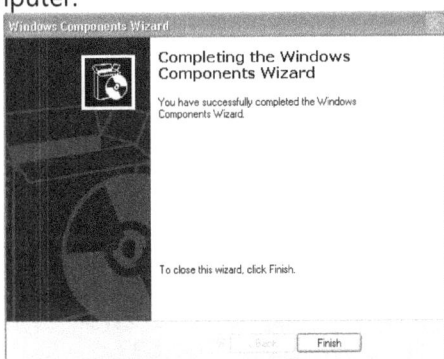

Fig. 4.16

Note: If the Windows XP Installer screen appears (which auto-runs from the Installer CD), click on the Exit button.

2.7 After a few minutes you will be advised that the IIS components have been installed
Click on the Finish button. Now you have successfully completed installation of ISS on your computer.

Fig. 4.17

2.8 Close the Add/Remove Software window

4.3 ASP Syntax, Variables, Procedures

4.3.1 ASP Syntax

- Server-side scripts resembles HTML tags. However some things about the ASP tag that sets it apart from normal HTML tags:

  1. An opening ASP tag is <% while an HTML tag normally looks like <tagname>

  2. A closing ASP tag looks like %> while an HTML tag normally looks like </tagname>

  3. ASP code can occurr anywhere, even within an HTML tag opening tag like this:

```
<html>
<body>
<% response.write("Hello World!") %>
</body>
</html>
```

- To use scripting language other than VBScript, We need to insert a language specification at the top of the ASP page:

```
<%@ language="javascript" %>
<html>
<body>
<%
....
%>
```

- Server scripts are executed on the server, and can contain any expressions, statements, procedures, or operators valid for the scripting language you prefer to use.

The response.write Command

- The response.write command is used to write output to a browser.

- There are two methods to write response.write

Method 1:

Program 4.1:

```
<!DOCTYPE html>
<html>
<body>
<%
response.write("Hello Sir!")
%>
</body>
</html>
```

Output:

```
Hello Sir!
```

Method 2

Program 4.2:

```
<!DOCTYPE html>
<html>
<body>
<%
="Hello Sir!"
    %>
</body>
</html>
```

Output:

```
Hello Sir!
```

Using VBScript in ASP

* You can use several scripting languages in ASP. However, the default scripting language is VBScript:

Program 4.3:

```
<!DOCTYPE html>
<html>
<body>
<%
response.write("Hello World!")
%>
</body>
</html>
```

Output:

```
Hello World!
```

* We can add comments to our VBScript code using a single quote.

   For example:

   'this is a comment

Using JavaScript in ASP

* To set JavaScript as the default scripting language for a particular page you must insert a language specification at the top of the page:

Program 4.4:

```
<%@ language="javascript"%>
<!DOCTYPE html>
<html>
<body>
<%
Response.Write("Hello World!")
%>
</body>
</html>
```

- JavaScript is case sensitive, You will have to write your ASP code with uppercase letters and lowercase letters when the language requires it.

- ASP is shipped with VBScript and JScript (Microsoft's implementation of JavaScript). If you want to script in another language, like PERL, REXX, or Python, you will have to install script engines for them.

Using HTML tags in ASP

You can use HTML tags for formatting

Program 4.5:

In below example we have used HTML tags to show heading<h2></h2> and to set text colour.

```
<!DOCTYPE html>
<html>
<body>
<%
response.write("<h2>Active Server Pages</h2>")
%>
<%
response.write("<p style='color:#0000ff'>This text is styled with the
style attribute!</p>")
%>
</body>
</html>
```

ASP Operators:

- ASP is programmed in VBScript by default, thus ASP's operators are VBScript operators by default.

- The mathematical operators in ASP are similar to many other programming languages. However, ASP does not support shortcut operators like ++, --, +=, etc.

Operator	English	Example	Result
+	Addition	myNum = 3 + 4	myNum = 7
-	Subtraction	myNum = 4 - 1	myNum = 3
*	Multiplication	myNum = 3 * 2	myNum = 6
/	Division	myNum = 9 / 3	myNum = 3
^	Exponential	myNum = 2 ^ 4	myNum = 16
Mod	Modulus	myNum = 23 Mod 10	myNum = 3
-	Negation	myNum = – 10	myNum = – 10
\	Integer Division	myNum = 9 \ 3	myNum = 3

Comparison Operators:

- Comparison operators are used when you want to compare two values to make a decision. Comparison operators are most commonly used in conjunction with "If...Then" and "do...While" statements, otherwise known as conditional statements. The items that are most often compared are numbers. The result of a comparison operator is either TRUE or FALSE.

Operator	English	Example	Result
=	Equal To	4 = 3	False
<	Less Than	4 < 3	False
>	Greater Than	4 > 3	True
<=	Less Than Or Equal To	4 <= 3	False
>=	Greater Than Or Equal To	4 >= 3	True
<>	Not Equal To	4 <>3	True

Logical Operators:

- A logical operator is used for complex statements that must make decisions based on one or more of these truth values.

Operator	English	Example	Result
And	Both Must be TRUE	True and False	False
Or	One Must be TRUE	True or False	True
Not	Flips Truth Value	Not True	False

string Operators:

- The only string operator is the string concatenation operator "&" that takes two strings and combine them together to form a new string. An example would be string1 = "Tim" and string2 = " is a Hero". The following code would combine these two strings into one: string3 = string1 & string2

Operator	English	Example	Result
&	String Concatenation	string4 = "Bob" & " runs"	string4 = "Bob runs"

ASP - if statement:

- ASP If Statement it is actually the same as programming a VBScript If Statement.

if statement syntax:

- ASP's If Statement is slightly different than the If Statement implementation in most other languages. There are no brackets, or curly braces, nor are there any parenthesis. Rather the beginning of the code to be executed in the If Statement when its true is marked with Then and the end of the If Statement is plainly marked with End If. Below is a very basic If Statement that will always be True.

Program 4.6:

```
<%
Dim myNum
myNum = 6
If myNum = 6 Then
    Response.Write("Variable myNum = 6")
End If
%>
```

Output:

```
Variable myNum = 6
```

- You might notice that the "=" operator is used to both set the value of myNum to 6 at first, then it is used to compare myNum to 6 in our If Statement. It is used to explain that in ASP you cannot set the value of variables within If Statements, which means that the "=" can only compare.

ASP - if else conditional statement:

- ASP IF Else works Just like other programming languages. Below is an example that will always be false, so that the Else portion of the If Statement is always executed.

Program 4.7:

```
<%
Dim myNum
myNum = 23
If myNum = 6 Then
    Response.Write("Variable myNum = 6")
Else
    Response.Write("Variable myNum = " & myNum)
End If
%>
```

Output:

```
Variable myNum = 23
```

Asp - elseif conditional statement:

- In ASP you can check for multiple conditions with ElseIf, which is the name given to an If Statement that depends on another If Statement.

- Below is an example whose second if statement (elseif) is always true.

Program 4.8:

```
<%
Dim myFastfood
myFastfood = "JBox"
If myFastfood = "McD's" Then
    Response.Write("Happy Meal!")
ElseIf myFastfood = "Dominos" Then
    Response.Write("Cheese Pizza!")
Else
    Response.Write("Foot-long turkey sub.")
End If
%>
```

Output:

```
Cheese Pizza!
```

ASP select case:

- ASP uses the Select Case statement to check for multiple Is Equal To"=" conditions of a single variable.For example
- The variable that appears immediately after Select Case is what will be checked against the list of case statements. These case statements are contained within the Select Case block of code. Below is an ASP Select Case example that only checks for integer values.

Program 4.9:

```
<%
Dim myNum
myNum = 5
Select Case myNum
    Case 2
        Response.Write("myNum is Two")
    Case 3
        Response.Write("myNum is Three")
    Case 5
        Response.Write("myNum is Five")
    Case Else
        Response.Write("myNum is " & myNum)
End Select
%>
```

Output:

```
myNum is Five
```

ASP select case - case else:

- In the select case example, you might have seen there was a case that was referred to as "Case Else". This case is actually a catch all option for every case that does not fit into the defined cases.
- It is a good programming practice to always include the catch all Else case. Below we have an example that always executes the Else case.

Program 4.10:

```
<%
Dim myNum
myNum = 454
Select Case myNum
    Case 2
        Response.Write("myNum is Two")
    Case 3
        Response.Write("myNum is Three")
    Case 5
        Response.Write("myNum is Five")
    Case Else
        Response.Write("myNum is " & myNum)
End Select
%>
```

Output:

```
myNum is 454
```

select case with string variables:

- In previous examples we have used integers in our Select Case statements, but you can also use a string as the variable to be used in the statement. Below we Select against a string.

Program 4.11:

```
<%
Dim myPet
myPet = "Tiger"
Select Case myPet
    Case "dog"
        Response.Write("I own a dog")
    Case "cat"
        Response.Write("I do not own a Tiger")
    Case Else
        Response.Write("I once had a cute cat")
End Select
%>
```

Output:

```
I do not own a Tiger
```

4.3.1 Variables

- A variable is used to store information.

Declaring a variable in ASP:

- In ASP you declare a variable with the use of the Dim keyword, which is short for Dimension. Dimension in computer terms refers to space in computer memory.
- Variables can be declared one at a time or all at once. Below is an example of both methods.

```
<%
'Single Variable Declarations
Dim myVar1
Dim myVar2
'Multiple Variable Declarations
Dim myVar6, myVar7, myVar8
%>
```

- ASP uses VBScript by default and so it also uses VBScripts variable naming conventions. These rules are:
  1. Variable name must start with an alphabetic character (A through Z or a through z)
  2. Variables cannot contain a period
  3. Variables cannot be longer than 255 characters (don't think that'll be a problem!)
  4. Variables must be unique in the scope in which it is declared (Basically, don't declare the same variable name in one script and you will be OK).

Assigning values to asp variables:

- Assigning values in ASP is simple enough, just use the equals "=" operator. Below we have set a variable equal to a number and a separate variable equal to a string.

Program 4.12:

```
<%
'Single Variable Declarations
Dim myString, myNum, myGarbage
myNum = 20
myString = "Hello User"
myGarbage = 99
myGarbage = "I changed my variable"
Response.Write("myNum = " & myNum & "<br />")
Response.Write("myString = " & myString & "<br />")
Response.Write("myGarbage = " & myGarbage & "<br />")
%>
```

Output:

```
myNum = 20   myString = Hello User
myGarbage = I changed my variable
```

Session Variables

- Session variables are used to store information about ONE single user, and are available to all pages in one application. Typically, information stored in session variables are name, id, and preferences.

Application Variables

- Application variables are also available to all pages in one application. Application variables are used to store information about ALL users in one specific application.

Program 4.13:

Assign your name to variable and display it.

```
<!DOCTYPE html>
<html>
<body>
<%
dim name
name="Sachin Joshi"
response.write("My name is: " & name)
%>
</body>
</html>
```

Lifetime of Variables

- A variable declared outside a procedure can be accessed and changed by any script in the ASP file.

- A variable declared inside a procedure is created and destroyed every time the procedure is executed. No scripts outside the procedure can access or change the variable.

- To declare variables accessible to more than one ASP file, declare them as session variables or application variables.

4.3.3 ASP Procedures

- Procedures are used for effective programming.

- In ASP you can call a JavaScript procedure from a VBScript and vice versa.

- A procedure can be included in the body of an HTML but to separate the script behavior from the rest of the file, it is usually a good idea to include the procedures in the head section of the file. The advantage of including a script in the head section is that it is more likely to be interpreted before the section it refers to is reached.

Program 4.14:

```
<!DOCTYPE html>
<html>
<head>
<%
sub vbproc(num1,num2)
response.write(num1*num2)
end sub
%>
</head>
<body>
<p>You can call a procedure like this:</p>
<p>Result: <%call vbproc(5,4)%></p>
<p>Or, like this:</p>
<p>Result: <%vbproc 5,4%></p>
</body>
</html>
```

Output:

```
You can call a procedure like this:
Result: 20
Or, like this:
Result: 20
```

- To write the procedure/function in another scripting language Insert the <%@ language="language" %> line above the <html> tag.
- There are two kinds of procedures in VBScript: A sub procedure and a function.

1. Sub Procedures

- A sub procedure is a section of code that carries a task but doesn't give back a result.
- The Sub procedure contains a group of VBScript statements which are executed when the sub is called. The Sub may take arguments but does not return a value. A sub is defined as follows:

```
Sub sub_name
    statement group
End Sub
```

- To differentiate the name of the sub procedure with any other regular name, it must be followed by an opening and closing parentheses.
- We can declare variables in the procedure.Using declared variables, the above procedure can be written as follows:

```
Sub DisplayFullName()
Dim FirstName, LastName
Dim FullName
FullName = FirstName & " " & LastName

End Sub
```

Calling a Procedure

- After creating a procedure, you can call it from another procedure, function, or control's event in the body section of an HTML file.

- To call a simple procedure such as the earlier DisplayFullName, you can just write the name of the sub procedure

- In the following example, the above DisplayFullName sub procedure is called when the user clicks the Detail section of the form:

```
Sub Detailer()
DisplayFullName
End Sub
```

- If you want the procedure to be accessed immediately as soon as the page displays, you can assign its name to the onLoad() event of the body tag.

2. Functions

Creating a Function

- A function is an assignment that a piece of code can take care for the functionality of a database.

- The main difference between a sub procedure and a function procedure is that a function can return a value.

- A function is created like a sub procedure with a few more rules.

- The creation of function starts with the Function keyword and closes with End Function. Here is an example:

```
Function FindFullName()
End Function
```

- The name of the function follows the same rules as sub procedures.

- To implement a function, remember that it is supposed to return a value. In the body of the function, describe what it is supposed to do. to return the right value, assign the desired value to the name of the function. Here is an example:

```
Function CalculateArea(Radius)
CalculateArea = Radius * Radius * 3.14159
End Function
```

Calling a Function

- If you want to use the return value of a function in an event or another function, assign the name of the function to the appropriate local variable.

- Make sure you include the argument(s) of the function between parentheses.

4.4 ASP Forms

- With ASP you can process information gathered by an HTML form and use ASP code to make decisions based on this information to create dynamic web pages.

The Request.Form Collection

- When you have an HTML form, like following:

```
<FORM METHOD="post" ACTION="process.asp">
<INPUT TYPE="text" NAME="FirstName">
<INPUT TYPE="text" NAME="LastName">
<INPUT TYPE="radio" NAME="Sex" VALUE="M">
<INPUT TYPE="radio" NAME="Sex" VALUE="F">
<TEXTAREA NAME="Address">
</TEXTAREA>
<INPUT TYPE="submit" VALUE="Send">
</FORM>
```

- You have within it a number of elements, each with a unique name. The fields in the form above are FirstName (Text), LastName (Text), Sex (Option: M or F), and Address (Multiline Text). The last input type is "submit" that is a button required to submit the user input to your script.

- On clicking the Submit button, the contents of each of these fields are posted to the script that you pecified in the FORM Action attribute. In the above example, it is

    ```
    "process.asp".
    ```

- The form processing script can access these input values as below:

    ```
    Request.Form ("FirstName")
    ```

    ```
    Request.Form ("LastName")
    ```

- Once you have this value, you can process it as you need – enter it into a database, mail it to yourself, - anything you want.

- Remember that the METHOD specified in the FORM tag must be POST if you want to use the Request.Form collection to process it.

The Request.QueryString Collection

- While surfing you may have seen page URL's like the one below:

    ```
    http://www.samplegreetings.com/show.asp?CardID=128762173676
    ```

- This is a direct link to a card that your friend sent you. You just need to click on the link, and the card shows up. You do not need to identify yourself or enter any code number anywhere. All the information that the site needs, is encoded in the string,

```
CardID=128762173676
```

- This is known as the Query String and forms part of a URL.
- You can pass multiple values too, using something like:

```
Page.asp?FirstName=Manas&LastName=Patil&Sex=M
```

- The Request.QueryString Collection helps you sort this stuff out and extract only what you need.
- So to access the data contained in the variable FirstName above, you would use:

```
Request.QueryString ("FirstName")
```

- This again, is a regular variable that you can assign to another, or do arithmetic on.
- The Request.QueryString collection gives you access to yet another class of variables – those passed via a FORM with it's METHOD = "get."
- However, there is a limit to the amount of data that can be passed on via the QueryString and you are expected to use a form for more data.

GET and POST

- There are two ways we may get info from users by using a form: GET and POST methods. Additionally, GET method may be used for other porpoises as a regular link. Let´s check both methods.

POST method

- This method will be indicated in the form we are using to get information from user as shown in the example below:

```
<form method="POST" action="">
Your name<BR>
<input type=text name=thename size=15><BR>
Your age<BR>
<input type=text name=theage size=15><BR>
<input type=submit  value="Send info">
</form>
```

Your name

Your age

Send info

- When submitting the form we will visit the URL bellow (will be different when using GET method):

```
http://www.samplegreeting/getinfo.asp
```

- When getting information from the form in the response page we will use **Request.Form** command.

Code	Output
`<%=Request.form %>`	thename=Dhruv&theage=30
`<%=Request.form ("`**`thename`**`")%>`	Dhruv
`<%=Request.form ("`**`theage`**`")%>`	30

`<%`
`Theage=Request.form ("theage")`
`Thename=Request.form ("`**`thename`**`")`
`Response.write("Hi " & Thename & ",`
`I know you are " & Theage & " years`
`old")`
`%>`
	Hi Dhruv, I know you are 30 years old

GET method

- This method may be used exactly as in the example above, but the URL we will visit after submission will be different.

- In the example bellow we have replace the word "POST" and "GET" has been written instead.

```
<form method="GET" action="getandpostgetinfo.asp">
Your name<BR>
<input type=text name=thename size=15><BR>
Your age<BR>
<input type=text name=theage size=15><BR>
<input type=submit  value="Send info">
</form>
```

- When submitting the form we will visit the URL bellow (will be different when using GET method):

        http://www. samplegreeting/getinfo.asp?**thename**=Dhruv&**theage**=30

- When getting information from the form in the response page we will use**Request.Querystring** command.

Code	Output
`<% =Request.Querystring %>`	thename=Dhruv&theage=30
`<% =Request.Querystring ("`**`thename`**`") %>`	Dhruv
`<% =Request.Querystring ("`**`theage`**`") %>`	30

contd. ...

`<%`	Hi Dhruv, I know you are 30 years old

```
Theage=Request.Querystring
("theage")
Thename=Request.Querystring
("thename")
Response.write("Hi " & Thename & ", I
know  you  are  "  &  Theage  &  "  years
old")
%>
```

4.5 ASP Session and Cookies

4.5.1 Session

- When you are working with an application on your computer, you open it, do some changes and then you close it. This is much like a Session. The computer knows who you are. It knows when you open the application and when you close it. However, on the internet there is one problem: the web server does not know who you are and what you do, because the HTTP address doesn't maintain state.

- ASP solves this problem by creating a unique cookie for each user. The cookie is sent to the user's computer and it contains information that identifies the user. This interface is called the **Session object**.

- The Session object stores information about, or change settings for a user session.

- Variables stored in a Session object hold information about one single user, and are available to all pages in one application. Common information stored in session variables are name, id, and preferences. The server creates a new Session object for each new user, and destroys the Session object when the session expires.

- A session starts when:
  - A new user requests an ASP file, and the Global.asa file includes a Session_OnStart procedure
  - A value is stored in a Session variable
  - A user requests an ASP file, and the Global.asa file uses the <object> tag to instantiate an object with session scope

- A session ends if a user has not requested or refreshed a page in the application for a specified period. By default, this is 20 minutes.

- If you want to set a timeout interval that is shorter or longer than the default, use the **Timeout** property.

- The example below sets a timeout interval of 5 minutes:

```
<%
Session.Timeout=5
%>
```

- Use the **Abandon** method to end a session immediately:

```
<%
Session.Abandon
%>
```

The only disadvantage of using session is

- The main problem with sessions is WHEN they should end. We do not know if the user's last request was the final one or not. So we do not know how long we should keep the session "alive". Waiting too long for an idle session uses up resources on the server, but if the session is deleted too soon the user has to start all over again because the server has deleted all the information. Finding the right timeout interval can be difficult.

Store and Retrieve Session Variables

- The most important thing about the Session object is that you can store variables in it.
- The example below will set the Session variable username to " mickey mouse" and the Session variable age to "50":

```
<%
Session("username")=" mickey mouse"
Session("age")=50
%>
```

- When the value is stored in a session variable it can be reached from ANY page in the ASP application:

```
Welcome <%Response.Write(Session("username"))%>
```

- The line above returns: "Welcome mickey mouse".
- You can also store user preferences in the session object, and then access that preference to choose what page to return to the user.
- The example below specifies a text-only version of the page if the user has a low screen resolution:

```
<%If Session("screenres")="low" Then%>
   This is the text version of the page
<%Else%>
   This is the multimedia version of the page
<%End If%>
```

Remove Session Variables

- The Contents collection contains all session variables.

- It is possible to remove a session variable with the Remove method.
- The example below removes the session variable "sale" if the value of the session variable "age" is lower than 18:

```
<%
If Session.Contents("age")<18 then
   Session.Contents.Remove("sale")
End If
%>
```

- To remove all variables in a session, use the RemoveAll method:

```
<%
Session.Contents.RemoveAll()
%>
```

Loop Through the Contents Collection:

- The Contents collection contains all session variables. You can loop through the Contents collection, to see what's stored in it:

Program 4.15:

```
<%
Session("username")=" mickey mouse"
Session("age")=50
dim i
For Each i in Session.Contents
   Response.Write(i & "<br>")
Next
%>
```

Output:

```
username
age
```

- If you do not know the number of items in the Contents collection, you can use the Count property:

Program 4.16:

```
<%
dim i
dim j
j=Session.Contents.Count
Response.Write("Session variables: " & j)
For i=1 to j
Response.Write(Session.Contents(i) & "<br>")
Next
%>
```

Output:

```
Session variables: 2
mickey mouse
50
```

Loop through the StaticObjects Collection

- You can loop through the StaticObjects collection, to see the values of all objects stored in the Session object:

```
<%
dim i
For Each i in Session.StaticObjects
  Response.Write(i & "<br>")
Next
%>
```

4.5.2 Cookies

- A cookie is often used to recognize a user. A cookie is a small file that the server embeds on the user's computer. Each time the same computer requests a page with a browser, it will send the cookie too. With ASP, you can both create and retrieve cookie values.

Create Cookie

- The "Response.Cookies" command is used to create cookies.The Response.Cookies command must appear BEFORE the <html> tag.

- In the example below, we will create a cookie named "firstname" and assign the value "Ahana" to it:

```
<%
Response.Cookies("firstname")="Ahana"
%>
```

- It is also possible to assign properties to a cookie, like setting a date when the cookie should expire:

```
<%
Response.Cookies("firstname")="Ahana"
Response.Cookies("firstname").Expires=#May 10,2016#
%>
```

Retrive Cookie Value

- The "Request.Cookies" command is used to retrieve a cookie value.

- In the example below, we retrieve the value of the cookie named "firstname" and display it on a page:

Program 4.17:

```
<%
fname=Request.Cookies("firstname")
response.write("Firstname=" & fname)
%>
```

Output:

```
Firstname=Ahana
```

A Cookie with Keys

- If a cookie contains a collection of multiple values just like array of cookies, we say that the cookie has Keys.

- In the example below, we will create a cookie collection named "user". The "user" cookie has Keys that contains information about a user:

```
<%
Response.Cookies("user")("firstname")="Priya"
Response.Cookies("user")("lastname")="Pande"
Response.Cookies("user")("country")="India"
Response.Cookies("user")("age")="25"
%>
```

Read all Cookies

- Look at the following code:

```
<%
Response.Cookies("firstname")="Ahana"
Response.Cookies("user")("firstname")="Priya"
Response.Cookies("user")("lastname")="Pande"
Response.Cookies("user")("country")="India"
Response.Cookies("user")("age")="25"
%>
```

- Assume that your server has sent all the cookies above to a user.

- Now we want to read all the cookies sent to a user. The example below shows how to do it. The code below checks if a cookie has Keys with the HasKeys property.

Program 4.18:

```
<!DOCTYPE html>
<html>
<body>
<%
dim x,y
for each x in Request.Cookies
  response.write("<p>")
  if Request.Cookies(x).HasKeys then
    for each y in Request.Cookies(x)
      response.write(x & ":" & y & "=" & Request.Cookies(x)(y))
```

```
      response.write("<br>")
    next
  else
    Response.Write(x & "=" & Request.Cookies(x) & "<br>")
  end if
  response.write "</p>"
next
%>
</body>
</html>
```

Output:

```
firstname=Ahana
user:firstname=Priya
user:lastname=Pande
user:country=India
user:age=25
```

- If your application deals with browsers that do not support cookies, you will have to use other methods to pass information from one page to another in your application. There are two ways of doing this:

1. Add parameters to a URL

You can add parameters to a URL:

```
<a href="welcome.asp?fname=John&lname=Smith">Go to Welcome Page</a>
```

And retrieve the values in the "welcome.asp" file like this:

```
<%
fname=Request.querystring("fname")
lname=Request.querystring("lname")
response.write("<p>Hello " & fname & " " & lname & "!</p>")
response.write("<p>Welcome to my Web site!</p>")
%>
```

2. Use a form

- You can use a form. The form passes the user input to "welcome.asp" when the user clicks on the Submit button:

```
<form method="post" action="welcome.asp">
First Name: <input type="text" name="fname" value="">
Last Name: <input type="text" name="lname" value="">
<input type="submit" value="Submit">
</form>
```

- Retrieve the values in the "welcome.asp" file like this:

```
<%
fname=Request.form("fname")
lname=Request.form("lname")
response.write("<p>Hello " & fname & " " & lname & "!</p>")
response.write("<p>Welcome to my Web site!</p>")
%>
```

4.6 ASP Global.asa

- The Global.asa file is an optional file that can contain declarations of objects, variables, and methods that can be accessed by every page in an ASP application.

- All valid browser scripts (JavaScript, VBScript, JScript, PerlScript, etc.) can be used within Global.asa.

- The Global.asa file must be stored in the root directory of the ASP application, and each application can only have one Global.asa file.

- The Global.asa file can contain only the following:
  - Application events
  - Session events
  - <object> declarations
  - TypeLibrary declarations
  - the #include directive

Events in Global.asa

- In Global.asa you can tell the application and session objects what to do when the application/session starts and what to do when the application/session ends. The code for this is addded in event handlers. The Global.asa file can contain four types of events:

  1. **Application_OnStart** - Occurs when the FIRST user calls the first page in an ASP application. This event occurs after the Web server is restarted or after the Global.asa file is edited. The "Session_OnStart" event occurs immediately after this event.

  2. **Session_OnStart** - This event occurs EVERY time a NEW user requests his or her first page in the ASP application.

  3. **Session_OnEnd** - This event occurs EVERY time a user ends a session. A user-session ends after a page has not been requested by the user for a specified time (by default this is 20 minutes).

4. **Application_OnEnd** - This event occurs after the LAST user has ended the session. Typically, this event occurs when a Web server stops. This procedure is used to clean up settings after the Application stops, like delete records or write information to text files.

- A Global.asa file could look something like this:

```
<script language="vbscript" runat="server">
sub Application_OnStart
'some code here
end sub
sub Application_OnEnd
'some code here
end sub
sub Session_OnStart
'some code here
end sub
sub Session_OnEnd
'some code here
end sub
</script>
```

- Because we cannot use the ASP script delimiters (<% and %>) to insert scripts in the Global.asa file, we put subroutines inside an HTML <script> element.

<object> Declarations

- It is possible to create objects with session or application scope in Global.asa by using the <object> tag.

  Note: The <object> tag should be outside the <script> tag

  Syntax:

```
<object runat="server" scope="scope" id="id"
                        {progid="progID"|classid="classID"}>
....
</object>
```

Parameter	Description
scope	Sets the scope of the object (either Session or Application)
id	Specifies a unique id for the object
ProgID	An id associated with a class id. The format for ProgID is [Vendor.]Component[.Version] Either ProgID or ClassID must be specified.
ClassID	Specifies a unique id for a COM class object. Either ProgID or ClassID must be specified.

Examples:

The first example creates an object of session scope named "MyAd" by using the ProgID parameter:

```
<object runat="server" scope="session" id="MyAd"
                                        progid="MSWC.AdRotator">
</object>
```

```
The  second  example  creates  an  object  of  application  scope  named
"MyConnection" by using the ClassID parameter:
```

```
<object runat="server" scope="application" id="MyConnection"
classid="Clsid:8AZ4067A-B3FC-11CF-A560-00A0C9081C21">
</object>
```

- The objects declared in the Global.asa file can be used by any script in the application:

```
GLOBAL.ASA:
<object          runat="server"          scope="session"          id="MyAd"
progid="MSWC.AdRotator">
</object>
```

```
You  could  reference  the  object  "MyAd"  from  any  page  in  the  ASP
application:
```

```
SOME .ASP FILE:
<%=MyAd.GetAdvertisement("/banners/adrot.txt")%>
```

TypeLibrary Declarations

- A TypeLibrary is a container for the contents of a DLL file corresponding to a COM object. By including a call to the TypeLibrary in the Global.asa file, the constants of the COM object can be accessed, and errors can be better reported by the ASP code. If your Web application relies on COM objects that have declared data types in type libraries, you can declare the type libraries in Global.asa.

Syntax:

```
<!--METADATA TYPE="TypeLib"
file="filename" uuid="id" version="number" lcid="localeid"
-->
```

Parameter	Description
file	Specifies an absolute path to a type library.
	Either the file parameter or the uuid parameter is required
uuid	Specifies a unique identifier for the type library.
	Either the file parameter or the uuid parameter is required
version	Optional. Used for selecting version. If the requested version is not found, then the most recent version is used
lcid	Optional. The locale identifier to be used for the type library

Error Values

- The server can return one of the following error messages:

Error Code	Description
ASP 0222	Invalid type library specification
ASP 0223	Type library not found
ASP 0224	Type library cannot be loaded
ASP 0225	Type library cannot be wrapped

- METADATA tags can appear anywhere in the Global.asa file (both inside and outside <script> tags). However, it is recommended that METADATA tags appear near the top of the Global.asa file.

Limitations of Global.asa

- Limitations on what you can include in the Global.asa file:
  - o You cannot display text written in the Global.asa file. This file can't display information
  - o You can only use Server and Application objects in the Application_OnStart and Application_OnEnd subroutines. In the Session_OnEnd subroutine, you can use Server, Application, and Session objects. In the Session_OnStart subroutine you can use any built-in object

Implementing subroutines in Global.asa

- Global.asa is often used to initialize variables.
- The example below shows how to detect the exact time a visitor first arrives on a Web site. The time is stored in a Session variable named "started", and the value of the "started" variable can be accessed from any ASP page in the application:

```
<script language="vbscript" runat="server">
sub Session_OnStart
Session("started")=now()
end sub
</script>
```

- Global.asa can also be used to control page access.
- The example below shows how to redirect every new visitor to another page, in this case to a page called "newpage1.asp":

```
<script language="vbscript" runat="server">
sub Session_OnStart
Response.Redirect("newpage1.asp")
end sub
</script>
```

- You can include functions in the Global.asa file.
- In the example below the Application_OnStart subroutine occurs when the Web server starts. Then the Application_OnStart subroutine calls another subroutine named "getcustomers". The "getcustomers" subroutine opens a database and retrieves a record set from the "customers" table. The record set is assigned to an array, where it can be accessed from any ASP page without querying the database:

```
<script language="vbscript" runat="server">
sub Application_OnStart
getcustomers
end sub
sub getcustomers
set conn=Server.CreateObject("ADODB.Connection")
conn.Provider="Microsoft.Jet.OLEDB.4.0"
conn.Open "c:/webdata/northwind.mdb"
set rs=conn.execute("select name from customers")
Application("customers")=rs.GetRows
rs.Close
conn.Close
end sub
</script>
```

Example of Global.asa

- In this example we will create a Global.asa file that counts the number of current visitors.
  - The Application_OnStart sets the Application variable "visitors" to 0 when the server starts
  - The Session_OnStart subroutine adds one to the variable "visitors" every time a new visitor arrives
  - The Session_OnEnd subroutine subtracts one from "visitors" each time this subroutine is triggered
- The Global.asa file:

```
<script language="vbscript" runat="server">
Sub Application_OnStart
Application("visitors")=0
End Sub
Sub Session_OnStart
Application.Lock
```

```
Application("visitors")=Application("visitors")+1
Application.UnLock
End Sub
Sub Session_OnEnd
Application.Lock
Application("visitors")=Application("visitors")-1
Application.UnLock
End Sub
</script>
```

- To display the number of current visitors in an ASP file:

```
<!DOCTYPE html>
<html>
<head>
</head>
<body>
<p>There   are   <%response.write(Application("visitors"))%>   online
now!</p>
</body>
</html>
```

4.7 ASP Objects- Request, Response, Application, Server

- ASP is a scripting environment revolving around its Object Model. An Object Model is simply a hierarchy of objects that you may use to get services from. In the case of ASP, all commands are issued to certain inbuilt objects, that correspond to the Client Request, Client Response, the Server, the Session and the Application respectively. All of these are for global use

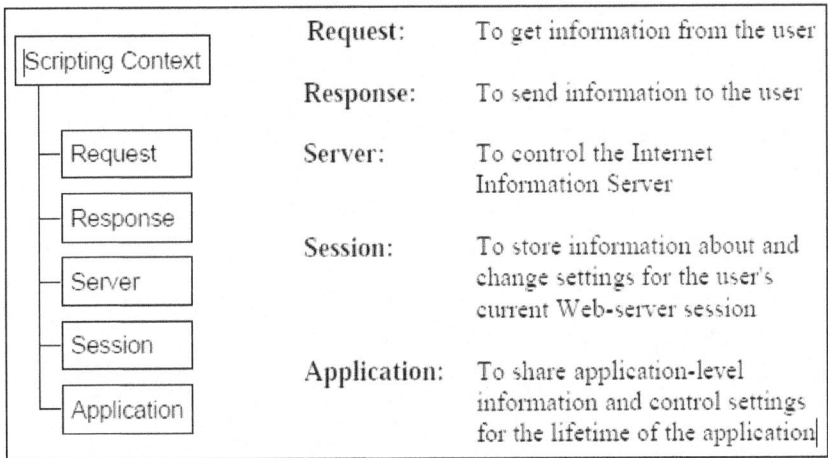

Fig. 4.18: ASP Objects

- The Request and Response objects contain collections (bits of information that are accessed in the same way). Objects use methods to do some type of procedure (if you know any object-oriented programming language, you know already what a method is) and properties to store any of the object's attributes (such as color, font, or size).

4.7.1 Request object

- The Request object retrieves the values that the client browser passed to the server during an HTTP request.

Syntax: `Request[.collection|property|method](variable)`

Collections:

- **ClientCertificate**

  To get the certification fields from the request issued by the Web browser.

- **Cookies**

  The values of cookies sent in the HTTP request.

- **Form**

  The values of form elements in the HTTP request body.

- **QueryString**

  The values of variables in the HTTP query string.

- **ServerVariables**

  The values of predetermined environment variables.

  Properties

- **TotalBytes**

  Read-only. Specifies the total number of bytes the client is sending in the body of the request.

Methods:

BinaryRead

- Retrieves data sent to the server from the client as part of a POST request.
- Variable parameters are strings that specify the item to be retrieved from a collection or to be used as input for a method or property.
- All variables can be accessed directly by calling Request(variable) without the collection name.
- If a variable with the same name exists in more than one collection, the Request object returns the first instance that the object encounters.
- It is strongly recommended that when referring to members of the ServerVariables collection the full name be used.
- For example, rather than Request (AUTH_USER) use Request.ServerVariables (AUTH_USER).

4.7.2 Response Object

- The Response object is used to send information to the user. It supports only Cookies as a collection (to set cookie values). It's object also supports a number of properties and methods.

  Syntax: `Response.collection|property|method`

- **Collections:**

  o **Cookies:** Specifies cookie values. Using this collection, you can set cookie values.

- **Properties of Response Object:**

Properties	Description
Buffer	Indicates whether page output is buffered.
CacheControl	Determines whether proxy servers are able to cache the output generated by ASP.
Charset	Appends the name of the character set to the content-type header.
ContentType	Specifies the HTTP content type for the response
Expires	Specifies the length of time before a page cached on a browser expires.
ExpiresAbsolute	Specifies the date and time on which a page cached on a browser expires.
IsClientConnected	Indicates whether the client has disconnected from the server.
Pics	Adds the value of a PICS label to the pics-label field of the response header/
Status	The value of the status line returned by the server.

Methods of Response Object:

Method	Description
AddHeader	Sets the HTML header name to value.
AppendToLog	Adds a string to the end of the Web server log entry for this request.
BinaryWrite	Writes the given information to the current HTTP output without any character-set conversion.
Clear	Erases any buffered HTML output.

contd. ...

End	Stops processing the .asp file and returns the current result.
Flush	Sends buffered output immediately.
Redirect	Sends a redirect message to the browser, causing it to attempt to connect to a different URL.

Write	Writes a variable to the current HTTP output as a string. This can be done by using the construct
	
	`Response.Write("Apple")`
	
	or the shortcut command
	
	`<%="Apple" %>`

4.7.3 Application Object

- The Application object can store information that can be perseved for the entire lifetime of an application (a group of pages with a common root). Generally, this is the total time that the IIS server is running. This makes it a great place to store information that has to exist for more than one user (such as a page counter).
- The drawback of this is that since this object isn't created anew for each user, errors that may not show up when the code is called once may show up when it is called 10,000 times in a row.
- In addition, because the Application object is shared by all the users, It is hard to implement threading.
- You can use the Application object to share information among all users of a given application.
- An ASP-based application is defined as all the .asp files in a virtual directory and its subdirectories. Because the Application object can be shared by more than one user, there are Lock and Unlock methods to ensure that multiple users do not try to alter a property simultaneously.

  Syntax: `Application.method`

Collections of Application Object:

Collections	Description
Contents	Contains all of the items that have been added to the Application through script commands.
StaticObjects	Contains all of the objects added to the session with the <OBJECT> tag.
Lock	The Lock method prevents other clients from modifying Application object properties.
Unlock	The Unlock method allows other clients to modify Application object properties.

contd. ...

Events	Application_OnEnd
	Application_OnStart
	Scripts for the preceding events are declared in the global.asa file. For more information about these events and the global.asa file, see the Global.asa Reference.
Remarks	You can store values in the Application Collections. Information stored in the Application collections is available throughout the application and has application scope.

4.7.4 Server Object

The Server object provides access to methods and properties on the server. Most of these methods and properties serve as utility functions.

Syntax: `Server.property|method`

Properties of Server Object:

Properties	Description
ScriptTimeout	The amount of time that a script can run before it times out.

Methods of Server Object:

Methods	Description
CreateObject	Creates an instance of a server component. This component can be any component that you have installed on your server.
HTMLEncode	Applies HTML encoding to the specified string.
MapPath	Maps the specified virtual path, either the absolute path on the current server or the path relative to the current page, into a physical path.
URLEncode	Applies URL encoding rules, including escape characters, to the string.

4.8 ASP Database Related Operations - Insert, Retrive, Update, Delete

- In this topic we will look at a practical example of using ASP & ADO to create a database-driven website.
- Let us have a running database example. Consider a database for a class of students.
- The database schema is as follows:

Table: Student

ID	Student ID Numbers; also the primary key of the table.
FirstName	First name of the Student.
LastName	Last name of the Student.
DateofBirth	Birth date of the Student.
Email	Email address of the Student.

4.8.1 Retrieving Data

- The SQL SELECT statement will be used for retriving data from a table.
- Consider, we want to display a complete list of all the students in the class.
- Here is a complete page that lists out all the student records in a Table.

Program 4.18:

```
<HTML>
<HEAD>
<TITLE>Student Records</TITLE>
</HEAD>
<BODY>
<%
Dim DB
Set DB = Server.CreateObject ("ADODB.Connection")
DB.Open ("PROVIDER=Microsoft.Jet.OLEDB.4.0;DATA SOURCE=" +
"C:\Databases\Students.mdb")
Dim RS
Set RS = Server.CreateObject ("ADODB.Recordset")
RS.Open "SELECT * FROM Students", DB
If RS.EOF And RS.BOF Then
Response.Write "There are 0 records."
Else
RS.MoveFirst
While Not RS.EOF
Response.Write RS.Fields ("FirstName")
Response.Write RS.Fields ("LastName")
Response.Write "<HR>"
RS.MoveNext
Wend
End If
%>
</BODY>
</HTML>
```

- Let's look at the example line by line.
- The first few lines are the opening HTML tags for any page. There's no ASP code within them. The ASP block begins with the statement,

```
Dim DB
```

which is a declaration of the variable that we're gonna use later on. The second line,

```
Set DB = Server.CreateObject ("ADODB.Connection")
```

- It does the following two things:
- Firstly, the right-hand-side statement, Server.CreateObject() is used to create an instance of a COM object which has the ProgID ADODB.Connection.
- The Set Statement then assigns this reference to our variable, DB.
- Now, we use the object to connect to the database using a Connection String. The string,

```
"PROVIDER=Microsoft.Jet.OLEDB.4.0;DATA SOURCE=" +
"C:\Databases\Students.mdb"
```

is a string expression that tells our object where to locate the database, and more importantly, what type the database is (Please remember that this is a Connection String specific to Access 2000 databases. This example does not use ODBC.)

- If the DB.Open statement succeeds without an error, we have a valid connection to our database under consideration. Only after this we can begin to use the database.
- The immediate next lines,

```
Dim RS
Set RS = Server.CreateObject ("ADODB.Recordset")
```

- Serve the same purpose as the lines for creating the ADODB.Connection object. Only now we're creating an ADODB.Recordset

```
RS.Open "SELECT * FROM Students", DB
```

is possibly the most important line of this example. This line executes the query, and assigns the records returned to our Recordset.

- Now, assuming that all the records we want are in our Recordset object, we proceed to display it.

```
If RS.EOF And RS.BOF Then
Response.Write "There are 0 records."
```

- In any scenario where it is expected that no records might exist, this is an important error check to be performed. In case your query returned no results, the Recordset.BOF (beginning of file) & Recordset.EOF (end of file) are both True at the same time.
- So you can easily write an If-statement to perform a very basic error check.
- We shall look at the next few lines as a complete block of code.

```
Else
RS.MoveFirst
While Not RS.EOF
    Response.Write RS.Fields ("FirstName")
     Response.Write RS.Fields ("LastName")
      Response.Write "<HR>"
RS.MoveNext
Wend
End If
```

- **RS.MoveFirst** is a method that moves the record pointer to the First record. By default, it may or may not be positioned correctly, so it is essential to position it before you begin any operations.

- Then we have a While-loop that iterates through all the records contained in the Recordset. The condition that we check is that RS.EOF should be False.

- The moment it is True, it can be inferred that there are no more records to be found.

- **RS.Fields("FirstName")** retrieves the value of the "FirstName" field of the current record. We use a Response.Write statement to write it out to the page. Similarly, we write the RS.Fields ("LastName") after the first name.

- After you're done displaying, you must advance the record pointer to the next record, so you execute a RS.MoveNext. And that's all you wanted to do within the loop, so you end the loop now. Just write Wend and the loop ends.

4.8.2 Inserting Data

- Although SQL provides us the INSERT INTO statement for inserting records into a database, we are going to use the **ADODB.Recordset** object for doing this to make things simpler.

- So here's how you insert a new record:

Program 4.19:

```
<HTML>

<HEAD>

<TITLE>Student Records</TITLE>

</HEAD>

<BODY>

<%

Dim DB

Set DB = Server.CreateObject ("ADODB.Connection")

DB.Mode = adModeReadWrite

DB.Open ("PROVIDER=Microsoft.Jet.OLEDB.4.0;DATA SOURCE=" +

"C:\Databases\Students.mdb")

Dim RS

Set RS = Server.CreateObject ("ADODB.Recordset")

RS.Open "Students", DB, adOpenStatic, adLockPessimistic

RS.AddNew
```

```
RS ("FirstName") = "Manasi"

RS ("LastName") = "Patil"

RS ("Email") = "Manasi@ManasiPatil.com"

RS ("DateOfBirth") = CDate("4 Oct, 1988")

RS.Update

%>

</BODY>

</HTML>
```

- The first few lines are the same as in the previous example. Note that we set the **Connection.Mode** to **adModeReadWrite** since we are going to insert data, which is a Write-operation. We also use the ADO constants, adOpenStatic & adLockOptimistic while opening the Recordset for it to be updateable.

- The lines, are what do the main processing. **RS.AddNew** adds a new, blank record to the database. Then you set the fields by assigning your data to the respective fields of the Recordset. Note the short-cut syntax used in this example.

```
RS.AddNew
RS ("FirstName") = "Manasi"
RS ("LastName") = "Patil"
RS ("Email") = "Manasi@ManasiPatil.com"
RS ("DateOfBirth") = CDate("4 Oct, 1988")
RS.Update
```

- Finally, when you're done assigning all the values, execute the Recordset.Update method to commit all changes to the record.

4.8.3 Updating Records

- If you know how to insert records, then updating them is a easy. As you can see in below example everything else remains the same.

Program 4.20:

```
<HTML>
    <HEAD>
    <TITLE>Student Records</TITLE>
    </HEAD>
    <BODY>
    Dim DB
    Set DB = Server.CreateObject ("ADODB.Connection")
    DB.Mode = adModeReadWrite
    DB.Open ("PROVIDER=Microsoft.Jet.OLEDB.4.0;DATA SOURCE=" +
```

```
"C:\Databases\Students.mdb")
Dim RS
Set RS = Server.CreateObject ("ADODB.Recordset")
RS.Open "SELECT * FROM Students WHERE FirstName = 'Manasi'",
DB, adOpenStatic, adLockPessimistic
RS ("Email") = "mynewemail@ManasiPatil.com"
RS ("DateOfBirth") = CDate("4 Oct, 1988")
RS.Update
%>
</BODY>
</HTML>
```

- Firstly, you need just position the current pointer to the record that you wish to update. Use a proper SQL statement to achieve this. (It is advisable to check if that record exists, prior to modifying it.)

- Then, as earlier, modify the records by assigning new values to them. You need not assign values to all fields; just modify the fields you need. Then execute the **RS.Update** statement to write the changes back to the database.

4.8.4 Deleting Records

- Use the SQL DELETE statement to delete one or more records satisfying a particular criterion.

Program 4.21:

```
<HEAD>
<TITLE>Student Records</TITLE>
</HEAD>
<BODY>
<%
Dim DB
Set DB = Server.CreateObject ("ADODB.Connection")
DB.Mode = adModeReadWrite
DB.Open ("PROVIDER=Microsoft.Jet.OLEDB.4.0;DATA SOURCE=" +
"C:\Databases\Students.mdb")
DB.Execute ("DELETE * FROM Students WHERE FirstName =
'Manasi'")
%>
</BODY>
</HTML>
```

- Implement the utmost caution while using the DELETE statement for two reasons:
  - Firstly, because there's no Undo available to restore your changes.
  - And secondly, because if you forget the WHERE clause, it proceeds to delete **all** of the records in the table.

4.9 Programs on Database Related Operations

Program 4.22: Create an ASP application which allows the user to generate a simple query based upon the value of some text entered into a form.

First the html page, format.html, looks like

```
<HTML>
<FORM METHOD="GET" ACTION="format.asp">
<H3>CD Search</H3>
Enter an artist:<BR>
<INPUT TYPE="TEXT" NAME="artist">
<P>Select format<BR>
Album <INPUT TYPE="RADIO" NAME="FORMAT" VALUE="Album">
Single <INPUT TYPE="RADIO" NAME="FORMAT" VALUE="Single">
Both <INPUT TYPE="RADIO" NAME="FORMAT" VALUE="Both" CHECKED>
<P><INPUT TYPE="SUBMIT" VALUE="Search">
</HTML>
```

Here we have added three radio buttons, grouped under the name format, to allow the user to select aCD format.

We need to vary the SQL query depending on the user's choice of radio button. For example, if the user were to select the album format then the SQL would read

```
SELECT Title,Artist,Format from CDs WHERE Artist LIKE '% artist%' AND
format='CDA' ORDER BY Artist
```

We can do this by using an If..Then... Elseif statement to add an extra part to the WHERE clause.

The Active Server Page, format.asp, starts as

```
<%
format=Request("format")
Query="SELECT Title,Artist,Format from CDs WHERE Artist LIKE '%"
Query=Query & Request("artist") & "%'"
If format="Album" Then
Query=Query & " AND format='CDA'"
ElseIf format="Single" Then
Query=Query & " AND format='CDS'"
End If
Query = Query & " ORDER BY Artist"
```

If both has been selected then no addition need to be made to the SQL query string. The rest of the Active Server Page will execute the query and output the results in a table as in the previous example.

The HTML page would look like

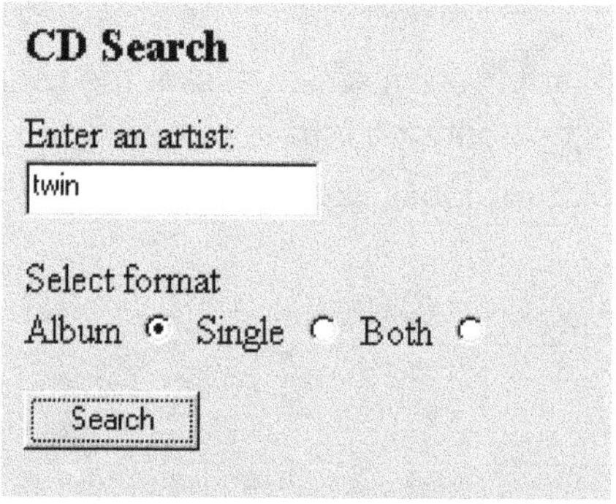

CD Search

Enter an artist:
twin

Select format
Album ⦿ Single ○ Both ○

Search

Fig. 4.19

And the HTML generated by the Active Server Page would look like the format.

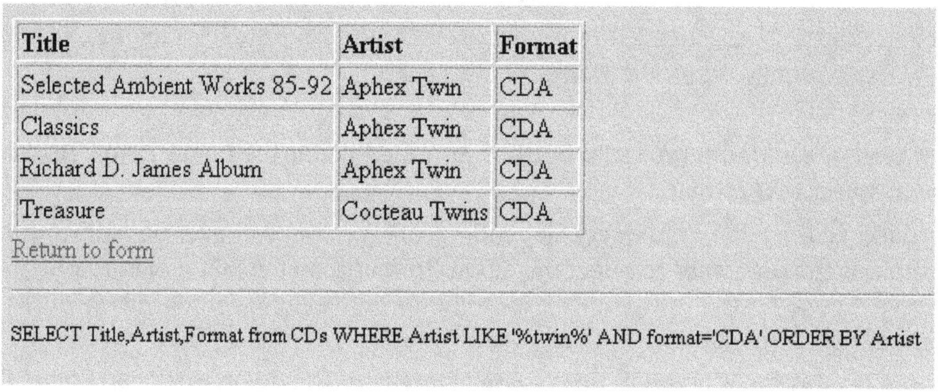

Title	Artist	Format
Selected Ambient Works 85-92	Aphex Twin	CDA
Classics	Aphex Twin	CDA
Richard D. James Album	Aphex Twin	CDA
Treasure	Cocteau Twins	CDA

Return to form

SELECT Title,Artist,Format from CDs WHERE Artist LIKE '%twin%' AND format='CDA' ORDER BY Artist

Fig. 4.20

Program 4.23: Create Application to Add/Modifey record in following table

ID	Title	Artist	Format
1	Second Coming	Stone Roses,	CDA
2	Singles	Smiths	CDA
3	Dummy	Portishead	CDA
4	Revolver	Beatles, The	CDA
5	The Times They Are A-	Dylan, Bob	CDA
6	Love Spreads	Stone Roses,	CDS

The HTML form, addcds.html, is straightforward

```
<HTML>

<FORM METHOD="GET" ACTION="addcds.asp">

<H3>Add CD to Database</H3>

<B>Artist</B><BR>

<INPUT TYPE="TEXT" NAME="artist" MAXLENGTH="50"><P>

<B>Title</B><BR>

<INPUT TYPE="TEXT" NAME="title" MAXLENGTH="50"><P>

<B>Format</B><BR>

<INPUT TYPE="RADIO" NAME="format" VALUE="CDA" CHECKED> Album<BR>

<INPUT TYPE="RADIO" NAME="format" VALUE="CDS"> Single<P>

<INPUT TYPE="SUBMIT" VALUE="Add to database"><P>

<INPUT TYPE="RESET" VALUE="Clear">

</FORM>

</BODY>

</HMTL>
```

The form would look like

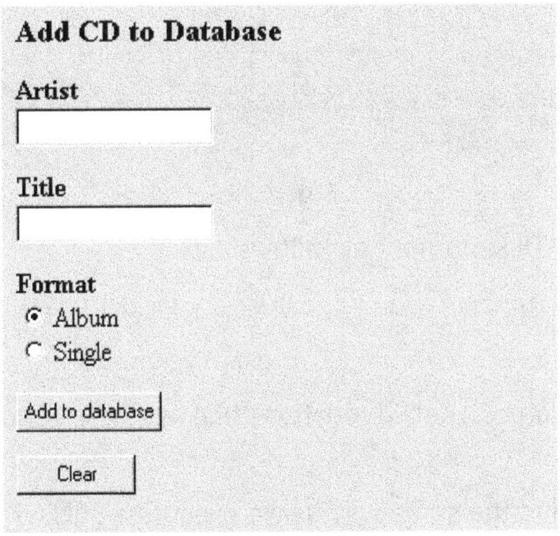

Fig. 4.21

The Active Server Page it calls, addcds.asp, is as follows:

```
<%
artist=Request("artist")
title=Request("title")
format=Request("format")
Query = "INSERT INTO CDs (artist,title,format) VALUES ("
Query = Query & "'" & artist & "','" & title & "','" & format & "')"
Set DataConn = Server.CreateObject("ADODB.Connection")
DataConn.Open "records"
Set RSlist = Server.CreateObject("ADODB.recordset")
RSlist.Open Query,DataConn,3
%>
<HTML>
<BODY>
<H3>CD Added To Collection Database</H3>
<HR>
<SMALL><%=Query%></SMALL>
</BODY>
</HTML>
```

On execution we would get the following HTML generated:

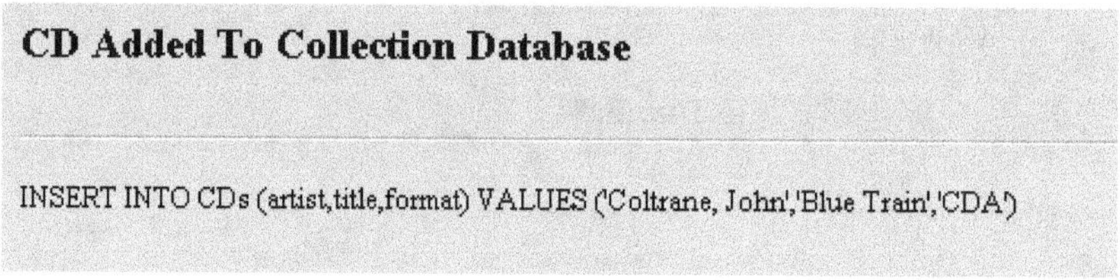

CD Added To Collection Database

INSERT INTO CDs (artist,title,format) VALUES ('Coltrane, John','Blue Train','CDA')

Fig. 4.22

We use the SQL UPDATE statement as follows:

```
INSERT INTO records (artist,title,format) VALUES
('value_of_artist','Value_of_title','Value_of_format')
```

Since all three fields are of data type text then we must enclose the values in single quotes.

The query is executed in the same way as we execute a SELECT query. Note however the username the Web server runs under must have write access to the database file.

Program 4.24: Write a program to delete records from a database using an Active Server Page.

The following Active Server Page, deletecd.asp, provides the user with a form to select a CD for deletion.

```
<%
Query="SELECT ID,Title,Artist from CDs ORDER BY Artist"
Set DataConn = Server.CreateObject("ADODB.Connection")
DataConn.Open "records"
Set RSlist = Server.CreateObject("ADODB.recordset")
RSlist.Open Query,DataConn,3
%>
<HTML>
<BODY>
<FORM ACTION="deleteme.asp" METHOD="GET">
<INPUT TYPE="SUBMIT" VALUE="Delete Selected CD"><P>
<TABLE BORDER=1>
<TR><TD><B>Title</B></TD><TD><B>Artist</B></TD><TD>Delete</TD></TR>
<%
Do While Not RSlist.EOF
%>
<TR>
<TD><%=RSlist("Title")%></TD>
<TD><%=RSlist("Artist")%></TD>
<TD>
<INPUT TYPE=RADIO NAME="record_ID" VALUE="<%=RSlist("ID")%>">
</TD>
</TR>
<%
RSlist.Movenext
Loop
%>
</TABLE>
</FORM>
</BODY>
</HTML>
```

When executed the Active Server Page generates the following HTML output:

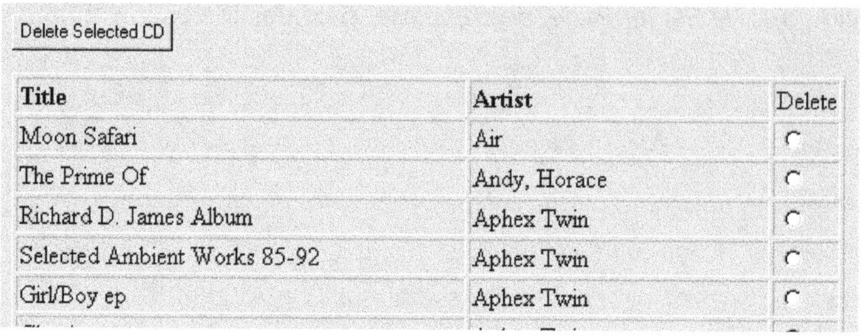

Title	Artist	Delete
Moon Safari	Air	◌
The Prime Of	Andy, Horace	◌
Richard D. James Album	Aphex Twin	◌
Selected Ambient Works 85-92	Aphex Twin	◌
Girl/Boy ep	Aphex Twin	◌

Fig. 4.23

Next to each entry is a radio button, called record_ID. The radio button takes the value of the ID number of the particular CD selected

```
<INPUT TYPE=RADIO NAME="record_ID" VALUE="<%=RSlist("ID")%>">
```

When the Submit button is selected the string record_ID=ID_number is passed to deleteme.asp

```
<%
Query="DELETE from CDs WHERE ID=" & Request("record_ID")
Set DataConn = Server.CreateObject("ADODB.Connection")
DataConn.Open "records"
Set RSlist = Server.CreateObject("ADODB.recordset")
RSlist.Open Query,DataConn,3
%>
<HTML>
<BODY>
<H3>CD Deleted from Database</H3>
<A HREF="deletecd.asp">Return to list</A>
</BODY>
</HTML>
```

Which uses the SQL DELETE statement to delete the required record.

Practice Questions

1. What does ASP stands for?
2. How do you write, "Knowledge is wealth" in ASP?
3. What is IIS? Explain steps to install IIS.
4. What is the default scripting language in ASP? Explain with syntax.

5. How do you get information from a form that is submitted using the "get" method?

6. If Page 1 has this link:

   ```
   <a href="page2.asp?color=green">Go</a>
   ```

   How can page2.asp get the "color" parameter?

7. Write a short note on:

   (a) ASP Syntax

   (b) Variables

   (c) Procedures

8. Which ASP property is used to identify a user?

9. Explain ASP Session with suitable example. Which one of these events is a standard Global. as a event?

10. State difference between HTML and ASP.

11. Write a short note on ASP objects.

12. Explain Globla.asa

13. Explain following database related operations with example for following database schema:

Table: Employee

ID	Employees ID Numbers; also the primary key of the table
FirstName	First name of the Employee
LastName	Last name of the Employee
DateofBirth	Birth date of the Employee
Email	Email address of the Employee
Designation	Designation of the Employee
Salary	Salary of the Employee

(a) Insert Data

(b) Retrieve Data

(c) Update Data

(d) Delete Data

■■■

www.ingramcontent.com/pod-product-compliance
Lightning Source LLC
Chambersburg PA
CBHW080957020726
47505CB00009B/2231